"I know why you'd let yourself touch me,"

Jack said. "Because I'd be safe. I'll be gone in a week. No expectations, no nasty surprises. You can't get left holding the pieces of your heart if you know going into it that there's no future, right?"

Carly finally met his eyes. Her chin tilted up. "Okay," she said softly. "So what if you're right, *cowboy?* I don't think you're the type who...sticks."

"Don't kid yourself. If I tried it once—" his eyes coasted deliberately over her again "—I'd sure be back for more."

Her pulse went wild. "In...in a physical sense, maybe."

"That's the part that counts, cowgirl."

Dear Reader,

Wow! What a month we've got for you. Take *Maddy Lawrence's Big Adventure*, Linda Turner's newest. Like most of us, Maddy's lived a pretty calm life, maybe even too calm. But all that's about to change, because now Ace Mackenzie is on the job. Don't miss this wonderful book.

We've got some great miniseries this month, too. *The One Worth Waiting For* is the latest of Alicia Scott's THE GUINESS GANG, while Cathryn Clare continues ASSIGNMENT: ROMANCE with *The Honeymoon Assignment*. Plus Sandy Steen is back with the suspenseful—and sexy—*Hunting Houston*. Then there's Beverly Bird's *Undercover Cowboy*, which successfully mixes romance and danger for a powerhouse read. Finally, try Lee Karr's *Child of the Night* if you enjoy a book where things are never quite what they seem.

Then come back again next month, because you won't want to miss some of the best romantic reading around— only in Silhouette Intimate Moments.

Enjoy!

Leslie Wainger

Leslie Wainger
Senior Editor and Editorial Coordinator

Please address questions and book requests to:
Silhouette Reader Service
U.S.: 3010 Walden Ave., P.O. Box 1325, Buffalo, NY 14269
Canadian: P.O. Box 609, Fort Erie, Ont. L2A 5X3

UNDERCOVER COWBOY

BEVERLY BIRD

Published by Silhouette Books

America's Publisher of Contemporary Romance

SILHOUETTE BOOKS

ISBN 0-373-07711-4

UNDERCOVER COWBOY

Books by Beverly Bird

Silhouette Intimate Moments

Emeralds in the Dark #3
The Fires of Winter #23
Ride the Wind #139
A Solitary Man #172
*A Man Without Love #630
*A Man Without a Haven #641
*A Man Without a Wife #652
Undercover Cowboy #711

Silhouette Desire

The Best Reasons #190
Fool's Gold #209
All the Marbles #227
To Love a Stranger #411

*Wounded Warriors

BEVERLY BIRD

has lived in several places in the United States, but she is currently back where her roots began on an island in New Jersey. Her time is devoted to her family and her writing. She is the author of numerous romance novels, both contemporary and historical. Beverly loves to hear from readers. You can write to her c/o Silhouette Books, 300 East 42nd Street, New York, NY 10017.

For George M. Harvey and his speedy and professional "editing service," for bucking me up and bailing me out more times than I can count.

Chapter 1

The bar was dark, too smoky, and the hum of conversation from the other patrons was a steady buzz punctuated by bursts of laughter. The big, balding man seated at a table far in the back did not contribute to the noise level. He tore the retirement application neatly in half without so much as a word.

Jack Fain frowned at the gesture, a quick knitting of his blond brows. "Come on, Paul. You and I both know it's dangerous to send out an agent who's lost his nerve."

Not that he considered it shameful for a man to lose his nerve. The only shame was in *not* admitting it and acting accordingly, he thought. He had spent six weeks in ICU and another six recuperating at home after the gut shot that had nearly killed him. As far as he was concerned, any sane man would be cautious after that. Any sane man would adjust his priorities.

But Paul Manning shook his head. "You could lose half your nerve and still have more than most."

"I'm forty-three years old. My reflexes are getting slow." Not to mention what was happening to his instincts, he thought.

"You've still got a few good years left in you."

"And I intend to spend them on a beach somewhere watching hard brown bodies stroll by in the sand." He signaled the waitress for a beer. Florida, he thought. Maybe it was time to go back to Florida. The thought was new and vaguely alarming. He justified it with thoughts of hard, brown bodies who could speak his name—his real name—without an accent, the kind of women he had grown up with before spending so many years out of the country.

"I could hold up your debriefing," Paul pointed out.

Jack shot him another impatient scowl. "I don't care as long as I'm inactive in the meantime. And you'll get tired of the games eventually."

"Can you honestly tell me you're willing to leave with Scorpion just . . . dangling?"

"He's not dangling. The game's over. Scorpion won."

A telephone rang from somewhere beneath the table. Paul held Jack's gaze for a moment, then he reached down for his briefcase. He removed a cellular phone and listened briefly.

"I'm with him right now. I'll ask him," Paul said after a moment.

Jack stiffened.

Paul placed the receiver back in the case. "Speak of the devil," he mused, then he gave a satisfied smile.

As far as Jack was concerned, there was only one devil. He was a political assassin whom the agency had code-named Scorpion. His strikes were lethal and fast, and he disappeared very well afterward. Jack had chased him for eleven years, roughly half his entire service. Three months ago, it had been Scorpion who had finally caught him.

It had happened in Brazil, in São Paulo. He'd received a tip from a previously reliable contact that Scorpion was visiting a back-alley brothel. He'd gone to the place and Scorpion had come up behind him, greeting him gently, urging him to turn around.

The gun . . . hard and cold in his gut. Pain flaring, exploding, driving him backward, red fire bursting into the night . . .

And worse than the pain, so much worse than the pain, was knowing that he had been played for a fool. That had never happened before. More than anything else, it told him it was time to quit.

Jack rubbed unconsciously at the scar on his belly. "You set this up," he snapped.

"No."

"Are you trying to tell me that Scorpion struck again now, while we sit here arguing about this? Cut me a break."

"Our boy's always had an excellent sense of timing."

That was true, Jack thought. "Where?"

"In the Caymans."

"The *Caymans?* What in the hell is he doing there?"

Paul shrugged. "You tell me. You're the man who's been on him all this time."

Jack ignored that subtle bit of coercion. "Who'd he hit?"

"A Judas in a money-laundering operation. Scorpion took the guy out, then he stole the jet and the money, and he disappeared again. Except this time Tony Esposito thinks he has the plane on radar. Sloppy, sloppy." Paul paused, seeming lost in thought. "Well, at least Tony has a rogue in the air, a Lear that hasn't filed a flight plan. That was him on the phone. He's thinking that maybe it's not Scorpion this time. Maybe we've got...I don't know, an impostor. Tony wants to know what you think." Paul outlined the gruesome details of the hit.

Jack scowled. It made no sense. "He stole the money that he was supposed to retrieve? No. No way." It wasn't Scorpion's usual scene, not his typical sort of work. There were no political overtones to it. There was no international intrigue. Scorpion had never worked for dirty American money, not since the first time he'd struck.

And then, suddenly, Jack understood. It was finally going to happen. Something inside him went hot, then cold. *The picture.*

"It's him," he said flatly.

The waitress brought his beer. He pushed it away without tasting it. "Turning renegade with the money forces him into retirement. His name will be mud after this."

"One would think so," Paul agreed.

"So he's finally reached the point where he wants to get out. Probably because he thinks I'm dead. Hell, he killed me. He saw me go down, stood over me...." Kicked him in the ribs, he thought, to watch for any sign of a grimace, any clue that he was still alive.

Jack had been beyond grimacing. It was the only thing that had saved him.

"So if you run off to a sunny beach somewhere, he's the world's most successful renegade," Paul pointed out. "He'll disappear one last time and that will be that."

The phone rang again. Jack finally reached for his beer, drinking deeply. His pulse started doing odd things as Paul talked and finally hung up again.

"Tony definitely has a trace on the plane."

"It's heading for the Midwest," Jack said flatly.

Something flared behind Paul's eyes. "There, you see? No other man would guess that."

Jack waved an impatient hand and put his glass down on the table with a sharp crack. "It only makes sense. Scorpion's first hit was in Dallas when Kenny LaFrancke recruited him for his nasty friends." He and Kenny had been in the service together. And then, Jack thought, they had gone bad together.

Actually, Kenny had been the first to turn. He'd gotten involved doing some dirty work for an American oil cartel, but he had balked at actually committing murder. Instead, he had recommended his old buddy from the Marines, Brett Peterson, a man with a fascination and proclivity for guns and all they could do.

The agency had gotten Kenny LaFrancke off the streets some time ago. The man had sung like a bird, trying to cop a deal for himself. That was how they'd learned that the cartel had paid Peterson to kill when Kenny found himself a little squeamish in that area. It had only been LaFrancke's word that that was how the whole thing had gone down, because the cartel had effectively erased all signs of their involvement by then and Peterson himself had vanished into thin air. But Jack tended to believe Kenny.

After that, Peterson had no longer used his real name. The agency had dubbed him Scorpion, but he had used any number of aliases. His original identity had died as his reputation and the demand for his services grew.

Still, Kenny's testimony, and that one link to a real name, had allowed the agency to learn that Peterson had been born in Dallas and that he had been involved with some small-scale criminal activity even before LaFrancke's friends recruited him. And then Jack had found one more link between Scorpion and the man who had once called himself Brett Peterson—the picture that had been haunting him for years now. He had waited a long time for that photograph to mean anything. Once again, he got the strong, frightening sense that that was going to happen now.

Now . . . when he had lost his nerve.

"It's all in his file," he went on hoarsely. "You don't need me. All you've got to do is put an agent on this who can read."

"Reading's a far cry from having been there."

"Having been there wasn't always so damned cozy, either," he snapped back. He and Scorpion had never really spoken, Jack thought, and only once, in São Paulo, had they looked fleetingly into each other's eyes. Still, there *had* been a certain intimacy involved. Jack had eaten the man's leftovers on occasion, and more than once he'd grabbed a catnap on the same sheets the man had just left.

He knew him. And right now, he was pretty sure that Scorpion was heading back to a woman with hair the color of night, a woman with hearth and home in her eyes.

Once, in Holland, Jack had been so hot on the assassin's heels that when Scorpion had reached his room at the Amsterdam Hilton, the man had had no choice but to keep going, right out the window. Even so, he'd left a handful of his hair behind, as well as a gym bag in the hotel closet. The bag had contained a razor, some cologne and a half dozen counterfeit IDs that Scorpion simply had never used again. But at the bottom of the bag there had been something far more curious and potentially useful. Jack had found a dog-eared photograph of a woman, standing in front of what looked like a barn.

That photograph was in Jack's wallet now, if only to remind him how deadly it could be for a man like Scorpion or himself to love so strongly. Then again, Jack rarely needed reminders. He more or less lived with the knowledge in the area of his gut, a squirming thing that hit him whenever a woman—whenever *anybody*—got too close.

Close was deadly. Close was fatal. Close hurt.

Still, he could fully understand why a more foolish man, a less wary man than himself, would be drawn back to the woman in Scorpion's photograph. Jack had allowed himself to get sucked into marriage once, too—and Zoe had not had all that many of the hinted qualities the woman in Scorpion's photograph seemed to possess. Still, he had liked Zoe enough to respect her, enough to let her go when it had become quickly and painfully clear that he could not, would not, give to her what she needed.

Scorpion had let go, too, but now he was going back to his woman, and that would be a fatal mistake even while Jack thought it was an understandable one.

There was something true and honest about the woman in Scorpion's picture. She was not actually beautiful, but there was a certain irresistible warmth about her. It was, Jack thought with rare sentimentality, like a banked fire, beckoning with heat and promise. The photo was black and white, flat, yet her image stroked something in a man's heart, lured him, called to him. He couldn't tell the color of her eyes, but her hair was long and rich and it looked very black. In her eyes was an offer of both simple pleasures and keen intelligence. She wore a white gauze dress and was endearingly barefoot.

She had been young in the picture, in her early twenties. She had certainly aged by now, but Jack had always known that sooner or later, Scorpion would have to go back to her, to touch her, to see her, to taste her, one more time. He hadn't carried her picture because she meant nothing to him, and Jack knew she was still alive.

The agency had identified her. Brett Peterson had been married once, very briefly, before he had disappeared into his Scorpion persona. Periodically, the agency checked on that woman's whereabouts, making sure she was still where she was supposed to be, making sure she'd had no apparent contact from the man. She never had. Scorpion seemed to have been . . . saving her.

Jack realized that Paul was watching him, waiting for him to go on.

"He'll go find her now," he said carefully. "That woman in the picture." Jack fought the urge to take it out of his billfold and examine it one more time. It wasn't necessary. He had long since memorized her face, and every limited detail of the background.

"So Tony Esposito should just walk up her rose-trimmed path, knock on the door and say, 'Excuse me, Mrs. Scorpion, but I'd like to arrest your husband now'?"

"No. He won't stay there. My guess is that he'll collect her and disappear. How much money did he come out of the Caymans with?"

"We're putting it at about fifteen million."

Jack whistled. "No," he said again. "He won't stay in Oklahoma."

"Oklahoma?"

"She was still there a year ago."

"Do you think she's been waiting for him all this time?"

"You mean, as in she's expected that he'd eventually come back for her? I don't know yet," Jack answered honestly. "*He* hopes so."

"Should I arrange a ride to the airport for you?"

Jack's eyes narrowed on him. He didn't comment.

Paul held his napkin up to inspect it in the dim, golden light. He'd folded it into a neat triangle while they'd talked. "Tell you what," he proposed finally. "Go after him this last time and wrap this thing up, and I'll sign your retirement papers without a peep. Hell, I'll even buy you a gold watch."

Jack sat back in his chair. His heart was racing too fast. It was wrong for all the right reasons. It was foolish, dangerous, and all his instincts told him to stop, here and now, with his guts once again tucked safely inside him where they belonged.

But he'd been waiting a long, long time for the assassin to make this move, to go after this woman.

"Yeah," he said finally. His voice was hoarse, almost a groan.

"Yes, as in you need a ride to the airport?"

Jack nodded. His adrenaline surged. The briefcase rang a third time. Paul talked and hung up.

"You're good, my friend."

"Where'd he land?" His voice still sounded too eager... too scared. This was wrong. But he had no choice, not really. He had to finish this. Otherwise, he realized, it would haunt him forever.

Like the woman with the long dark hair had haunted Scorpion.

"He's in Oklahoma City," Paul answered. "We've put men from the Tulsa office throughout the airport. They'll keep him in sight until you can get out there and take over. My God, he walked right into our hands this time." He hesitated. "Are you *sure* it's him?"

"I'm sure. He's not thinking straight. He's too eager. He's retired now, and he wants her. Also keep in mind that he doesn't think I can come after him this time."

"He's got to know we'll send *somebody*. For that matter, so will the guys he turned on."

"It'll take them a week or more. They won't panic right away. Scorpion's been reliable, the cream of the crop, for eleven years. They'll assume something happened to make him change his flight plan, that he's just being cautious. When he doesn't show up *next* week, that's when it'll occur to them that he might have turned on them." He paused, thinking. "As for us, well, he probably doesn't think any of our other agents are good enough to nail him."

Jack stood abruptly. "You might want to start shopping for that watch."

"My word is as good as gold," Paul said grandly.

"On second thought, skip the gold. Just make sure that baby's water- and sand-proof." Florida, he thought again. Soon now. And that, too, was a good way to wrap things up, to come full circle.

He left the bar, whistling a tuneless version of the national anthem.

Carly Castagne dropped the first piece of toast on the floor. She scorched the second. Her sister watched as she grabbed it and hurled it, still smoking, in the general direction of the kitchen sink.

"You're going to be fine," Theresa said soothingly. "Just go out there and tell them hello, and that we're glad they're here, then teach them all how to ride."

Carly shot her sister a disbelieving look. Theresa was almost childlike in her innocence and optimism. She amazed her, because Carly, on the other hand, had never failed to see bogeymen lurking in shadows in all her thirty-three years. She was a realist, she thought. Life was hard, so you did whatever you had to do to survive. Even when it hurt.

This hurt. Or, at least, it pinched very uncomfortably.

She crossed the kitchen to look out the window. Four tourists were standing beside the first cattle pen, grinning like fools. Two had arrived last night, and two had come this morning, and so far Theresa had dealt with them, showing them to their rooms and getting them settled. But now Theresa was looking at her expectantly, and it was time for Carly to take up the reins.

She pressed her fingers to her temples. "I'm really not very good with people," she muttered in a last, halfhearted protest.

"You're not good with *men*," Theresa clarified.

Carly winced and dropped her hands. It was a fine point, but indisputably true. She'd already lost a husband and a father. Granted, her father had died on her. There was little she could have done about that.

"You'll be fine," Theresa said again.

Carly took a deep breath and squared her shoulders. The thing was, she had no choice. Either her beloved ranch ran as a dude operation for the summer, or it would go to the highest bidder.

She stood a moment longer, her gaze flicking over the ramshackle fences and outbuildings of Seventy Four Draw. The cattle ranch had been in their family for generations. Cholesterol-conscious America was trying to make sure it didn't last generations more. The fact of the matter was that people just weren't eating as much beef as they used to, and Seventy Four Draw was good for very little else but producing beef. The ranch just wasn't bringing in enough money anymore to cover costs and pay Uncle Sam, too.

Damn the IRS. But she knew that damning them wasn't going to help in the least. Unless she started making payments to them, they were going to force a tax sale on her by September.

Oh, Daddy, how could you do this to me? I'm only one person. I can't do it all. I need you now and where are you? Planted six feet under without a care in the world.

Their parents had passed away within six months of each other, and it had been her father's dying wish that Carly take care of his ranch. But it was much more than a one-woman job, she thought, especially with beef prices plummeting and the IRS breathing down her neck.

Theresa was no help. She was seven months pregnant, and in the middle of a divorce. She had come running home from Tulsa, expecting that the Draw would take care of her as it always had. As for Michael, their brother, he worked in Oklahoma City and rarely set foot on the ranch at all. He was their idea man. It had been his brainstorm for Carly to take tourists along with her the next time she drove cattle up to auction in Kansas.

"Okay," she whispered aloud, forcing her feet to the kitchen door. "I can handle this." Then she veered suddenly for the back stairs instead.

"Where are you going?" Theresa asked, startled.

"I can't go out there like this, smelling like calf poop." She had spent the better part of the morning wrestling with an orphan who had been born last night, trying to get him to nurse from a bottle when all his instincts told him to insist upon the real thing.

"You're procrastinating, Carlotta," Theresa chided.

Carly winced. *Carlotta*. Where had her father been on the day her mother had decided to name her that? It was just another classic example of him letting her down.

She bounded up the stairs, but when she reached the hallway there, she hesitated. She lifted a hand to knock on her daughter's closed bedroom door, then she lowered it again reluctantly. There really wasn't time now. If she knocked, she really *would* be procrastinating.

At the moment her daughter, Holly, was just another bogeyman in the shadows, she thought, sighing. A beloved bogeyman, but a problem all the same. She wanted so badly for Holly to go on this next cattle drive with her. At seven, eight, even ten years old, Holly had loved going on the auction trips. Then eleven had come, and suddenly, it wasn't cool to go on trail rides with your mom anymore. It *was* cool to wonder who your father was and why he'd left you. But Carly couldn't tell her that. The truth of the matter was that Brett Peterson had taken off after the first buxom blonde to cross his path, and how did you explain that to an eleven-year-old?

You didn't, she thought, her heart squeezing.

To be fair, Brett hadn't known she was pregnant when he'd gone trotting off after the blonde. And she had never thought it was worth the bother to chase him down and tell him. She had filed for divorce, had taken back her maiden name and had given the same one to her daughter, and she had put the whole marriage behind her. It was, after all, the sensible way to deal with bogeymen. And it had never been an issue until Holly had grown up enough to blame her mother for the fact that Brett hadn't stayed.

Oh, honey, if life were only that one-sided, that easy.

Against all her better judgment, Carly knocked. Without waiting for an answer, she opened the bedroom door and stuck her head inside.

"Hey."

Holly was sitting Indian-style on the bed, a Walkman in her lap, the cord trailing up and around her neck, disappearing beneath her long, sable hair. She looked up at Carly and pried off one earphone.

"What?" she demanded.

Carly cleared her throat. "Those people are here. The guests."

"So?" Holly asked sullenly.

"So I was wondering if maybe you wanted to come downstairs and take a look at them."

"What for? They're stupid."

Carly realized she'd have a hard time arguing with her on that score. She kept her mouth shut and shrugged.

"Why would anybody pay *money* to sweat and get dirty and drive a bunch of steers to Kansas? That's *stupid*," Holly repeated.

"Yeah, well, maybe when they start getting sweaty and dirty, they'll realize that." *And then maybe they'll all go home,* she thought. *And then I'm right back to square one with the IRS.*

Carly groaned aloud. "It might be good for a laugh," she tried.

Holly only shook her head and dropped the earphone back into place.

A realist knew when she was beaten, Carly thought. *Temporarily* beaten. She'd try again later.

She left Holly's door and went on to her own room. She struggled out of her jeans and her T-shirt as she headed for her closet, then she stopped dead as she passed in front of her vanity mirror.

Had what had happened with Brett been her fault?

She crossed her arms over her chest and scowled. She had no hips to speak of, she thought. It was a moderately small wonder that her underwear stayed up. She tugged on her panties and that was a mistake because without her arms crossed over her breasts she was faced with a good look at them as well.

What there was of them. She sighed, dropping her arms to her sides.

She was too thin. There was no flesh on her—she was all muscle and lean lines. And she was flat-chested. Except for her long, dark hair and the green eyes she'd inherited from her Irish mother, she thought she could easily pass for a boy—one who badly needed a haircut and who had pretty eyes.

Would Brett have stayed if she had been some-how... different? Would he have stayed if she had been softer, more feminine, more pliant?

"Carlotta!" Theresa's voice floated up the back stairs. "They're waiting!"

Carly dragged a clean shirt and a fresh pair of jeans out of her closet. She thought she should probably put a bra on as well, although God knew there wasn't much there to jiggle around. She dressed again, then she leaned sideways for one last glimpse in the mirror.

The sad truth of the matter was, when you were only one woman and you had sixteen hundred cows, thirty-four horses, eighteen chickens and three roosters, four ranch hands, a pre-pubescent daughter and a pregnant sister all looking to you for answers, who had time to be worrying about their appearance? *Don't forget the IRS,* she reminded herself darkly.

She smoothed her hair back from her forehead, flattening all the little wisps that had already come free from her braid. She licked her finger and rubbed at a smudge of dirt on her forehead. She ran for the stairs and hit the kitchen again at a jog, then she glanced out the window again and skidded to a stop.

"*Now* what?"

"What do you mean?" Theresa asked. She had been washing dishes, and she dried her hands to come look out the window herself.

The four original tourists were still there, but now there were two strangers as well, two men. They'd come out of nowhere. Either they were tourists with twelve hundred dollars apiece in their pockets, dropping into her barnyard like manna from heaven, or they were drifters looking for work.

Well, they'd have no luck here, Carly thought. She could barely pay the people she had, and had dropped two of them to part-time just last week.

She yanked open the back door. Suddenly she was doubly convinced that her world was going to hell in a handbasket.

Chapter 2

The reality of Carlotta Castagne hit Jack like a wrecking ball in the solar plexus.

She came through the back door, almost bouncing with energy. That was his first impression. His second was that age had not detracted from her beauty at all.

Her innocence was gone, he realized, but the *sense* of her was the same, and so much stronger than in the photograph. It was something rich yet simple, honest and good. Her eyes told stories now, where they had simply been bright and eager in that photograph taken so many years ago.

She was smaller than he would have expected, and thinner. She moved like a hot, summer wind, and she made him want things he had always been very sure no man could ever have.

At least, not a man like himself.

Jack felt a subtle change in Scorpion's stance and forgot the woman for a brief moment. There was suddenly a hunger and an alertness about the assassin, and Jack felt it like a physical touch. He realized that his own heart was beating hard as he waited for something to happen.

Nothing did. Not yet.

He hooked a finger over the brim of the battered cowboy hat he had bought off a stranger in the airport. He eased it down a little farther on his forehead. The only thing he figured Scorpion might recognize about him was his eyes—and then only if he stared directly into them. Jack thought it would pretty much be an instinctual thing, but even so, he wouldn't risk it.

"Did either of you talk to Michael?" Carlotta demanded, looking at him and Scorpion.

Michael?

"Of course," Scorpion lied smoothly. Then again, Jack thought, maybe he had.

"You did?" Carlotta repeated, clearly startled. "He didn't tell me. Did you pay him?"

"I did," Jack offered quickly.

"Me, too," said Scorpion.

In that moment, Jack knew that if the assassin had come back here to collect this woman, she didn't know it. She didn't seem to recognize him, anymore than Scorpion recognized Jack with his eyes shadowed—a near impossibility since this was the first time Jack had ever entered the field looking like himself. Scorpion knew that the agency had had a man on him all these years, but he had met that man in too many guises to be sure which one was real.

Jack hoped.

He had tailed the assassin in the form of a shaggy, blonde surf bum in Honolulu, and a scar-faced mercenary in South Africa. Scorpion had "killed" a louse-ridden Brazilian peasant in São Paulo. As busy as Jack had been changing his appearance, Scorpion had been even more industrious—he had endured cosmetic surgery several times over the years, and now not even Carlotta Castagne seemed to see past the changes. Jack watched her closely as she looked at the assassin and all her expression revealed was a little harried annoyance, too genuine to be forced.

Then again, maybe he was being gullible again, as in São Paulo.

Jack found himself hoping strongly that that wasn't true. Not only because harboring such doubts about his own impressions said a great deal about his nerve and his foolhardiness in pursuing this chase, but because it would shatter his preconceived image of her. He realized that he *wanted* her to be honest.

"Well, then," she went on, looking around at the others. "Welcome to Seventy Four Draw. I'm Carly Castagne, and I'm going to explain what you can expect over the course of the next week or so."

Carly, Jack noted. She didn't use Carlotta. It suited her.

He listened with half an ear, still paying more attention to Scorpion. He had taken over the assassin's tail in a small motel on the outskirts of Oklahoma City at three o'clock yesterday morning. At dawn today, Scorpion had finally made a move, arranging for a rental car, coming here. Jack was both relieved and chagrined to find other people hovering in the barnyard. Something was going on, and with any luck he could slide right in as though he had always intended to be a part of it.

That was the up side. The down side was that it made locking horns with Scorpion this last and final time a far more dangerous proposition with so many innocent people underfoot. It changed things, made them hairier. Gone was the possibility of a short wrap-up to this thing, like a shoot-out in Carlotta Castagne's corral. He doubted if so many people would all manage to neatly duck, if one of them wouldn't manage to get him- or herself shot.

Gone, too, was the possibility that he could just stroll into their bedroom with his gun drawn, since Carly didn't even seem to know the man and Jack doubted if Scorpion was going to make it into her bedroom any time soon. He'd have a few problems to work out with her first.

Damn it.

Jack turned his attention to his surroundings. The ranch was a cluster of barns and outbuildings that had seen better days. He recognized one of them from the photograph—at least he was reasonably certain it was the same barn. The eaves were the same. The buildings were locked together like puzzle pieces by a series of weathered three-board fences and gates. Inside the paddocks, dusty, orange-red earth showed through scrubby patches of grass. The air felt as if it hadn't rained in a long time.

The house was big and white with peeling paint. There was an old, idle windmill out on the horizon. It looked for all the world as he had imagined Oklahoma to look. Odd, he thought, that of all the places he had been and seen over the years, the Dust Bowl had never been one of them.

"I figure it's going to take us five days to get the cattle into Kansas," Carly Castagne was saying, "and I have to make sure you all can ride first. Still, with a little effort, we should be able to squeeze it all into eight days."

Jack looked her way again sharply. *Cattle? Kansas? Ride?* What the hell had he walked into?

"Uh, what's the big deal?" he asked, fishing cautiously. "Just put us on some horses and off we go. Right?"

Her eyes narrowed again. They could do that in a flash, he realized, giving a sensation of heat again. They were green, as it turned out, and they were easily the prettiest thing about her. She seemed to study him for an inordinately long time.

"Going is one thing," she said finally. "Getting there is another. If I just 'put you on some horses,' I doubt very much if any of you would even get so far as the ranch boundaries. So what we're going to do is begin with some intensive riding lessons, and hopefully you'll all learn enough that we'll be able to leave here on Friday morning."

"For Kansas," he clarified.

She looked at him impatiently. "Of course, for Kansas."

"On horses."

"It's a long walk otherwise."

"Right."

"I've never even been near a horse before," Scorpion said. "What happens if it takes us longer to learn to ride and we can't leave until Saturday?"

Jack stiffened.

What is it, buddy? Do you want an extra day to touch base with your ladylove and whisk her off into the sunset with you? Then again, that idea had some merit. If Scorpion whisked her off, none of them would be going anywhere on horses.

"I have to get these cattle into Fort Dodge by Wednesday," Carly Castagne explained. "Saturday just doesn't leave me enough margin for error."

"Just out of curiosity, how many cows are we talking about here?" Jack asked.

Her gaze shot his way again. "Three hundred and seventy-two. But most of them aren't cows."

Jack lifted a brow. "No?"

"No. They're steers, or at least they will be shortly. My men are castrating them now."

He'd had to ask.

"Is it healthy for them to travel after such surgery?" someone asked.

"It's not surgery," Carly Castagne answered. "We just push them into chutes and brand them and give them their vaccines at the same time. Slice underneath and punch and burn the top. It's over with before they know it. Any other questions?"

"Yeah," Jack said. "How fast will we travel and how far?"

She swore under her breath. "Didn't Michael tell you *anything?*"

"Not nearly enough," he answered emphatically.

Carly sighed. "Well, it's about two hundred and fifty miles to the stockyards. Normally, I make about sixty-five miles in a very long day with a herd. Under the circumstances, with all you guys underfoot, I'll settle for fifty, and even that's going to practically kill you. I hope you all brought aspirin."

Jack stretched lazily, knocking his hat brim back just a little. "So what do we do first?"

She looked at her watch. "We've got enough time before lunch that I can teach you how to tack up a horse. And you'll need to know how to care for one. You'll each be responsible for your own, and you've got about three more days to get to know them as well as you know your worst nightmare."

Jack nodded absently. He was beginning to formulate a plan—a loose one, depending uncomfortably upon Scorpion making any and all first moves. But he was sure that whatever the assassin did now, Carly Castagne would be in the thick of it. He wouldn't need to stick close to the assassin, he decided. That was too risky. If he got too close for too long, the man would almost have to wonder what he was doing. Scorpion didn't know who he was exactly, but the assassin *did* know that an agent code-named Gemini had been playing cat and mouse with him for a whole lot of years. Scorpion knew that in the end, he had finally shot him, but it wouldn't be out of the question for the agency to have sent someone else.

No, he'd just keep close to the woman, Jack decided. He looked at her again. He had little doubt that when Scorpion made contact with her, she would, in some way, let it show. She was a pawn, an innocent, an amateur, as clear as a pane of glass.

Carly Castagne set off toward the barn. Jack let his eyes continue to follow her. She wore gratifyingly tight jeans and a bright red shirt. Her hair was all caught up in a long, heavy braid that bounced when she moved.

She moved purposefully now, with a neat, little sway to her hips. She flipped the braid over her shoulder as she went, and it danced against her back. He found himself staring at the little rubber band there at the end of it, found himself thinking of tugging it free, found himself wondering about all that long, dark hair—not quite as black as in the photograph, he realized, but more of a mahogany color. He wondered what it would feel like spilling into his hands.

He realized what he was doing and felt his heart kick.

She was Scorpion's woman, whether she knew it yet or not. She was Scorpion's weakness, not his own. He was too smart. Too wary. Too jaded to ever believe in happily-ever-afters again.

He dragged his eyes away from her. He had to get through to Paul, he thought, had to put the home office onto the chore of finding out who Michael was and how much money the man would need to smooth the seams of two unexpected tourists showing up for this little roundup.

A cattle drive, for God's sake.

"Can I help you?"

Jack turned sharply to find a heavily pregnant woman standing on the back porch. He fished out his wallet and held it up. "I need to make a phone call. It's long distance but I'll use my calling card."

"Certainly. Come on in."

Jack jogged up the steps and followed her inside. At the last moment, he glanced back over his shoulder, toward the barn. Then he realized that he was not keeping an eye on the assassin, but trying for one last glimpse of Carly Castagne.

Jack swore silently. Maybe he hadn't just lost his nerve. Maybe he was losing his mind.

Carly leaned against one of the stalls and watched the guests work on the horses she had assigned them. It was the first chance she'd had to assess all of them.

There was a short, stocky woman named Myra. She said she was a schoolteacher, and she fluttered a lot. Carly wasn't quite sure how she was going to manage on a horse without sending it into a blind bolt. And, as luck would have it, there was a well-endowed blonde. Her name was Leigh Bliss—appropriate, Carly thought, if the looks the men were giving her were any indication.

One of those men was so bumbling and urgent he set her teeth on edge. His name was Winston Meyer and he reminded her of a very large, very eager puppy, inclined to act before he thought. Carly let her gaze wander away from him to Reggie Toppman. Compared to Winston, he was compact and solid, but he was taciturn and grimly watchful.

Then there were the Johnny-come-latelies. Well, *one* of the Johnny-come-latelies, she amended. The other one was still back at the house. She'd get to him later.

"Excuse me." She stepped closer to the one she had at her disposal. "I didn't get your name."

The man turned away from his horse and gave her a slow, knowing smile. It made her skin pull into gooseflesh.

Someone walked over my grave, she thought. She shook her head to clear it and looked down at her clipboard.

"Your name?" she repeated impatiently.

"Can you guess?"

Oh, God, was he some kind of nutcase? She looked up at him again. "No time," she explained, trying hard to keep her voice mild and polite.

The man nodded, but he didn't answer her. Carly made a sound of exasperation and turned away.

"Brad Patterson."

Her heart skipped a beat. She spun back to him. *"What?"*

"Brad Patterson. That's my name."

"I . . . oh." She shook her head, feeling foolish.

She had been dwelling far too much on her ex-husband lately, and that was purely Holly's doing. She had stopped missing him a very long time ago. She wrote this man's name, so similar to Brett's, on her clipboard, then she stuck her pencil behind her ear when she heard another sound behind her.

She turned around again and found the other newcomer entering the barn alley. "What about you?"

"What about me?" Jack paused, looking concerned.

"I didn't catch your name."

"Oh. Jack. Jack Fain." He smiled—almost.

The instinct she'd felt when she'd first seen him in the barn-yard came back to Carly hard and fast. There was something off about this guy, too, she thought despairingly. Why couldn't Michael have just sent her a bunch of nice, normal city folks?

A niggling, uncertain feeling came to the pit of her stomach when she looked at Jack Fain. He was supremely confident—maybe that was all it was. She sensed that he was a man who needed no one, and she had a hunch that he would prefer it if no one needed him either.

He was attractive in a rough sort of way, she allowed. Well, okay, he was *very* attractive, and she felt a subtle physical pull toward him. But she simply didn't have time for that, so she clamped down on it, trying to judge his face dispassionately.

His were the kind of looks that had probably been arrest-ingly handsome ten years ago. Now his face was handsome *and* it contained character. What kind remained to be seen. His eyes were an odd color, a sort of leonine gold, and they said that he'd seen it all and found most of it humorous, albeit in a dark and twisted way. His smile was a slow, incomplete quirking of his mouth. There were faint lines at the corners of his eyes. All in all, she thought, he looked rough, hard, capable . . . and somehow dangerous.

"Is this mine?" he asked, stopping beside the last available gelding.

Carly nodded, still watching him pensively.

"What's wrong with his ear?" He stepped closer to examine it.

"He had a run-in with some barbed wire last summer." Her voice sounded defensive, and that annoyed her. "Don't worry. It won't affect his performance."

Jack muttered something she couldn't hear.

She explained what she wanted him to do with the horse and he set about grooming it. As she watched, his horse planted its left front hoof stubbornly, refusing to allow him to lift it and clean out the shoe. Carly stiffened out of pure instinct as he moved around in front of the animal, but he only closed one strong-looking hand over the beast's muzzle, bringing its eyes on a level with his own. He said something to it in an under-tone and the horse lifted its foot.

Carly's mouth twitched, and then she frowned again. "Mr. Fain?"

He looked up at her.

"Just out of curiosity, have you ever been within spitting distance of a horse before?"

"Nope. Never."

"You certainly have a . . . uh, way with them."

"Just a natural talent, I guess." His mouth went halfway into that grin again.

Carly played with the end of her braid. He went on working with the animal with absolutely no trace of the skittish wariness that most people displayed the first time they came nose to muzzle with an animal so much larger than themselves. Winston, on the other hand, was clearly terrified. She glanced over at the big man and thought that it was going to be a very long week.

"Okay," she said finally. "Now that you've got them all cleaned up, we're going to tack them." She lifted her own Western saddle from the portable rack she had wheeled into the barn alley. "First, just watch me."

She began explaining what she was doing as she stepped into her own mare's stall and put the saddle on her. Then she had the guests do the same thing with their own horses. Winston more or less threw his in the general vicinity of his mount. His gelding shot out with one irritated hoof, just missing him.

"Gently," she clarified, rubbing her eyes. She should be over at the chutes helping with the castrating and the branding. She should be bringing in the last of the cows from the far pastures, the ones who wouldn't calve this year but were going to Kansas anyway. She should be—

"Can we get hurt doing this?" Winston asked.

"Well, sure, if you're stupid," she answered, startled. She'd thought that was pretty much a given.

"I think I made a mistake," Leigh piped up. "My horse doesn't look like yours."

Carly groaned silently. "Move over."

She went to the blonde's horse, nudging her out of the way. She started to fix her saddle for her, then she felt warm breath on her nape where her braid left her skin exposed. She whipped around and found Jack Fain.

The fact that he had moved from his own horse to Leigh's so fast, so silently, unnerved her all over again. Or maybe it was just the tickle of his breath on her nape. God knew it had been a long time since she'd felt such a thing.

She fought the urge to shiver with the memory of it. Even the fact that the urge was there for her to fight left her mildly shaken.

"You want to give me some room here?" she demanded too harshly.

Jack stepped back a little. A very little. "Sorry. I couldn't see what you were doing."

For the life of her, she couldn't remember what she had been about to do next.

She forced herself to turn her back on him again. She did it with a last slow, wary glance.

She finished with Leigh's horse and stepped away just as the dinner gong rang out from the house. "Lunchtime," she announced breathlessly.

She left the barn without looking back to see if they followed her. By the time she reached the porch, she heard them chattering like a flock of crows as they streamed after her. She held the door open for them, then Jack Fain passed her. She found herself inching backward to give him a wider berth.

It was Brad Patterson she ought to be keeping an eye on, she thought, catching that man watching her again with a strange, intent smile. She was starting to think he was definitely a loose cannon.

They all moved into the kitchen, and she stepped in behind them. Her great-great-grandfather had built the house with an extended family in mind, and the kitchen table seated twenty in a pinch. The little knot of tourists looked lost as they gathered at one end.

Carly went to the head of the table and they all grabbed chairs and sat. Theresa brought a platter of fried chicken and a large pitcher of iced tea. Carly filled her plate and her glass, then she felt Jack's eyes upon her.

He had taken the seat directly to her left. After a moment, his gaze moved from her face to her plate.

"Hungry?"

"If you don't grab it fast, you might have to do without," she explained shortly.

One of his brows went up, but then the back door creaked open again and Plank and Gofer, the two full-time cowboys she still managed to employ, came into the kitchen. Then there was a soft thump on the back stairs and Holly joined them as well.

"Ah," Jack said. "He who hesitates goes hungry."

Under other circumstances, she might have smiled. "Now you're catching on."

He reached for the chicken platter with no more apology than she had displayed. Carly watched Holly. Her daughter's eyes stayed sullenly on her plate, and it made her throat squeeze. Theresa followed the chicken with a steady stream of biscuits, corn and mashed potatoes. Carly realized that Jack was watching her sister now.

"Is she coming with us on this trip?" he asked.

"Yes." Carly bit hungrily into a leg.

"Can she ride a horse in that condition?"

"No."

He looked back at her quizzically. "So. . ." he prompted.

"So she drives the ones that pull the cook wagon."

"Drives?"

She paused in midchew to mime the snapping of a whip over a team of horses. "Giddy-up."

"Oh." He was silent for a moment. "You don't let much stand between you and your food, do you?"

Carly deliberately swallowed a mouthful of corn before she answered him. "Lunch is for eating, not for inane conversation."

She heard Holly suck in an appalled breath at her rudeness, conveniently forgetting that *she* didn't think much of the tourists either. Then again, Jack was a man, and Holly was more than a little critical of her mother's interaction with anything in pants.

Carly reached for her tea, feeling suddenly cornered, as if any step she took was wrong. Jack Fain closed a hand over her forearm before she could touch her glass.

Something happened to her. She was aware of a frisson of heat shooting through her. It was much stronger than the shivery flutter that had gone through her when he'd breathed on her neck in the barn.

"What do you think you're doing?" she gasped.

"Mom!" Holly cried.

"We're going to have to try to get along a little more amicably here, cowgirl," Jack said quietly.

Carly tried to pull her arm back. He wouldn't let her go. "Why?" she demanded.

"Well, I'm your guest, for one thing. I don't want to be locking horns with you all week."

That was certainly reasonable, but her temper was beyond caring. "I haven't locked *anything* with you yet," she snapped, "but keep it up and I'll be more than happy to oblige."

Holly groaned. Theresa jumped in brightly, sensing trouble at the other end of the table.

"So what brings all of you to the Wild, Wild West?"

Jack finally released her arm. Carly pulled it back, rubbing it, frowning at him angrily.

"I have my own electronics firm," Reggie said quietly when no one immediately answered. "I wanted to go somewhere where there wouldn't be any phones."

Winston stopped chewing long enough to nod. "Same here," he said urgently. "I've got a meat-packing company. You've no idea how the smells can get to you after a while. I wanted fresh air. At least here the cattle are alive."

Theresa looked quickly at Winston, obviously trying to get Winston off the subject of his factory smells and dead animals while everyone was eating. "What about you?"

"I have a birthday this week," said Myra. "No, I won't tell you how old and I won't tell you which day, but just once, before I get too old, I want to do something. . . ." She trailed off to shiver. Carly stopped chewing again to stare at her. "Something *wild*," she finished.

"I want a cowboy," Leigh contributed.

Gofer leaned across the table toward her. "You've found yourself one, ma'am."

There was a chorus of nervous laughter, then everyone looked pointedly at Jack and Brad, the only two who hadn't answered.

"I'm taking the long way to nowhere," Brad said finally, enigmatically, and the odd comment made Carly's skin pull tight. Then he smiled sheepishly. "I'm a poet," he explained.

"What about you, Mr. Fain?" Theresa asked.

Carly paused with her next piece of chicken halfway to her mouth. She angled her gaze toward him. She was very interested in hearing this.

"Call me Jack," he said after a moment.

Carly waited.

"I'm hiding from an ex-wife," he added finally.

"Is she big and mean with a double-barreled shotgun?" Carly didn't really intend that anyone should hear her, but Jack answered fast and easily.

"Nope. She's a redhead."

Laughter rippled across the table again. It was more relaxed this time. Six strangers were becoming friends.

"My lawyer's serving her with the divorce papers this week," Jack went on. "I thought it would be a good idea for me to get out of town."

"I hear Acapulco's lovely this time of year," Carly drawled.

"Then you hear wrong. It's too hot."

She pushed her chair back abruptly. "If we're going to get everything done by Friday, I have to get you people on horses ten minutes ago."

They all looked up at her, surprised. At least half of them were still chewing.

"Carlotta..." Theresa chided, but Carly had no intention of listening to a dissertation on her manners right now. Her manners could be damned. Manners weren't going to keep these fools on horses across two hundred and fifty miles. There would be strays to chase down, rivers to cross and who knew what else. She wouldn't be able to baby-sit them once they set off. They were going to have to be able to handle their mounts reasonably well on their own.

Besides, she thought, Jack Fain was making her nervous.

Jack watched her slam her way through the back door. She ate like a fullback, he thought, but there wasn't a spare piece of meat on her. He was relatively sure that if he ever peeled those jeans off her he would find lean, fluid muscles beneath satin skin. And it shook him again to realize that he was even thinking of peeling those jeans off her.

Scorpion's woman, he reminded himself. And that was only the first of the reasons why it was probably a good idea to leave her jeans the hell alone.

He stood up to follow her, and for one brief, deadly moment, he forgot where the assassin was. The man came in on him from his left. Jack stopped short, the hairs on his nape lifting. The assassin gave him an odd look at the way he froze. Jack hooked his hat down over his eyes and waited for some flare of understanding or recognition on the man's face anyway.

Nothing happened.

Scorpion passed him, brushing close enough to him that Jack could smell his madness—a sour, lingering sort of thing that was perhaps purely in Jack's imagination. He went outside and Jack followed him, watching a moment to make sure he stayed with the others. Then he lengthened his stride to catch up with Carly Castagne.

"Hold up there, cowgirl."

She spun back to him. "Don't call me that!"

"Sorry. Carly." He paused. "Carlotta doesn't suit you," he realized again, aloud. He thought she almost smiled.

"That's the first sensible thing you've said yet. No one but Theresa and Michael call me by my full name, so don't get into that habit, either."

She started walking again. He fell into step beside her.

"Look," she went on, flashing those eyes up at him. "I've really got to get you folks practicing your riding so I can run over to the chutes. I don't have time to chat with you, Mr. Fain."

"Jack. And I'd like to go with you."

That stopped her again. "To the chutes? What for?"

"It sounds like something it might be interesting to see."

Scorpion was four steps behind him, still to his left. He was talking intently to Myra. It made Jack uncomfortable for Myra's sake, but there wasn't a thing he could do about it. He let his attention drift back to Carly and his grin spread more fully this time.

"Is it me you don't like," he heard himself ask, "or is it men in general?" And even he wondered what this could possibly have to do with Scorpion.

Carly gasped, hearing an echo of so many of Holly's accusations. It hurt. Then there was the fact that she really *had* been trying to be reasonably polite, at least until he had ticked her off at lunch.

"What have I done?" she cried.

"It's subtle," he allowed. "Sort of a grudge with nothing to hang it on."

"Well, even if I *had* a grudge, I can't think what business it might be of yours."

"Humor me."

She decided to do it, just for the hell of it, just to see what his reaction would be. "Okay. I don't like you."

He'd expected her to be honest, and he wasn't disappointed. He half smiled. "I can't think of anything I've done to set you on edge."

"How about that business back at the house?" Suddenly she was angry. "I don't trust you, Mr. Fain." And she didn't, she realized. But it was just a feeling...with nothing to hang it on. He just seemed dangerous. Cold and calculating and... different somehow.

She went on doggedly, admittedly fishing. "If you've got a redheaded ex-wife, then my father is going to come walking into this barnyard at any moment. And let me tell you, *that* would startle a few people, myself included."

"Why?"

"Because Dad died eleven years ago."

Jack felt a knock of surprise. She said it so flatly—but then he saw her eyes change, going darker.

"I'm sorry."

"Don't be. I'm over it. Now."

"Are you?"

"Sure. He's gone. I'm here. And he left a lot of responsibility on my shoulders, so if you'll excuse me, I'll go see to some of it."

There was some strong bitterness there, he realized. He would think about that later. For now he wondered where Scorpion fit into this. Coincidentally, the assassin had first killed in Dallas at roughly the same time this woman's father had died.

Jack began walking after her again.

"Who's Michael?" he asked, probing. He already knew, of course. When he'd called Paul earlier, he'd found out. "Your husband?"

Carly glanced over her shoulder at him. "No. My brother." She meant to leave it at that. But there was something intrusive about him, some edge that genuinely seemed to want to know more. "My *ex*-husband went scurrying off after someone who looked very much like Leigh, as a matter of fact, tripping over his tongue the whole way. She showed up on a Tuesday looking for a job. On Thursday, they were both gone."

Ah, Jack thought. So that was how it had ended for Scorpion in Oklahoma. There was a *lot* of bitterness there, Jack amended. He realized again that Scorpion was going to have his hands full if his plan was to tell Carlotta who he was so that he could get in her bed. He'd have a hard time even if he *didn't* tell her who he was, if he just tried to start up with her from scratch. The bastard had left some scars behind.

"We're not all that bad," he heard himself answer.

Carly pulled ahead of him. "Who?" she asked.

"Men. In general."

She shook her head. He wasn't sure if it indicated denial or disinterest. "I've got work to do."

"Well, we're not."

She grabbed her hat from a fence post and plunked it back on her head so that he could no longer see her eyes. "Not all of us wander off after we've committed ourselves to something," he went on.

One of her brows disappeared beneath her hat brim. "You couldn't prove it by me."

Jack went on the offensive. He told himself he was doing it to gather information. He told himself he wanted to know for sure how she'd react if Scorpion revealed himself to her. "So it's safer for you to stay ticked off at men than to give another one a chance to let you down?" he said, guessing. "Is that it?"

Her face closed down. "Will you please excuse me?"

She told herself she was definitely going to walk away from him this time. But then his eyes moved strangely, slanting a little toward the other guests. Carly followed his gaze, frowning. None of them appeared to be especially impatient.

"What are you doing here?" she asked suddenly, following her instincts. They were fairly clamoring now. "You could have gone a million places if you just wanted to escape an ex-wife. Why Oklahoma?"

His golden eyes came back to her and he tipped his hat. "I wanted to learn how to ride a horse and castrate steers, ma'am."

He went to join the others. She watched him go, her eyes narrowing.

"And pigs can fly," she muttered, her heart thumping.

Chapter 3

Carly left the guests in the paddocks to practice their riding. She organized them in a buddy system, hoping to prevent any major misadventure or injury. She put Winston and Leigh in one pen, with Reggie and Brad in the next. She put Jack Fain with Myra in the last one, not sure why she felt so smug about separating him from the blonde.

She'd asked Theresa to watch over them from the house. She wasn't overjoyed at leaving them to their own devices, but she couldn't figure out any other way to do everything she had to do today. If the calves weren't castrated by dusk, it wouldn't matter how well the guests learned to ride. They wouldn't be going anywhere.

There was also the matter of Holly, she thought. While she was working with the guests, she had noticed her daughter striding purposefully down the driveway, her long brown hair swinging, her hands shoved with too-deliberate insouciance into the pockets of her shorts. As soon as she was able, Carly swung up on her mare and cantered after her.

"Where are you headed?" she asked when she caught up with her.

Holly continued walking. "Becky's."

Carly swallowed a groan. Becky was trouble with a capital *T*. She was fourteen, and had just finished her freshman year at high school. Carly hadn't yet figured out why Becky would want to hang around with an eleven-year-old, but nothing she could think of was good.

Still, she refrained from saying so. She could already hear Holly's response. *You have to make something bad out of everything. Why do you have to ruin everything? I'll bet that's why my dad left.*

And Carly would have to fight herself against telling her that she had never *had* a dad, that she'd had a biological father who'd been gone by the time she was born. It tore Carly's heart out every time they had the fight, and she avoided it whenever possible.

"I really could use your help around here today," she said finally, instead.

"Becky's *dad* is taking us to the roller rink."

And there it was. The gauntlet was thrown. Carly stepped carefully over it.

"Not today, honey. It's just not possible. I need you here."

Holly stopped and looked up, her eyes on fire. "*Why?* You said—"

"Please," Carly interrupted. Then she heard her own pleading tone, and she was angry at herself.

The kid was eleven years old! Holly *needed* parental authority, not some woman who was tiptoeing around her, wary of starting a fight! So why did Carly always feel so guilty for laying down the law?

Because you can't give her a daddy.

"Not today," she said again, tightly. "Aunt Theresa's watching the guests to make sure nobody falls off. But if they do, there's not a lot she'll be able to do about it in her condition. So hang around for a while just in case she needs your help. I'll drive you to the rink myself, tomorrow."

She turned her mare around before Holly could protest any further. How she was going to find the time to drive into town tomorrow was anybody's guess.

Holly watched her mother go. Her throat hurt. She *hated* this place! All anybody ever did was work. What her mom needed was a foreman—she had heard her and Aunt Tee talking about that a lot. Then maybe she wouldn't be so busy all the time.

Maybe she'd be nicer. Maybe she'd find a husband. Maybe they'd be *normal*.

Holly felt tears burn at her eyes. As far as she was concerned, there was nothing worse in the world than being different.

Then, suddenly Holly's thoughts broke off as something interesting happened back at the paddocks. One of those goofy tourists—the one who was kind of handsome, even if he was old—left the place where he was supposed to be riding and went after her mom.

Holly started walking back toward the house. Something strange and squirmy happened to her heart. Something like hope.

Maybe hanging around this afternoon wouldn't be so bad after all.

Carly passed the paddocks and took off down a well-worn path that ran beside them. Jack let her go maybe a hundred yards before he went after her.

She had expressly warned them not to do anything other than walk their horses and get used to them. She'd said she'd be back within the hour and they could speed things up then. But by the time Jack cleared the fences, she was nearly out of sight. The rutted trail wound its way past a huge oak that spread out its ageless branches to shield the sun from that part of the path. He lost her in the shadows there.

There was no help for it.

"Giddy-up," he muttered to his horse, feeling foolish. "Come on, you old beast, get the lead out." The horse twitched its ugly, split ear and plodded along obstinately.

Well, when in Rome, Jack thought. He didn't have spurs but he figured he could make up for that with impact. He thumped his heels hard into the animal's sides.

The horse bolted.

It happened so abruptly that Jack almost toppled backward. He grabbed the saddle horn to keep himself from falling. He lost his hat, but it didn't matter because Scorpion was back in the paddocks and with any luck he would stay there. Luck was half the game, after all.

Jack had almost reached her when he finally made some sense of the horse's rhythm and instinctively began moving his hips along with it. It didn't matter. Carly Castagne was hot as a hornet anyway.

"Let's get one thing straight, *cowboy,*" she snapped when he sawed on his reins, stopping beside her. "When I say jump, *then* you jump. If I say stand still, you don't move a muscle. Got it? There are five other people in this group and I won't let you put them in danger of getting hurt. If you had done this stupid, imbecile, macho act while they were still close to you, every one of their horses would have taken off after you! And maybe *they* wouldn't have had your thick-brained luck and stayed on!"

Jack wiped the back of his wrist over his forehead. She had a point and he wouldn't argue with her.

"Sorry. I have a few questions."

Impossibly, suddenly, Carly felt like crying. She did *not* need this. There was so much work to be done between now and the time they left, it was mind-boggling. And she had just added another errand to the list.

By next week this feeling of helpless desperation would pass. She knew that. It always did after the dust settled from these auction trips. But right now the last thing in the world she needed was six tourists on her hands, one of whom was arrogant, hardheaded and looking at her with golden eyes that made her feel ... entirely too much like a woman again.

Her heart constricted as she realized that that was what had been bothering her about him from the start. It was the *way* he looked at her, as if he knew her. As if he knew every good, sweet thing about her. And to hear Holly tell it, there were precious few of those.

But her mind was reluctant to stay on Holly now.

He had lost his hat. His hair was golden, too, she noticed for the first time. He must have spent a good bit of time outdoors in the not-too-distant past, because it was sun-bleached, almost two-toned, with streaks of rich brown near the roots.

She didn't have time to be noticing this.

She didn't *want* to notice, she thought, panicked. She had been alone for a very long time now, and she had learned that the best way to handle that was to avoid the ache that inevitably came when she allowed herself to think about what she was missing.

Jack watched her lay her calves ever so gently against her mare's ribs. Her horse started moving again. He followed her lead and his own horse began walking sedately beside hers. Easy enough, he thought, if you knew what you were doing.

"What do you want to know?" she asked wearily.

He'd meant to ask her about the terrain they'd be crossing and heard himself wonder instead, "Don't you have *anyone* to help you around here?"

Her chin came up a notch, almost as though she was warding off the world. Alone. He had seen her eyes change for a moment there, going vulnerable, looking overwhelmed for the space of a heartbeat. For the first time he wondered what her life was like. It struck him that it probably wasn't easy, and it was about to get worse. He felt an alarming, amazing shaft of regret.

A pawn. She's just a pawn.

"Plank and Gofer," Carly answered flatly. He had almost forgotten his question. "And two other part-time guys on those rare occasions when I can pay them."

"You're the owner, right?"

"One-third. Along with my sister—Theresa—and my brother, who you probably won't meet. There hasn't been enough money in recent years to hire too much help."

She rode with easy grace, just slouched enough to appear thoroughly relaxed . . . or very tired.

"I didn't realize Theresa was your sister," he said idly, digging.

Carly shrugged. That startled everybody. Theresa was so voluptuous and feminine, even when she wasn't pregnant, and she had those big, dark eyes. They didn't look much alike.

"She takes after my father," Carly said. "She got all the Spanish genes. I caught a few from my mother's side."

"So where's your mother?"

"Dead, like Dad."

Jack's brows shot up.

"Cancer got Mom," she went on, reading his expression. "Then Dad just . . . died. He wasn't much without her."

"And you were left to hold everything together," Jack guessed.

Carly scowled at him. "It wasn't like that," she said defensively. *Yes, it was.*

"Whose idea was it to take in tourists?"

She flinched visibly. "The IRS."

Ah, Jack thought. "And Holly's your daughter?"

She slanted her eyes his way again. "Well, aren't you just smarter than the average bear?"

Jack's mouth quirked halfway to a grin. "She looks like you."

"No. She looks like her father."

Not really, Jack thought, not if they were talking about Scorpion. Still, it had been a very long time since Scorpion had looked like himself, and Jack wanted to make sure.

"The guy who went after the blonde?" he asked. "So Holly is . . . what? About eleven?"

Carly nodded.

They were coming up on the chutes. Jack could see a knot of people working in the distance. "So how rough is this country we're going to be crossing?" he asked suddenly.

Her spine straightened a little at the change of subject. "Don't worry. I'll get everyone over it, man and beast alike. I always do."

"Describe it to me."

Carly scowled at him. "Why? You'll see it when you see it. I wouldn't take you anywhere that I didn't think you could get through, believe me."

"Call it inherent caution."

A sensation like butterflies fluttered briefly in her tummy. It didn't have anything to do with the way he looked at her this time. It was all well and good to take his money, she thought, to drag him across Oklahoma and Kansas and deposit him at the other end of the trail. But for the first time she wondered if it was going to be that simple.

His curiosity seemed . . . inordinate. Then again, she reasoned, she really *wasn't* good with people, she had never run a dude ranch before, and she couldn't have said with any certainty just how a tourist was supposed to act and how many questions one could be expected to ask.

She finally decided there was no real harm in telling him what he wanted to know.

"The first hundred, maybe hundred and fifty miles, are rough," she began. "The land rolls a lot. There are chasms, some deep ones the closer we get to the Kansas border. We've

got to cross both the North Canadian and the Cimarron rivers, and that's no treat.''

"Trees?"

She looked at him oddly. "Around the rivers. The rest of the
way is pretty barren."

"What kind of chasms?"

"The soil around here is rocky. Rain doesn't get absorbed
very well. It runs off to lower ground. Fast. So what you're left
with is a lot of natural erosion."

"What happens at the border?"

"Everything flattens out and the soil turns more loamy. Then
we're pretty much into prairie and it's only maybe a hundred
miles the rest of the way to the auction yards at Fort Dodge."

"What can we expect by way of weather?"

Carly grimaced. "Absolutely anything at all. It's June."

"What does that mean?"

"It means we're into tornado season. Even short of twisters, the weather's unpredictable around here in the summer. We
usually get our fair share of storms. We just hope that there's
no cold front coming in to clash with the heat. And if one *does*
come in, then we pray that it comes slowly."

"Or what?"

"Or we find ourselves a long way from Kansas, Toto."

He let out a rumble of laughter. The sound played seduc-
tively over her skin. Carly looked at him sharply.

"Anything else?" she asked shortly.

They had reached the chutes. He could barely hear her now
over the bawling and bleating of the calves, and the shouts of
the men. The air stung his eyes. It was thick and grainy with
dust.

"It hasn't rained lately," he observed.

"No. It's been pretty dry all spring, and that worries me.
Usually when it's been dry for a while, we have a lot of storms
in a short period of time as though to make up for it."

Jack nodded. He watched her gaze dart to the men, and her
green eyes darkened as she saw something that didn't please
her.

"I'd better get back and practice my riding," he said finally.

Carly's mouth widened slowly, tantalizingly, until it became
the first true grin he'd seen from her. It transformed her face,

he realized, made her look much, much more like the girl in the photograph.

It also did odd things to his breathing.

"Why bother?" she countered. "I guess you're just about stubborn enough to hang on to that pony even if one of those twisters carried you both a mile."

Jack felt his own mouth twitch. "It's entirely possible, cowgirl."

"Don't call me that!" But she wasn't sure he heard her. He turned his horse around and set off at a neat canter.

Carly watched him go until someone called out to her from the chutes. "I'm coming!" she shouted back. She pulled her mare around and picked her up into a trot.

Jack's heart doubled, then tripled its rate as he headed back to the paddocks. For a while, talking with the cowgirl, he had relaxed, had almost forgotten about Scorpion. Now he wondered what the assassin had been up to while he was gone.

It wasn't unusual for him to actually lose sight of the man. He could hardly sleep with him, couldn't watch him every moment without the assassin becoming dangerously aware of him as well. Jack had always made do with creeping along behind him, sometimes into his hotel rooms after he'd left them, moving through twisted streets and blackened alleys, chasing the rumor of his presence. More than once he'd actually been able to interfere with a hit, saving the unsuspecting mark once he'd figured out who it was. But then São Paulo had changed everything.

Now, when he couldn't actually see Scorpion, he had to wonder if the assassin was behind him. It brought an itchy, hot feeling to the back of Jack's neck.

This time there was the added disadvantage that Scorpion could, theoretically, disappear into thousands of empty, arid miles at any given moment. Jack felt nervous perspiration slide down his back at that prospect before he reminded himself that it was a long shot. Now that the assassin had come here, it was highly unlikely that he would move on without Carly Castagne. Besides, there seemed to be something about leaving on Saturday that appealed to him.

Unless that had been a red herring.

There were too damned many variables here, Jack thought again, grimly. He felt as if he was floundering, groping, in a way he never had before. He rubbed his scar.

He would revise his game plan, he decided. Carly Castagne had enough on her mind, apparently including problems with her daughter, if that scene he had witnessed down on the drive was any indication. He decided suddenly that he wasn't going to let Scorpion make contact with her after all. It had nothing to do with the possibility that she might succumb to the man all over again, even with a different face and name. It had everything to do with wanting to get in and out of her life fast, before she even felt the ripple.

She didn't need any more ripples.

It didn't strike him to wonder why he felt so protective of her. He didn't want to wonder if he was actually protecting himself, that maybe, just maybe, his scattered instincts had nothing to do with a new scar... and everything to do with his fascination with the woman who was supposed to bring the other guy down.

He turned into the paddock again and rode behind Myra, then flinched at a voice behind him. He didn't like voices behind him.

"Hi there."

He looked around. It was Carly's daughter. Scorpion's daughter. And hell, *there* was a whole new worry. How long before the bastard realized that the kid was eleven years old? How long before he put two and two together? Jack realized that the assassin hadn't spared the kid much attention. So far.

There was yet another thing he'd have to dig up an explanation for.

"Hi yourself," he answered warily. He had never been real comfortable with kids. Maybe because he had never been one himself.

"Were you talking with my mom?" she asked.

"Uh . . . yeah."

"What about?"

"Stuff."

"What kind of stuff?"

"The trail."

"Oh." She seemed disappointed. What the hell did she think they'd been discussing?

"She's not really mean," Holly went on. "Not really."

Jack scowled. "I don't think she's mean." And why was he discussing this with a kid?

"You don't? Did she do that thing with her chin?"

"What thing?" Jack asked cautiously.

"You know." The kid tipped her own up. She did a remarkable imitation of Carly's eyes narrowing with determination. Jack realized with some surprise that he was on the verge of laughing. In that moment, she looked exactly like her mother.

And *that* made Jack wonder what Scorpion's reaction to such a sight would be. He stiffened and gave a careful look in the man's direction.

"Don't you have something better to do than bug me?" he asked shortly. Something in the house, he thought. Something as far away as possible from the man who was her father.

Holly's chin came down. Then her eyes widened. Then she smiled. "Wow."

"Wow *what?*" Jack demanded.

"You're just like her."

Chapter 4

It was full dark and the moon was a perfect white ball in the sky when Carly was satisfied enough with their progress to call it a night. Faces were grim all the way around when she finally told them to stop riding.

She stood waiting for them beneath a rusty lantern hanging on the barn wall. It threw a yellow oval of light down that ringed her like a spotlight, the central character in a play she didn't even know was about to unfold.

Jack was surprised by another faint stirring of regret in his gut.

"Okay, everybody, take your horses into the barn and un-saddle them," she called out. "Lay the saddle pads *up* so the sweaty sides can dry overnight. Otherwise you're going to have an itchy horse in the morning, and he's going to be none too pleased to have you climb aboard again. After you've done that, you've got to walk them down. Put your hands on their chests a second. Feel how hot and damp they are? When your horse is cool to the touch and perfectly dry, *then* you can brush him and put him back in his stall.

"After that, your time's your own," she finished, "but I'd recommend getting some sleep. We'll start up again with the rooster tomorrow morning. Leigh, you'll be bunking with

Myra. Jack, you'll be in with Brad. Sorry we don't have private rooms, but I don't guess Michael promised you the Ritz. Any questions?''

She watched them, working the rubber band out of the end of her hair as she waited. Jack felt something catch him about the throat and squeeze.

When she got the band out, her hair fell clear to her waist and it was the color of a midnight sky. She worked her fingers through it but it was still wavy from the braid. It transformed her, making her look exotic and hauntingly beautiful. The moonlight and the lantern cast shadows across her face. They marked her cheekbones, darkened her eyes.

Carly glanced his way and saw the way he was looking at her. Her breath stopped halfway into her lungs and a feeling of expectancy, of need, hit her out of nowhere.

Need for something you can't have, an unbidden voice whispered nastily. She took an automatic step backward, feeling too shaken.

Jack Fain wasn't interested in her, at least not that way, she reminded herself. No matter what his eyes said, he called her cowgirl, and the implication was clear. There was Leigh—all woman—and then there was her—all workhorse. She didn't want to admit that it hurt.

"What's your problem?" she managed finally. Her voice lacked a lot of its usual spunk.

Jack shook himself, managing half a grin. "Don't have one, cowgirl. Not a one."

"Well . . . good." Carly breathed again carefully and forced her legs to carry her back to the house.

Jack moved his eyes deliberately to the temperamental beast who was his companion for the duration. He had lied. He had two *big* problems. He had to start keeping his mind off the cowgirl, at least in the carnal way it was starting to wander. And the sleeping arrangements were another major snafu.

He led the horse into the barn and untacked it, working over the pros and cons of this new possibility of bunking with Scorpion—Brad, he called himself this week. Was it better to keep close to him, or would the assassin somehow recognize him if he did? His horse felt only marginally cooler by the time Jack made his decision. He pushed the animal into its stall, and its big, brown eyes came around to him reproachfully.

"Too damned bad, buddy," Jack muttered. "I've got things to take care of here. You're just going to have to itch."

He left the beast and hurried into the house. Theresa was in the kitchen, but there was no sign of Carly. The others were still outside, walking their horses down dutifully. The cowboys had retired some time ago.

"Where's Carly?" Jack demanded.

Theresa looked startled. "I'm not sure. She passed through here a moment ago like her tail was on fire."

Jack let himself wonder about that for a moment. He thought of the way she had looked at him before she had demanded to know what was on his mind. For a brief moment, so lightning fast he thought now that he might have imagined it, the yearning on her face had touched him in a place he hadn't been aware of having.

He cleared his throat carefully, and couldn't think of a single response.

"What happened out there?" Theresa went on. "She seemed angry."

Jack didn't think angry was precisely what she had been.

Once again, he got a slow, careful grip on himself. Protecting her, keeping Scorpion from making contact with her, was one thing. Letting her get under *his* skin was something else entirely.

"Where does she usually go when she comes in for the night?" he asked neutrally.

"Usually to the parlor for a brandy. Then she takes it upstairs and unwinds before she takes a shower. Sometimes she comes back down to the office and works a little longer on the books, but you can't ever count on that." Theresa grimaced. "It depends on how upset she's been about finances lately."

"Is she upset now?"

Theresa hesitated, then nodded.

"How bad are they?" *Cool it.* It was enough to know that they were in trouble with the IRS. He could use that if he had to as leverage to get them to cooperate with him on the off-chance that this chase deteriorated into chaos.

Theresa seemed reluctant to talk about it anyway. He was a guest, after all.

She finally shook her head. "Carlotta will fix it."

Jack was a little astounded by her blind, naive trust.

"Where's the parlor?" he asked after a moment. "Maybe I can still catch her."

Theresa pointed him in the right direction.

He found the room with no difficulty, but then he went still in the door. There was only one light. It was perched on the fireplace mantel and it cast a soft glow. Carly stood at a window beside a sideboard that held a few crystal decanters and some glasses. Her hair was still long and free, and the side of her face that he could see was vulnerable again.

He must have made some sound because she stiffened and looked over her shoulder at him, straightening away from the window fast. "*Now* what?" she asked a little breathlessly.

Jack moved into the room and nodded at the sideboard. "Do I get a glass of that for my money?"

"No." Then the fight seemed to drain out of her. "I don't care. Help yourself."

"What's wrong?" he asked, pouring.

"Where would you like me to start?"

That almost-smile haunted his face for a moment, then was gone. "Everything seems to be going all right with your guests," he pointed out. "Winston ought to be riding bulls by tomorrow at the latest."

Carly startled herself by chuckling. She wouldn't have thought she had it in her tonight.

Jack sipped, then he put his glass on the sideboard again. "Listen, I need a couple of things from you."

Carly scowled, then she nodded. She didn't seem pleased, he thought, but being needed clearly didn't surprise her in the least.

"First of all, I need to change my room," he went on.

She surprised him with a sudden, intense look. "There's something off about Brad, isn't there?"

Jack felt his gut clench. "Why would you say that?"

"Why don't you want to room with him?" she countered.

He said the first thing that came into his mind. "Because he has a strong case of body odor."

Her jaw dropped, then she laughed outright. It was a full, rich sound, exactly as he would have imagined from her picture. She had so many layers, he realized suddenly. He hadn't anticipated her wary bitterness toward men, yet he wasn't surprised by these transient bursts of warmth, either. Unfortunately, the problem with layers was that getting to the bottom of them meant digging. And the concept of depth had always bothered him.

It implied roots, he thought, clinging, tenacious things that held you only as long as they chose to. Then they abandoned you, leaving you tumbling, free-falling, alone. He knew that all too well. And even if he had been a man who was willing to risk it, he sure as hell couldn't start digging with *this* woman.

Scorpion's woman.

"There are bathrooms upstairs, too," Carly finally pointed out, and Jack dragged himself back to the conversation.

"Are *you* going to tell him he needs to wash?"

Carly sobered. "I'd rather not. What's the point? I guess we'll all smell pretty ripe by the time we get to Kansas."

"So can't I just change rooms?"

She shook her head. "Not easily. Not without making a big fuss and embarrassing him. I can't put you in with Winston because there's only one bed in there. Unless you want to cuddle up with him real cozy-like."

"I'll pass."

"I thought so."

"So what about Reggie?"

"Same thing. One bed. Except his is only a twin. This was never meant to be a hotel," she said, and the tight set to her jaw made him feel almost sorry for her. Then her chin came up, and he was just impressed.

"Two weeks ago, it was just my home," she went on. "And the only rooms with twin beds are the ones Leigh and Myra are in, and yours and Brad's. Sorry, but I couldn't special-order new furniture for this shindig."

Okay, Jack thought. He'd work around it. Now it was time for the thing that was *really* going to get a rise out of her.

"The other thing is that I'd like to leave on Thursday."

He got pretty much the reaction he expected. First there was disbelief that he should make such an outrageous request. Then anger flared in her eyes. He'd decided to tell her that he'd gotten an urgent message from home, and hope that she didn't check it out with Theresa to find out that he hadn't received any calls. He'd tell her that he had to go home sooner than he'd planned, and he was concerned about fitting the whole trip in.

Given her problems with the IRS, he was willing to gamble that she'd acquiesce rather than refund his money.

Now he wasn't so sure.

"Look," he began, ready to cajole, then he broke off. There was a distant, buzzing, cracking sound from somewhere at the back of the house. He heard her incredulous cry just as the light on the mantel went out, plunging them into darkness.

"I don't believe this!" Carly burst out.

Jack's heart stumbled. He had the sneaking suspicion that the assassin was trying to fix it so that they would leave when he wanted to leave, on Saturday. And Scorpion had beaten him to the draw.

"Move!" Carly gasped. "I have to—"

He grabbed her hand instead and dragged her into the foyer. That was as dark as the parlor had been. Carly began to feel oddly disassociated, lost in her own home.

"Where's the generator?" Jack demanded.

Surprise kicked through her. How could he know that that was what had happened?

"Out back," she managed. "Behind the kitchen, beside the porch."

He began running. "Good place for a fire."

She flinched and went after him. "Isn't it, though?" *All that wood.*

They reached the kitchen. Carly realized with a sick, sinking sensation that she could see here. She could see because orange flames were already licking up the outside wall. They had consumed the kitchen door.

"No," she moaned. "Oh, God, no."

"Where's a fire extinguisher?" Jack shouted over the live, hissing sound of the fire.

Carly was wildly certain that using an extinguisher would be akin to spitting on the flames to put them out—the fire was that bad. She flung open the pantry door anyway, grabbing the extinguisher, and he snatched it out of her hand.

Where were the others? Oh, God, Holly was upstairs in bed, and she had guests all over the ranch!

Carly hesitated, her eyes going helplessly to the back stairs. She and Holly were sharing a room this week, and it was all the way at the front of the house. She'd be safe—*please, God, let her be safe*—because surely this fire could be handled before it went that far. Probably Holly would even smell the smoke and run out the front door on her own. Either way, it would take Carly only a short time to get things under control here, and she had to get things under control here first, *had* to, because there was no one else to do it. Theresa was waddling, pregnant, useless, and nowhere to be found, she realized. If Carly went for Holly first, then the whole house would burn to the ground.

She heard her daughter's name and realized it was her own voice wailing it.

Something angry and violent clawed suddenly at her throat. Damn the ranch! She was sick to death of always putting it first, before her own needs. *Oh, God, just let it burn, then I'll be quit of it.*

Strong hands caught her from behind, pulling her around. "Go on!" Jack shouted. "I'll get Holly. Get out of the house!"

The porch roof collapsed outside. It fell with a *whoofing* roar, and the fire at the door flared brighter.

"Snap out of it!" he yelled. "Go on!"

Carly finally stumbled to the door. She put her hand on the knob and bright pain seared across her palm. She gasped and flinched back.

"Not that way!" Jack hollered. "Open that door, and your kitchen's gone!"

The pain cleared her head. Carly dragged in a deep breath, then coughed as smoke filled her lungs.

She went for the window over the sink instead. She hoisted herself up into the basin even as she heard the hiss of the fire extinguisher behind her. Jack was quickly cooling off the interior surfaces before he went upstairs, keeping all points of combustion wetted down.

Someone to help. Someone to lean on, a precious, extra pair of hands.

She couldn't allow this, she realized, couldn't let him put himself at risk. He was a guest. She looked over her shoulder at him, but he was already gone.

She scrambled out through the window, landing awkwardly. Pain shot up from her ankle, but it wasn't so bad that she couldn't ignore it. She limped around the corner of the house to the back porch. It was already engulfed in flames, but she had known it would be.

She wasn't going to be able to get to the dinner gong to alert Plank and Gofer in the old bunkhouse. She ran, hobbling, for the first barn instead. The guests were still there, gathered outside. Only Jack seemed to have finished with his horse. They were all staring, aghast, at the house, and Theresa was with them.

Carly grabbed the hose there, twisting the spigot, then she thought shakily, *Thank God, Tee's out here*. That left only Holly inside. She thrust the hose at Winston. She was fresh out of nonpregnant family and employees. The guests would have to do.

"Haul it up to the house and start spraying," she told him.

He stared down at it as though a snake had somehow appeared in his hands.

"Now!" Carly cried.

The big man lumbered off. She left and half ran, half hopped, to the next barn, her ankle throbbing now. She grabbed Brad's arm as she passed him and pulled him along with her.

"Here," she gasped. "You can take this other hose."

"What took you so long to get out?"

The question was just strange enough to stop her for a moment. As she stared at him, he took the hose.

"Were you with Jack? What were you doing?"

Her heart started thundering even harder. He seemed angry. Dangerously so. His expression dragged icy fingernails over her skin.

Why? What was it to him?

Before she could pursue it, he dragged the hose away. Carly got the last one available and limped more slowly after him. Winston was aiming a pathetic stream at the house from his nozzle. Almost impossibly, it actually seemed to be doing some good, she realized dazedly.

Then Carly saw that it was *Jack* who was making a difference.

She stumbled and stared at him. He had gotten Holly. Her daughter was helping with the bucket brigade. He'd long since sprayed out the first extinguisher he'd found, and as she watched, he sent Myra to the barns for more. Now he took the hose from Winston and did something to the nozzle. The water sprayed in a more forceful arc.

There was nothing left for her to do.

Nothing.

She forced herself to walk again. By the time she reached the others, the ground was thick, clinging mud. Water dripped from the eaves. The back door was charred and the generator and the porch were unrecognizable. But the fire was out.

She looked dazedly at Jack. A livid burn streaked across his left cheek. That side of his hair was singed, too.

She tried to remember if she had been able to make the last insurance payment on the house.

The adrenaline went out of her fast. She dropped the hose from her nerveless hand and sat in the mud where she stood. Her tears came in a rush, shocking her.

Chapter 5

Carly couldn't remember the last time she had actually cried. She hadn't done it when Brett left, and she'd been much too angry to do it when her father died. In that magical moment when Holly was born, she had laughed.

But now, now that her house clearly wasn't going to burn to the ground after all, she fell apart. It was cumulative, she realized, trying to catch her breath. It was the fire and the IRS, the auction trip and the six tourists. And if she'd had to handle the fire on her own, the way she did everything else, she knew she would have held herself together until she got to her room. By then, enough time would have passed that she would have been shaky, but she wouldn't have . . . well, *blubbered*.

But it hadn't happened that way because Jack Fain had put the fire out, because Jack was here, hunkering down in front of her, reaching a hand toward her face, and something inside her spasmed with need, and that terrified her.

What was he doing? Drying her tears? Nobody had dried her tears in so long, she suddenly found herself crying harder.

"Knock it off," she gasped, turning her face away.

"Let me see your hand." Oh, God, his voice was too gentle.

"No!"

"You touched the door."

"I'll take care of it." *Leave me something to take care of.*

"Suit yourself." His voice turned short. He stood up again, and her heart hitched, almost as though she was disappointed.

"Theresa, are you okay?" he called out.

"I'm fine," her sister answered tremulously.

Carly finally looked up, swiping her hands over her cheeks. She combed her fingers through her hair. Holly came to sit beside her, leaning in to her for comfort as she hadn't done in a very long time.

"Wow, Mom," she whispered. "That was something."

"Yeah," Carly said shakily. "Wow." She held her too tightly for a moment, then she tipped her daughter's face up to look at her. "Are you all right?"

Holly nodded. "I was sleeping. That guy came and got me." She straightened away from her, looking at Jack. "He's *awesome.*"

Well, he's something, Carly allowed. She just didn't know what yet.

She realized that Leigh was missing. She twisted around to find the blonde standing beside the henhouse, looking rooted to the spot.

"Somebody ought to go get her," she muttered, "and remind her how to walk." But no one was listening to her. They were all watching Jack, waiting for guidance. If it seemed odd to them that it was coming from one of the other guests, no one seemed to notice.

"Theresa, can you make some coffee without electricity?" he asked.

Her sister nodded. "The range is gas, and I think the tanks are okay."

"Good. Dig up some candles, too. Come on, everybody, let's go inside and sit down."

They all began moving. Holly got up and Carly struggled to her feet as well. Jack caught her good hand and hoisted her the rest of the way.

"Thanks," she said stiffly, pulling away from him as soon as she was upright.

"You're welcome. Where's the first-aid kit?"

"In the kitchen. I said I'd take care of it." She looked at her burned palm again. Her ankle was beginning to put up a steady howl, too.

"I was thinking more along the lines of this welt on my face, cowgirl."

Carly stumbled.

What was he doing to her? It wasn't like her to think of herself first! Then again, it wasn't like her to feel hot awareness slide through her at a stranger's look, either. And having someone else take over her responsibilities *definitely* wasn't the norm.

It wasn't like her to fall apart.

"Right," she managed hoarsely. "I'll take care of that, too."

Jack started to argue, then he decided against it. She looked as though she badly needed something to do.

She negotiated the burned steps and went into the kitchen. Holly followed on her heels. The others had settled down at the kitchen table. They were all present and accounted for. Someone had thought to get Leigh after all. Carly went to dig the first-aid kit out of the pantry, then she came back and pushed at Jack's shoulder.

He sat and she studied the burn on his cheek in the dim candlelight, trying to avoid his eyes. How could anyone have eyes that color?

"It's not really that bad," she murmured.

"Hurts like hell."

"Don't be a wimp."

She patted at the burn, cleaning it, and was unsettled to realize that her hands were shaking. *Of course they're shaking. Your house just damned near burned down with your daughter in it.* But even as she thought about it, she knew that that wasn't entirely what was making her tremble.

She hadn't gotten this close to him before.

Jack sat with his legs splayed and it hit her suddenly that she was standing between them, that her right knee was flush against his thigh, and that in spite of everything the day had held he smelled good. A little sooty and sweaty, sure, but somehow, indefinably male. Her throat closed hard because it had been so long since she had been aware of such a thing, since she'd been close enough to a man to have it fill her head and her senses and make her want.

Oh, yes, she was definitely beginning to want. *No, please no, I can't let that happen.*

She finished up quickly, stepping away from him, and noticed that Holly was watching her closely.

"Did anyone see what happened?" Carly asked quickly.

Jack clenched his hands and dragged his mind back to the problems at hand. When she had begun working at his burn, he had expected her ministrations to be as fast and capable as everything else about her. He hadn't been prepared for her touch to be gentle, like a kiss of breath. When she had stepped back from him, he'd had the almost overpowering urge to grab her hips and pull her back to him.

She settled down in the chair beside him to tend to her own palm. There were murmurs to her question but no one really answered. Jack had lost his hat somewhere in the confusion. He didn't dare look at Scorpion, but he felt him, was so sharply aware of the assassin right now it was almost a physical hurt.

Finally, Carly looked up again. "I think something hot must have hit the generator," she said suddenly. "That's the only explanation I can think of. Once, a long time ago, lightning struck it, and it sounded just like it did tonight. But..." She trailed off, looking out at the clear sky through the open kitchen window.

Too close, cowgirl. There was no lightning tonight, Jack thought, but there *had* been a very small, low-percussion bomb. He'd bet good money on it. It had been one of those that were ignited by heat, he thought. The fire had to have started first. He could think of no other way the flames could have spread so far, so fast, in the short time it had taken them to get from the parlor to the kitchen.

He watched the others' faces covertly. He wondered if any of them might possess the kind of knowledge necessary to figure that out for themselves.

"I'd guess there was probably a short in the wiring or something," he offered finally.

Carly opened her mouth to argue but Theresa cut her off. "It must have been. Except that I just had it serviced last month and—"

"Well, there you have it," Jack interrupted.

"She does?" Carly asked warily. "*I* don't."

"While the technician was tinkering around in there, he must have crossed wires or something."

"And it took a whole month for it to go berserk? No way."
Then, suddenly, her mouth went dry.

She didn't like the look in his golden eyes. She couldn't quite
define it, and she scowled at him harder. He was trying to tell
her something. *Shut up and let it go.*

But *why?* What was going on here?

Carly shut her mouth slowly. For some absurd reason, she
trusted him even as she knew with fresh conviction that it might
be smarter not to. Maybe it was because he had saved Holly, she
thought, because he had interceded so that she wouldn't have
to make the agonizing choice of letting the house burn so she
could go to her daughter. But for whatever reason, she decided to give him the benefit of the doubt.

For now.

God, she was tired. Too tired to think clearly. Almost too
tired to care. And maybe it really was all her pessimistic imagination.

She stood up carefully. "Okay, everybody. The excitement's
over. The house is still standing. The rooster crows early in the
morning and we've got a big day ahead of us, so I suggest we
all get some sleep."

Jack risked a fast glance at Scorpion, then he stood as well.
"Sounds like a good game plan to me."

There were murmurs and yawns all the way around. Theresa
handed out more candles so the guests could find their way to
their rooms. They each leaned over the ones on the table to light
them, but Jack noticed that Carly only stood where she was,
flipping hers from hand to hand.

Holly kept hovering curiously in the kitchen as well.

"Go on," Carly said quietly, glancing at her. "I'll be up in
a minute."

The girl's eyes moved between them. "Sure," she answered,
and grinned.

Carly's heart skipped a beat. *Oh, no.* She couldn't let Holly
get her hopes up that something was happening between her
and Jack. It would be devastating to her when she realized that
it was all in her imagination again, yet another dead end. How
in the world had she gotten such a thing in her mind in the first
place? Carly wondered wildly, then she sighed.

Holly's hopes in that department were legendary. She had
tried to play matchmaker before, more and more often in the

recent past, but she'd always had fertile ground to plow before. Someone would flirt with Carly at a county social, or *something* Holly could grab and run with. And when Carly just didn't have time for the man, when there was nothing about him to entice her to *make* time, then Holly would go through a period of even worse withdrawal.

Carly just couldn't face another one.

She smiled weakly back at her, and Holly finally left the kitchen. Carly watched her, hurting, then her gaze slid back to Jack. She had bigger problems here than Holly's perception, she realized.

"Why do I feel like you know a lot more about what happened tonight than you're letting on?" she asked finally, slowly.

Jack kept his voice idle. "I have no idea."

For a second, her temper tried to flare. Then she thought that arguing with him would require more effort than she had in her right now. She felt as though every ounce of her adrenaline, every bit of her strength, all her *will*, had been suctioned right out of her.

A fire. This was too much.

She turned mutely for the stairs. That bothered Jack more than anything. He'd been prepared for her to try to grill him. Instead, he felt as though he were dropping a few more pounds onto her shoulders.

"Carly."

"Never mind," she managed. "I honestly don't care right now. Thanks for helping."

"Look—"

She glanced back at him. He met her eyes. Something happened in the exchange.

Carly felt sensation rush through her again, the kind she had put out of her mind long ago, yet had never really felt before now. The tantalizing twitch of awareness that she'd felt while fixing his face quickened into an ache at the very core of her. Titillation became longing. And longing hurt.

She curled her hands carefully into fists and tucked them beneath her arms. She didn't even *know* him.

And he called her cowgirl.

Something flared and heated inside Jack in response. There was a moment of suspended anticipation, a catch of breath, a waiting. He knew she was thinking again of that moment when she had stood between his legs. And so, impossibly, was he.

Hell. He raked a hand through his hair and looked away first. He couldn't get personally involved with her. He *couldn't.* She would take everything far too seriously, he thought, more seriously than he knew he was capable of. And he already knew that the worst thing he could ever do to this woman was let her down. She'd been hurt too much in the past.

Carly finally turned away again. He felt her movement rather than saw it. He told himself he was relieved.

"I'm going to sleep," she said softly.

"Good idea." He was startled to find that his voice was vaguely raw.

"Yes. It is."

So they agreed on that much, at least. But as she left the kitchen, he looked at her back, and her long hair was wilder than ever now.

Jack felt a spasming moment of regret.

She didn't come to breakfast the next morning.

Jack's eyes felt crusty and his neck hurt as he took his place at the table. He thought again that he was too old for this. He'd spent most of the night on the lumpy parlor sofa, getting up to investigate each time the old house had creaked and settled. And it had creaked and settled a lot. Sometime after midnight a dry wind had blown up to rattle branches against the eaves. By five o'clock this morning, he'd been profoundly grateful that there was only a handful of trees near the house.

He hadn't dared to sleep anyway. Not really, not deeply. He couldn't risk Scorpion catching him doing it.

He'd moved once or twice, into the barn for a short while, then to his car for a quick catnap. He'd been gambling that his roommate would think that he had a romantic liaison with one of the women and that was why he didn't come to bed. Judging by Scorpion's dark, furtive looks this morning, not only had the play worked, but he thought the woman was Carly.

That, he thought, could come in handy. Maybe. He'd have to see how it played out.

All in all, however, it had been a night of wasted vigilance. The assassin himself hadn't stirred. Only Theresa had roamed uncomfortably, too pregnant to sleep, and she had finally come downstairs to start breakfast at five-thirty. At six, Jack had heard Carly in the kitchen. He had peeked into the hallway to see her take a cup of coffee and two large muffins into her office.

Jack imagined that she was still in there now. It didn't take a rocket scientist to figure out what she was doing. One look at the kitchen door was all it required, that and the burned-out generator beyond it.

In spite of the fact that he knew he would use the Castagnes' financial problems to his advantage if he had to, a new hatred flamed in him for the man who called himself Brad Patterson, for causing her this added measure of grief.

Hell of a way to show you love her, buddy.

Carly pushed back from her desk. She put her boots up on the blotter, balanced her empty coffee mug on her knee and closed her eyes.

It wasn't even seven-thirty yet, and already her head hurt as if a little man was in there whaling away with a tiny sledgehammer. A tiny *hard* sledgehammer, with nails sticking out of it.

The door opened. Carly opened her eyes again as her sister came into the room.

"So what are we going to do?" Theresa asked. She stood against the bookcase, resting her arms atop her belly.

"There's only one thing we can do," Carly answered flatly. "We'll have to float a check. We can't live without electricity."

"Won't the insurance pay for it?"

"They would if I'd had a bunch of other stuff go wrong this year." She'd paid the premium, thank God, but she'd just discovered that it didn't do her any good. "We've got a huge deductible."

Theresa looked appalled. "Why did Michael get us a policy like that?"

"Well, the premiums are cheaper. And theoretically, we could go years and years without needing that insurance, so it's smarter to keep the monthly payments down." Carly got to her feet. "Okay," she went on, "here's what we're going to do. We'll tell the guests that the repairman's tied up for a couple of days and he can't get out here. We'll apologize six ways to

Sunday. That'll buy us at least enough time for me to get them off the ranch. Then electricity won't be quite so urgent. You can stay behind this trip to take care of getting it fixed.''

"Then who's going to drive the cook wagon?''

"I'll have to use Mazie Montoro full-time this week.'' He was one of those cowboys who preferred to roam and play it loose, working only when he had to. "I can't spare Plank and Gofer from their horses,'' she thought aloud. Not with six tourists adding to the already raucous confusion of a cattle drive. "This makes more sense even without what happened to the generator, Tee. I wasn't too keen on you bouncing along with us in your condition anyway.''

Theresa nodded. She hadn't particularly wanted to go, but remaining behind bothered her also.

"There's *nothing* in the checking account?''

"Not now,'' Carly answered. She knew her sister hated writing checks, she'd once said it felt so criminal. "The money from the first guests already went to the IRS, and Michael hasn't deposited the fees from those last two yet. Call him and make sure he has the money, *then* you can write the check. It'll just be a matter of holding our breaths long enough for the checks to clear from Brad and Jack.''

Jack.

She turned quickly away from Theresa, not wanting her to see her expression. She didn't want to and couldn't quite stop herself from remembering the way he'd looked at her before she'd gone upstairs last night. But he hadn't done anything about it. The only conclusion she could come to was that he'd decided she held no great allure after all.

She was relieved. Of course, she was. It was the only emotion she would allow herself.

He was attractive. She could admit that. But a voice in her head had been yelling loud and clear all morning—*watch out!* She'd sat here thinking about him long after she'd figured out what to do about the generator, and now she knew what to do about Jack Fain, too.

Assuming she could work up the nerve.

"Where are the guests?'' she asked suddenly, looking back at her sister.

"I told them to go out and tack their horses,'' Theresa answered, startled. "Wasn't that what you wanted?''

"It's perfect. Can you go keep an eye on them?"

"Sure. Where will you be?"

"Darling sister, you do *not* want to know." If a slightly elastic check worried her, Carly couldn't even imagine what she might think about this.

"Carlotta . . ."

"Go on," she urged. "Everything's fine. Just . . . uh, don't let anyone come back in the house. For *anything.* Tell them I'll be there in just a minute."

"What are you doing?" Theresa cried, thoroughly alarmed now.

"I'm going to try to get a little extra insurance." Or *assur*-ance, as the case might be, she thought.

She waited until she heard Theresa go outside. Oh, God, this was so horribly, morally wrong! Or *was* it? Thanks to Michael's flea-brained tourist idea, Jack Fain was living in her home. She was going to be at his mercy across a good many isolated, empty miles on the way to Kansas. If there was something funny about him, then she had to know. For her own protection, and for everybody else's.

It had nothing, *nothing,* to do with the fact that she was curious about him on a personal level.

Except . . . well, he hadn't really *done* anything to make her suspicious, she admitted. Nothing except ask her to leave a day early, but he'd never really had a chance to explain that. And then there was the way he'd taken charge last night with the fire. That just wasn't something she'd expect a guest to do, but for all she knew he had some kind of job where he was accustomed to authority. Maybe he was just used to taking charge. For all she knew, he *was* a fire fighter.

Okay, so explain that look. Explain why it seemed like he was warning you to shut up about the generator.

Carly groaned. She was trying to justify this to herself, she realized, and it was unnecessary. This was her home, she thought again, her ranch, her ride. She was simply acting on gut instinct to protect herself and her family.

She slipped up the stairs and went quietly down the hall to the room that Theresa had given to Jack and Brad. She glanced back over her shoulder guiltily and stepped inside.

The first thing she noticed was that he hadn't slept in his bed last night—or at least one of them hadn't, and she doubted if it was Brad. *He* was supposed to be the one with body odor.

A suitcase sat on the floor at the foot of the made-up bed. Carly took a deep breath and grasped it by the handle, setting it gently on the dresser. The sound of the locks springing open shot into the quiet room like gunfire.

Inside were jeans, oxford shirts, underwear, socks. There was a bottle of cologne. It brought vivid images to her, images of his face and of his callused hand taking hers. They were so clear and palpable that she looked warily over her shoulder yet again, half-expecting to find him standing right there in the doorway.

There was an electric razor. A lot of good that was going to do him on the trail, she thought. Where had the man's head been when he'd packed? Just where exactly had he thought he was going? There was a bottle of aspirin. Carly ran her hands inside all the little side pockets. She found some loose change, and a pack of matches from a bar in Bangkok. *Bangkok?* A world traveler, and now he was on a ranch in *Oklahoma?*

Finally she sighed. In all honesty, there was nothing really strange about any of it, she admitted. Outside of the matches, all his possessions seemed perfectly normal. And for that matter, she supposed a dude ride was something of a different vacation as well, so perhaps the matches fit.

Impulsively, she moved to Brad's suitcase on the opposite dresser. It was lying open. Glancing in, she saw that every single item still had a price tag on it, even his underwear and his toiletries.

Now *that* seemed strange.

Carly groaned. No, what it seemed like was that she was seeing big, bad bogeymen in shadows again, in *all* the shadows, and probably all they really were were dust bunnies. She went back and closed Jack's suitcase, putting it on the floor again.

"Mom?"

Carly squealed. She jumped, clapped a hand to her heart and spun around. Holly was standing in the door, watching her with that wide, wide grin again.

Oh, this was bad. Holly's imagination would take flight with this.

"What are you doing here?" Carly demanded inanely.

"I live here." Holly took a step into the room and looked around with exaggerated innocence. "Isn't this Mr. Fain's room?"

"I . . . is it?"

"Sure it is," Holly said happily.

"I thought I saw a mouse run in here. I was just checking."

"In his *suitcase*?"

Carly's heart kicked: "You didn't see that."

"Yeah, I—"

"No. You didn't." Carly gripped her daughter by the shoulders and turned her deliberately around, toward the hall again. "Promise me you won't mention this to anyone. Not even Aunt Tee. Cross your heart. *Please*, Holly, I mean it."

Holly shrugged and stepped out into the hall. "Noooo problem," she drawled, then she ran down the stairs.

Carly scowled after her a moment, then she left the room as well, her knees fairly knocking together from the fright her daughter had given her. She went back downstairs to the kitchen, peering out the window. The guests were all in the paddocks, practicing their riding. Theresa stood watch over them like some kind of swollen gestapo.

"Holly!" Carly called out, turning back into the downstairs hallway. She thought maybe she'd better have one last, quick word with her and explain . . . something, somehow. *What?*

Holly didn't answer anyway. Carly wandered toward the front of the house, glancing into rooms as she passed them. When she got to the parlor, she noticed that the sofa cushions were wrinkled and the bolster pillows were slightly askew.

So *this* was where he had slept last night.

She went in to adjust the pillows, then she noticed something brown sticking up from behind one of the cushions. She frowned and reached for it.

His wallet.

No, don't, there was nothing upstairs, so leave it alone. This is a hundred times worse than peeping into his suitcase. But it was as if her hands had minds of their own.

Carly opened the wallet. There was a driver's license from Arlington, Virginia. Roughly three hundred dollars in cash. Assorted credit cards. An AT&T calling card, and a few receipts from an automated teller machine. She glanced at the balances and her heart skipped. He certainly wasn't destitute.

She was about to close the billfold again, feeling almost nauseated with guilt, when she noticed the crumpled, smudged edge of a photograph sticking out from the little plastic section for pictures. She flipped the plastic open and all the teller receipts fluttered out. The picture was way, way in the back.

She scooped up the receipts again hurriedly and slid out the picture. It was old, black and white, and there were palm trees and water in the background. Florida, she thought. Or maybe the Caribbean. The man's hair was combed in a style reminiscent of the early sixties. He wore baggy khakis and a T-shirt. A pack of cigarettes was stuck into one rolled-up sleeve. He had a wide, infectious, boyish grin.

A kid stood beside him, holding a small fish. Carly looked closer and her heart kicked. The boy was Jack.

For that matter, now that she thought about it, the man looked a great deal like him also.

There was no woman in the picture, and there were no other pictures in the wallet. Despite the fact that both the man and boy were smiling, Carly felt an overwhelming sadness.

She replaced the picture carefully and slid the wallet back behind the cushions again. She felt oddly shaken, even as she felt relieved.

Chapter 6

Jack felt eyes on the back of his head as he rode around the paddock. He had lost sight of Scorpion a moment ago when he had turned a corner—the assassin was somewhere behind him, and he didn't like that much at all. Now he was sure that the man was watching him, perhaps wondering if and where he had seen him before.

Cold spilled through him. Jack stiffened. The split-eared gelding felt it and moved faster.

"Whoa, there, you ugly old beast."

Then they turned another corner, and he realized that it was Carly's daughter sitting on the fence, staring at him. "Hey," he said as he passed her.

"Hi."

He reined in. "What's up?"

"Oh, nothing," she said too fast, too innocently.

"You coming with us to Kansas?" he asked, because he couldn't think of anything else to say, and it was easier to keep Scorpion in sight if he was sitting here instead of riding around with him.

Holly wrinkled her nose. "It's boring."

"Maybe you shouldn't tell that to somebody who's paying a whole lot of money to do it."

"Oh." She thought about it, then she scrunched her face up. "Anyway, my mom's probably going to make me."

Jack managed not to laugh at her expression, and was a little startled to find that he even wanted to. The kid was a pistol. "It's rough being young, isn't it?" he said finally. "Having to do all those things you don't want to do?"

Holly's eyes widened into full-blown adoration. Uh-oh, Jack thought. If there was one thing he knew about himself, it was that he was nobody's hero.

"You got any kids?" she asked suddenly.

Jack scowled. "No."

"No?"

"What's wrong with that?" he asked, feeling absurdly defensive.

"Well, you're old."

"Thanks a lot."

"What I mean, is, almost everybody your age has kids."

"Well, I don't."

"How come?"

Because I'd never do to a kid what my parents did to me. The thought flashed at him for the first time in a very long time, and it still brought a tense, residual pain.

"Because I'm not married," he said shortly.

Holly brightened. "That's good."

"Yeah?" he asked warily. "How come?"

Because if he didn't have a wife, Holly thought, and if he didn't already have kids, then maybe he would want some. She grinned, thinking about finding her mom in his room, and about the way they'd both hung out in the kitchen last night after everybody else had gone to bed, except they hadn't stayed there very long. But still, she thought, it was a start.

"I think my mom likes you," she blurted.

Double uh-oh. There was no way to tell her that *liking* wasn't exactly what was going on here, Jack thought. Nope, it was just good, basic, sexual attraction rearing its provocative little head in the wrong place at the wrong time.

"Your mom's doing just fine without liking anybody," he said flatly, gathering up his reins again. On that note, he thought, it was probably best to end this little tea party.

Holly looked crestfallen and he felt a stir of absurd guilt for dashing her pipe dreams.

"I wish she wasn't, is all," Holly went on wistfully. "I just wish I had a dad."

Jack shifted uncomfortably in his saddle. "Sometimes it's better not to have one," he said finally.

"Like when?"

"It's better never to have one than to have one and lose him." He finally managed to turn his horse away from her. "You can't miss something you never had, right?"

"Is that what happened to you?"

This had all started when people had begun sending their kids to preschool before they were even five, Jack thought sourly. Now the little urchins were way too smart for their own good.

"Nothing happened to me," he said shortly.

"Do you have a dad?"

"No."

"Ever? Did you *ever* have one?"

"Until I was ten. Listen, kiddo, your mom's going to come out here any minute and she's going to be fried if I'm not going around in these silly little circles. Catch you later."

His heart was moving hard. Too hard. When was the last time he had spoken about his father? How come kids couldn't figure out when something was off-limits? And the hell of it was, you couldn't really snap at them for it, either.

"You got a picture of him?" Holly called out.

"If I show it to you, will you leave me alone?"

She looked crushed for a moment, then she brightened. "Sure."

Jack swung the ugly-eared gelding back to the fence. He reached into his jeans pocket, and his heart slugged his ribs.

His wallet was gone.

For a moment the cold feeling came back, drenching everything inside him. He shook it off. There was nothing in there that could come back to haunt him. That old picture of Carly Castagne was in a small pocket sewn into the inside of his left boot, though God only knew why he had felt compelled to bring it along. His agency credentials were in a similar pocket in his right boot. No sweat. No problem.

What bothered him was that he had lost his wallet in the first place.

It was sloppy, unforgivable. It wasn't like him. He had never, *ever,* done such a thing before, not while on a job, not while it mattered. *God, he really was losing his edge.* He no longer had any idea whether it was thoughts of the woman or worries about a new scar that were unfocusing him. He just knew that he wasn't himself, and that that was dangerous.

He'd been a fool to let Paul talk him into this.

"What's the matter?" Holly asked.

"I left my wallet in my room," he said tightly.

"Want me to go get it?"

He was saved from answering by Carly herself. She slammed out the back door and came toward them, and for a moment he thought she looked alarmed when she noticed them talking. Then, almost visibly, she forced herself to relax and she turned away to look at the others.

"Okay, everybody," she called out. "Come on over here where I'm standing. Let's see how much you've learned."

Before an hour had passed, Carly decided that at least half the guests wished they had never heard of Seventy Four Draw. At the very least, they were all beginning to wonder why they had spent perfectly good money for the pleasure of killing themselves. But she wasn't as pleased as she thought she'd be.

There was certainly no question that she needed this ride to be a success. But now she realized that she was beginning to take Michael's whole crazy idea as some kind of personal challenge as well. Could she keep these people on horses and get them into Kansas without losing any cattle on the way? Could she pull it off without it costing the ranch anything beyond what the guests were paying them? Could she pull it off *period?*

Maybe.

At ten-thirty, Winston finally fell off his horse. It had pretty much the effect that Carly had hoped for. Sure, it hurt. Sure, it jarred his teeth. But he'd broken no bones and there wasn't a scratch on him. His fear of the animal eased considerably.

At eleven, Myra's horse ran off with her. That was a godsend, too, Carly figured. Myra learned her lesson in a hurry. If she fidgeted too much while she was astride, the animal was going to take it as a cue to run.

At noon, Brad called out to her. "Are we stopping for lunch?"

Carly scowled at her watch. "Not yet."

She wanted to use the lunch hour to take Holly to the roller rink. She had decided that she wasn't going to back out on the promise. If nothing else, that fire last night had driven a few precious truths home to her. The ranch just didn't give her back enough to sustain her if she lost Holly, or even Theresa. They were all she had left, all that mattered.

Sorry, Daddy. The thought she'd had standing in the kitchen last night came back to her again. *Let it burn.* It had been right from her heart, she realized now. The truth was, the Draw had become like a cruel, selfish lover, sucking the lifeblood right out of her, leaving her hollow.

When had it happened? When had she started wanting, needing something more? She looked at Jack and realized that she didn't think she liked the answer to that. It had been recent, she realized. Very recent.

"No?" Jack repeated.

"What?" She couldn't seem to bring her thoughts back together.

"You said, no, we're not stopping for lunch."

"I said not yet," Carly corrected. "We lost half an hour getting Myra back from the next county. We have time to make up."

"What is this? Boot camp?" Jack demanded.

"We've still got a lot of work to do," she answered, unperturbed.

"The scenery sure makes it a lot easier," Brad said suddenly.

Carly glanced at him sharply. She could swear he was flirting with her today. Even now he was sending her a sly, sideways grin. Then again, for all she knew, he had decided that aliens were invading the earth and had started by taking control of her. Those sales tags on his clothing continued to bother her. They were just . . . weird.

She dug a firecracker out of her back pocket, lit it and tossed it roughly in Jack's direction. When it went off, his horse skittered and reared.

"What was that for?" he shouted.

Her heart thumped as she realized that he was genuinely angry. "Easy, cowboy. If Gofer or Plank or I should have to discharge our guns on the trail for some reason, then I want to make sure you all stay on your horses when it happens." None of their mounts was especially gun-shy, but there were exceptions to every assumption, and she was pleased to see that they had all weathered the explosion very well.

"You might have warned me," Jack muttered. There was still an edge to his voice, even though gun-broken horses weren't a bad idea, he thought, all things considered.

"That would defeat the purpose," Carly pointed out sweetly. She wondered why he was in such a foul mood today. "I might not be able to tell you first if the real thing happens," she went on. "Come on, everybody, keep riding."

Jack didn't, at least not right away. He gave her a long, measuring look before he finally cued his horse onward again.

He kept one wary eye on her in case she had another firecracker in her pocket, trying to keep his other eye on Scorpion at the same time.

At two o'clock she let them stop for lunch. Jack noticed that Holly looked pleasantly stunned when Carly grabbed a set of keys off a nail beside the stairs and waved her daughter outside. She was gone for nearly an hour and came back without Holly.

She worked the guests until five o'clock before she finally called out to them to stop riding. She'd put them through hell today, Jack thought. The firecrackers had been the worst of it, but then she'd forced their horses through some drainage ditches and a sizable trench to the east of the house. She said she wanted to prepare them for the rough terrain. He was beginning to think she was just sadistic.

Everyone, including Scorpion, watched her warily as she motioned to them to gather around her. Carly read their expressions and actually laughed again.

"Oh, come on. I'm not *that* much of an ogre. I'm even going to let you stop now so that you can all get some time to clean up before dinner. We only have two bathrooms, as you've probably already noticed, so don't anyone hog them. Wash up, do what you have to do, then find your way back to the dinner table. We'll eat at six-thirty."

She started for the house.

"Are we still leaving on Friday?" Scorpion called out. "Did you decide?"

Carly looked back at the man and her mouth quirked into another smile. It made Jack's skin crawl even as he thanked

God that she didn't seem to know who or what she was grinning at. And then something happened to him, something so unexpected and alien that he might have fallen off his horse if he hadn't already dismounted.

It started as a tightening in his gut. It moved to his throat, squeezing. Then it rushed, hot, up into his temples. And it hurt.

He was jealous.

Carly nodded. "We've made good progress," she answered, "and I've decided there's no reason I have to stay here to oversee the generator repairs. It makes more sense for Theresa to do it. I don't see why we can't leave on schedule."

She finally went back to the house. Jack's gaze swerved back to Scorpion.

The man was watching her intently, and suddenly Jack realized that he *did* have an instinct, a strong and clear one that hadn't been muddied by the events three months ago in São Paulo. Scorpion was going to make contact with Carly Castagne tonight.

And there was no way Jack was going to allow it.

It had nothing to do with the way she had smiled at the man, he told himself. It had nothing to do with the fact that he could count her smiles—her *true* smiles—on one hand, and now at least one of them had been earned by Scorpion, a man she had once been *married* to. It had everything to do with the fact that it just made more sense to get this game over with as expeditiously and with as few additional complications as possible.

If he prevented Scorpion from getting Carly Castagne alone, then there was no way the assassin could involve her in this. Sooner or later, the man would simply have to take his money and go, or all chances would be lost to him. Scorpion had to know that the longer he delayed, the more certainly he would be pursued, if not by the agency, then by the guys he had turned on.

Jack was reasonably sure now that the assassin's move would be to tell Carly who he was. He'd been flirting with her mildly all day, but not so much that he'd be able to sweep her off her feet all over again and get her to run off into the sunset with him. No, Jack thought, that was not something a woman like Carly Castagne would easily do, and Scorpion had to know, or have relearned it, by now.

Unfortunately, Jack thought, he really had no idea what Carly *would* do if Scorpion managed to tell her the truth. She had just smiled at the bastard. What would her reaction be after her shock and anger wore off? Would she realize she was still in love with him?

No, Jack thought, no way. He wasn't going to take the chance.

Jack didn't find his wallet in his room. He retraced his innumerable steps of the night before and finally located it in the parlor sofa.

Someone had rifled through it.

He always kept one automatic teller receipt between the third and fourth plastic picture windows. If the wallet was opened, there was no way it could not fall out. He, of course, always put it back between the proper windows. A stranger would not.

It was in the front now, with two other receipts, not anywhere near the picture windows at all.

Something clammy moved over his neck. Scorpion? Or Carly? It could even have been Holly. But if it was her mother or the assassin, then one of them had figured out enough to be suspicious, and that bothered him.

As a result of his search, Jack was the last one to get into a bathroom. He made quick work of it, while the question of who had snooped through his wallet continued to nag at him. Still, by the time he had showered and shaved, his mood had improved somewhat. There was comfort in knowing that whoever it was hadn't found anything important.

Then he pulled open the bathroom door, and all thoughts of the job at hand fled from his mind. Carly came out of the bathroom directly across from him. Her eyes were down on the towel and the clothing she carried. She didn't immediately notice him.

Her hair was free again, wet and sleek this time from her shower. She was barefoot. She had tiny, narrow feet. And she wore white. It was some little robe that barely touched her thighs. It couldn't be called sheer, not by any stretch of the imagination, and he suspected that Leigh Bliss had far more potent clothing in her arsenal. But if he squinted and angled his head just right, when she turned to flip off the light switch behind her, Jack could just make out the outline of brief bikini panties beneath the cotton.

He could *not* make out any trace of bra straps.

His breath snagged as completely and suddenly as if he were a teenager. Desire, that heat of hunger, ambushed him. Suddenly he could *feel* her wet hair sliding through his hands. He could *smell* the faint trace of soap on her body.

She turned around and this time she noticed him standing just inside the other door. He dragged his gaze up to her eyes again.

"You're going to be late for dinner," she managed, her voice sounding breathless. Faint, delicious color came to her cheeks.

"So are you." She was beautiful, he thought. God help him, she was Scorpion's woman and he couldn't be noticing things like whether or not she'd immediately put on a bra after she got out of the shower. He couldn't get into a contest with his nemesis, with this woman as the prize, because it was too twisted, too sordid, and there were far too many other issues at stake as well. She wasn't right for him. He was all wrong for her.

"What?" he asked hoarsely.

"I said, see you downstairs," she repeated.

Jack watched her mutely as she made her way to her room. "Yeah, right," he finally remembered to answer, but she was too far away to hear him.

He clenched his jaw and went to his own room to comb his hair and get some kind of grip on himself. Then they reached the kitchen at the same time, Jack from the front stairs and the hallway, Carly by way of the back stairs.

He wasn't sure, but he thought he saw her hesitate when she saw him.

Good, basic, sexual attraction, he reminded himself. He was sane now, in control, and he knew that that was all it was. And such a thing could certainly be handled with common sense and restraint by two sane adults who didn't need to get tangled up in each other's lives. Still, he was barely aware of the hum of the conversations around him as he sat down.

"What kind of wildlife might we expect to find?" Myra asked.

"I have a deck of cards in my suitcase," Reggie volunteered. "Does anyone feel like a game?"

"Do we have to use candles again tonight?" Winston wondered.

Carly looked at Theresa. "Were you able to do anything about the generator?" she asked.

Theresa shook her head and stammered. "I—I called the repairman. I—he'll be out tomorrow. No, maybe Friday. I mean, he's busy. We'll just have to rough it again tonight and tomorrow," she finished lamely, looking miserable.

Jack felt something in his gut harden warily. What had all that been about?

Then Holly burst in through the charred back door, and he heard a car take off outside.

"Did you have fun?" Carly asked her, and Jack shut out the distractions again, trying to think. Besides, the flushed look of happiness on the kid's face touched something in him, something he really didn't want touched, and Carly's answering smile made him tell himself harshly that he definitely did not care, didn't wonder, what had happened to make each of them so damned happy. It wasn't any of his business. He wasn't involved.

He thought about the generator. The arrival of the repairman was all the more reason to get them out of here as soon as possible, he decided. He didn't want Scorpion around when the guy noticed that an incendiary device had been installed in the box. He looked at Scorpion, wondering if this had occurred to the assassin as well. The man kept his eyes on his plate, eating diligently. His expression revealed nothing.

Dinner was scarcely over when Carly stood up. "I need to look at the books again," she said to no one in particular. "Excuse me."

Jack watched as she slipped into the hallway. She had changed into shorts and a T-shirt. He studied her legs briefly, then he caught himself and pulled his attention back to the others.

The cowboys were easily cajoled into a card game. They cleared the kitchen table and sat down to deal the first hand. Leigh complained of a headache and went to lie down. Jack suspected she was just disgruntled at being excluded from the hub of male activity, though by her own admission, she knew nothing about poker. Myra wanted to know if she could peruse the library at the front of the house, maybe take something to read up to her room.

Jack waited.

When the poker game was well under way and the sky outside was deep purple and mauve, Scorpion leaned back in his chair, stretching. The assassin watched one more hand idly, then he, too, excused himself to go upstairs.

Jack felt something hot and ready scoot through him, and this time it had absolutely nothing to do with wanting Carly Castagne.

Oh, yeah, he thought, Scorpion was going to make contact with Carly tonight. He waited until Scorpion had gone, then he begged out of the game as well. He went up the hallway, looking into the various rooms as he passed them. He wondered if he would have to go upstairs to Carly's bedroom to find her, but then he located her in the parlor again.

She was pouring at the sideboard, and he wasn't sure if he was disappointed or relieved that he wouldn't have to track her upstairs to her room. He wondered what she slept in.

"Hey," he said from the hallway.

Carly's head snapped up. She reached for another snifter and filled it halfway with brandy without commenting. She handed it to him as he stepped into the room.

Jack shut the door carefully behind him. She didn't comment on that either.

"Expecting me?" he asked finally, sipping.

"Resigned to it, more like."

You could have been upstairs in your room half an hour ago, he thought.

She could probably have gone upstairs half an hour ago, Carly thought. She could have avoided all this. She did feel much, much better about him now that she had snooped through his wallet and his suitcase. But she was still curious about why he had wanted to leave a day early, and she wondered if he would bring it up again if given the chance.

That was what she told herself. She didn't want to consider that maybe she just wanted to give him a chance to look at her that way again, the way he had last night and outside the bathroom.

She leaned her elbows on the sideboard behind her, waiting. Jack sat on the sofa, stretching out his legs with a laziness that belied his tension. He rolled his brandy around on his tongue and the silence stretched out.

Carly began to feel uncomfortable. "Did you want something in particular?" she asked.

He let his gaze roam purposefully over her legs again. He heard the tempo of her breath change, and he felt like a heel because at the moment he was just using that good old, basic attraction between them to stall.

He shifted his weight on the lumpy sofa. For the life of him, he didn't know what to say. He knew what he wanted to *do*. And it would sure as hell fill the time nicely until Scorpion made his appearance.

Come on, buddy, come on, he urged the man silently, *let's get this over with*.

"So," Carly went on finally, unaccountably nervous, fumbling. "Uh, do you really have a redheaded ex-wife?"

Jack was startled, then relieved that she'd brought up a relatively safe topic of conversation. "Yeah. I do."

"What's her name?"

He scowled. "Zoe."

"Does she really have a temper?"

"It comes and goes."

"Did you love her?"

That jolted him. "Why would you ask that?" he asked warily.

"Just trying to fill up the silence while you get around to telling me why you came in here." Carly paused. "Besides, you got a funny look on your face just then when I asked about her."

He'd been thinking that Zoe was an example of the last time his instincts had failed him. He'd thought—Zoe had *said*—that she was a woman who would be content with the little he could give her.

They'd both been wrong.

"So?" Carly prompted.

"So what?"

"Did you love her?" She couldn't have told why she was pushing it. Maybe because *he* was the one to seem uncomfortable for a change.

"I guess so. The mistake was more mine than hers."

"You *guess* you loved her?"

"Well, what do you want me to say?" His voice sounded defensive, even to his own ears, which made no sense because he was fully aware of and accepting of his own shortcomings.

At least, he always had been before.

"I married her, didn't I?" he went on grimly.

Carly shrugged. "Did you really leave her, or was it the other way around?"

"Actually, she left me." Jack's pulse moved warily. What was she getting at? "So she's not really going to be ticked off when she gets those divorce papers."

Actually, *he* had gotten the papers. Eight years ago. Then he remembered his comment yesterday at lunch and realized she'd been baiting him.

Was it she who had gone into his wallet?

Jack got up to pace; he thought pacing revealed entirely too much agitation, yet was unable to stop himself. He decided to change the subject.

"You're really not in a position to act virtuous about it, are you?" he countered.

Carly blinked at him. "Who? Me? Virtuous about what?"

"About love and marriage, all that garbage."

"*Garbage?* How romantic."

"Can you stand there and tell me that you loved Holly's father?" Good, he thought, now he was back on an even keel. He needed to know everything there was to know about Holly's father, he reminded himself. First and foremost, he needed to know if the man *knew* he was a father. And if he had to provoke Carly Castagne a little bit to get the information, then so be it.

Tit for tat, he thought narrowly. He'd shaken her up, he realized.

She answered stiffly. "Of course I did."

"So how come I haven't noticed him around here playing Daddy?"

She gave him a smug half smile. "Because you've only been here a couple of days."

"When was the last time *he* was here?"

Her smile vanished. "I never told Brett he was a father because I was damned if I was going to prolong contact between us if he didn't want contact. Which, apparently, he didn't, once he spotted that blonde. I never heard from him again."

Brett, he thought with a feeling close to satisfaction. The circle of proof had just neatly closed. No matter what a background check told him, it was always nice to hear verification right from the horse's mouth, especially in this day and age of computers. Anyone with a modicum of knowledge could hack in and alter records.

"So it was ego," he said finally, more relaxed, not sure what his excuse was for pushing it now.

Her eyes sparked. "Pride."

"Goes before a fall. Isn't that what they say?"

"I'm not falling. I *didn't* fall. It all worked out."

"For who? You or Holly?"

He said it without thinking, on a hunch, or maybe with the memory of his last conversation with the kid. Maybe he'd done it with the intention of putting in a plug for a child who was more or less too young—and definitely too emotionally involved—to do it herself.

Except, hell, he didn't want to get involved.

And then he really wished he hadn't.

Carly's look turned so abruptly stricken that he moved off that subject fast. "So how come you're all alone now?" he went on, and knew *that* question had nothing to do with Scorpion, or Holly, or anyone but himself. His heart thumped.

"I want to be," Carly muttered.

"Didn't seem that way when you were staring at me across the kitchen last night."

Shock and hurt flashed through her. "That was low," she breathed. She moved fast for the door.

"Wait."

She had meant to leave. She *had* to leave, Carly thought wildly, but she found herself turning around warily to look at him again. "What?"

"I'm sorry," he said quietly. "That was unnecessary. And probably irrelevant."

"I *want* to be alone," she insisted again, but even she heard that her tone had lost some of its conviction.

Jack's voice dropped an octave. It alerted her. It became soft, and then it roughened.

"If I touched you right now," he said slowly, "you wouldn't even put up half a fight, cowgirl."

Her heart whaled so hard against her chest it took her breath away. "I don't play games," she answered, her voice hitching. "*If* I wanted it, I'd take what was offered." And there was an invitation if she'd ever given one, Carly thought wildly. But he didn't do anything with it. Her skin flamed and she looked away.

Suddenly Jack wanted to dig through a few more of the layers, whether it meant getting deep or not. He wanted to *know*. "Yeah," he said. "You do play games. I'll bet you hate your ex-husband because he walked out on you, when you were pregnant, no less, but you tell yourself—"

"He didn't know!" she snapped.

"I guess telling him, letting him know, would make the slap in the face so much worse. I mean, what if you told him and he *still* didn't hang around? Ouch."

"*I won't beg!*" she shouted too loudly, then she lowered her voice deliberately. "Not with anyone, not for anything."

No, she wouldn't. "So what about your father?" He remembered that she'd been awfully bitter in that area, too. And he wanted to know why.

Carly went very still. "Leave him out of this."

"*He just... died.*" He mimicked her tone, her explanation, yesterday at the chutes. "Hell of a nerve."

"Stop it."

But he wanted it all, wanted to get to the bottom of her. "Loving you wasn't enough to keep your dad alive after your mother died. He left you the ranch, but you didn't mean so much to him that he didn't go and die on you."

Carly began shaking. Was she that transparent? "Damn you," she breathed.

Jack saw her eyes shine and he backed off. A little.

"Yeah," he said quietly. "And you'll be damned if you're going to let anyone do anything like that to you again, either die on you *or* run off on you, right?"

"That's my choice," she gasped.

"Sure it is. And I'll bet that's why you'd let yourself touch *me*. Because I'd be safe. I'll be gone in a week. No expectations, and no nasty surprises. You can't get left holding the pieces of your heart if you know going into it that there's no future, right?"

Carly finally met his eyes. Her chin tilted up. God, she was tough, he thought, impressed all over again.

"Okay," she said softly. "So what if you're right, cowboy? You wouldn't be a threat to me even if you lived on the next spread."

"What do you mean?"

"I mean that I don't think you're the type who . . . sticks."

She had that right. He wasn't sure why he felt compelled to argue the point.

"Don't kid yourself. If I tried it once—" his eyes coasted deliberately over her again "—I'd sure be back for more."

Her pulse went wild. "I . . . in a physical sense, maybe."

"That's the part that counts, cowgirl. I don't see the physical bodies of your father and your husband anywhere around here." That was a lie, but he went with it without his tongue stumbling. Once, before he'd lost his nerve, he'd been good at lying.

"It's *half* of what counts," Carly insisted stubbornly. "And you're not venturing too much of the other half yourself. You can't even look me in the eye and tell me that you honest-to-God loved your wife."

Correction, Jack thought, *I'm not fool enough to try.*

He turned away from her abruptly to look out the window. Carly snorted behind him.

"You can dish it out, Jack," she said softly, "but you sure can't take it, can you? Your *body* isn't with your wife right now, is it? Why'd you let her go?"

Suddenly he was mad. He felt cornered, accused, righteous. He moved dangerously close to her again and put his face near hers.

"Because I'm rarely home. I travel a lot. And it wasn't fair to her."

"Sounds like you just didn't love her enough to hang on."

"Watch it, cowgirl." He backed away from her carefully. What difference did any of it make anyway? Carly thought, suddenly tired. She went to the sideboard, drained the last of her brandy and moved for the door.

"Where are you going?" he asked sharply.

"To bed."

"I can't let you do that, cowgirl." It came out before he could think how to best phrase it, how to nudge her along rather than order her about.

Carly whirled back to him, astounded. "*Let* me?" she repeated, disbelieving. "Just who do you think you are?"

He couldn't risk it, he thought. She was going to have to stay right here where he could make sure Scorpion didn't get to her. And he realized that there was no way he was going to be able to talk her into it without playing his cards. Not this woman. He'd just have to sidetrack her a little longer.

That was the practical reason he had for moving past her quickly to block her way to the door. The purely personal reason was that he was pretty sure what her reaction would be.

Suddenly, recklessly, he decided to risk it. He'd work out the twisted, sordid angle of her being Scorpion's woman later. He wanted her. Was it possible that he had, in some measure, ever since he'd laid eyes on that picture?

Yes, he thought, yes, and the reality of her hadn't eased the steady ache at all. The reality of her had turned out to be warmer, smarter, kinder, more intriguingly complicated than he could ever have imagined.

For a brief moment, just a brief one, he let himself believe, pretend, that somehow it could all work out.

Carly came at him angrily. When she started to veer around him, he caught her arms and brought his mouth down hard on hers.

Chapter 7

Carly wondered if the groan she heard was his or her own.

In the space of a heartbeat, Jack's gaze had looked the way it had last night in the kitchen, and maybe, she thought, just *maybe* she was ready to grab any excuse to get close to him again, to touch him again, to *feel*.

He dropped her arms and caught her hips instead, pulling her to him hard and suddenly, and delicious shock crashed through her. His body was as male as the scent of him. And his kiss was as hard as his body. He wanted her, he really did want her, and that was so heady, so intoxicating, so good.

And then she got scared.

All the things he had said earlier started to echo in her head again. *I'm safe.* Oh, no, he wasn't. *I'll be gone in a week anyway.* Was that what she wanted? If she let herself touch him now, she knew somehow that she would ache for him when he was gone.

"This won't...I can't...don't make me..." It was all she could manage.

He looked her in the eye. "*Am* I making you, cowgirl?"

She took a fraction of a second too long to answer. His mouth covered hers again, then some of the pressure eased, but she knew it wasn't because he wanted her less. He slanted his head to the side so that he could taste her more fully, and his tongue invaded, forcing her mouth wider.

Something caught on fire inside her, something reckless and crazy. She wanted to deny it and couldn't. Need rocked her.

His hands relaxed but he didn't let her go. He maneuvered her backward without breaking the contact of their mouths until she felt the sofa touch the back of her knees. Then she went down, pulling him with her.

"Jack," she managed, without any true idea of what she wanted to say.

He stopped kissing her and went still. "Say it again," he whispered after a moment.

"What?"

"My name. Just like that." *In English. Without an accent.*

"Jack," she whispered. She didn't understand but she did it anyway because he seemed to need it, as much as she needed him to keep touching her. He covered her mouth again, and his kiss was deep and urgent. He swallowed her voice, and drove his hands into her hair.

It was as he imagined, he thought, thick and rich with the scent of her shampoo, something dark and warm and vaguely herbal.

He braced some of his weight on his elbows, and Carly wriggled beneath him until she felt his hardness against her, all temptation and promise. Something both scared and eager, hot and defiant leaped inside her. *More. Take it all.* She wanted everything he could give her, here, now, just in case the ranch and all her responsibilities swallowed her alive, in case she never got another chance.

Carly cried out. *Who was this man?* How could he do this to her?

He moved his mouth to her neck and she tilted her head back to give him better access. She shuddered at the wet heat as his tongue traced a line there. He dragged at the front of her T-shirt, and finally she felt his hands on her skin. They were calloused and relentless, sliding up over her belly.

He had capable hands, not gentle but demanding. One of them slid up beneath her bra, pushing it away to expose her breasts. He covered one with his hand, and she shuddered as his thumb moved deftly over her nipple, sure and teasing. There was no hesitation in him. He wanted, he took. Sensation plunged through her from that spot, then gathered hot and wild at the core of her.

Danger, her mind screamed. But she felt helpless against her own flaming need.

She pulled frenziedly at his shirt until it was free of his jeans. She finally found his skin as well, sliding her hands up his back beneath his shirt. It was smoother than she would have thought, and his muscles were as hard as she had imagined.

She had to stop this, and she would...she would...soon.

He had been right about her skin, too, Jack thought. It was like satin, fluid muscles sliding beneath it. And she *was* as hot and honest in her responses as her picture had made him think.

She melted. She burned. She moved beneath him just right, instinctively seeking out and finding a million connections of flesh, pushing his shirt back off his shoulders, her own mouth sliding hot and wet over his neck. Yes, he would deal with the repercussions later, but now he was very, very glad he had thrown caution to the wind.

He closed his mouth over one of her breasts, teasing her nipple with his tongue even as his other hand moved down to her belly.

No apologies, she thought. Just wanting, taking, giving, without games. It was the most incredible aphrodisiac she had ever known. Then Jack froze.

He went still so suddenly and completely that Carly didn't even realize it for a moment. Then his body turned to stone beneath her hands and she opened one eye warily to look up at him.

He was staring at some spot over her head, his head tilted just a little bit like a curious cat who had seen movement in shadow, a cat who was waiting for the prey to show its face.

"What is it?" she whispered, confused, instinctively frightened. "What's wrong?"

He didn't answer but placed one hand over her mouth. In contrast to his loving, the gesture was slow and gentle.

Then she heard it, too—the tread of a single footstep outside in the foyer. She couldn't quite decide if it sounded furtive or just hesitant, but she stiffened because he had.

Something cold washed through her, because she realized that at least one part of this man had not been involved in touching her. Some part of him had been detached, holding

back, listening. Otherwise he would never have sensed someone out there so soon. And why should he even care that
someone *was* there? There were people all over the ranch!

Oh, God, what had she done? What had she been *about* to
do, with a man who clearly hadn't needed even half as much as
she had? *When would she ever learn?*

Carly groaned aloud.

"Shhh," he cautioned.

A soft rap came at the door.

Jack eased off her. He slid his hand down his left calf and she
followed the gesture with her eyes.

"What are you—"

He shook his head hard and fast, silencing her again. He
motioned to the door. Another knock sounded. He wanted her
to answer it.

Well, of course she would. She got up, trying desperately to
pull her clothing back into place, and her hands fumbled.

She had been an utter fool in so many more ways than one,
she realized. Her face burned. She had convinced herself that
Jack Fain was just an average tourist because she had wanted
him to be so badly, because from the beginning some part of
her had wanted what had just happened between them to happen. She had wanted something for herself, so she had needed
to justify it, to be able to tell herself it was okay.

She crossed unsteadily to the door, unable to look at him.
But as she reached for the knob, she felt him move past her,
behind her. She whipped around again and saw him step behind the door so that when it opened he would be out of sight
of whoever was knocking.

He had a gun!

Oh, God, oh, God. The room tilted and seemed to spin
around her. Her emotions were too vulnerable, still too close to
the surface. Her body still ached and yearned. This was crazy,
like a nightmare.

He motioned that she should open the door and she finally
did, her hand shaking badly. Jack heard Scorpion's voice.
There had never been any doubt in his mind that he would. He
felt a sweet rush of exhilaration that his hunch had been right,
that the man had made a move tonight.

I'm not washed up, just a little shaky. He was still strong
enough to give this bastard a run for his money. Starting now.

"I'm sorry to disturb you," Brad said quietly. "Am I interrupting something?"

"I—no," Carly managed.

"It took you a moment to answer the door."

"Yes, well, I—" She broke off again, taking a breath. "Did you need something?"

"I was wondering if you had any aspirin. I know you said we were supposed to bring them, but I forgot and my muscles are sore."

She had seen aspirin in his bag. Or had that been Jack's bag? Her head hurt. She couldn't remember now.

"I—sure. They're, uh, there should be some in the first-aid kit."

Still the man hesitated. "Are you alone?" he asked finally. "There's something else I need to ask you about."

Not in this lifetime, buddy.

Jack pushed his gun into the back of his jeans before Carly could answer. He left his shirt untucked, doing the bottom button again fast. Then he stepped around the door into Scorpion's view.

The man's brows touched. It was a dangerous look.

Carly's heart boomed. She took a quick, instinctive step away from him and turned hard and fast to look at Jack.

At first she appeared incredulous, then her temper sparked in her eyes. Jack spoke before she could.

"I was the last one out of the kitchen last night," he said evenly. "I put the first-aid kit back in the pantry. It should be right there on the top shelf at the front."

Scorpion hesitated only a moment longer. He'd back off and regroup, Jack thought. *And when he comes back at her a second time, by God, I'll be here then as well.*

Scorpion clearly wouldn't be happy about that, but there was nothing he could do about it without tipping his hand. When he spoke again his voice was tight and clipped with control.

"Sure," he said finally. "Thanks."

Jack reached over Carly's shoulder and pushed the door shut gently. She waited only until the man's footsteps had receded down the hall.

"*What* is going on here?" she cried.

Carefully and deliberately, Jack sat down on the sofa to put his gun back where it belonged, in the holster around his left ankle.

"What *are* you?" she went on shrilly. *"Why do you have a gun?"*

"Shhh!" His nape prickled. He could only pray that Scorpion was far enough down the hall that he hadn't heard her.

He had to try to mop up this mess, he thought. Somehow. He raked a hand through his hair.

"*You* keep a gun," he pointed out reasonably. "Two of them, in fact. There's a shotgun in a rack in the cab of your truck. I also noticed a revolver in that little office in the first barn."

It wasn't the thing to say. Her face grew redder.

"While you were snooping about, did you happen to *notice* that I'm a rancher, that there are snakes and sick cows and any number of other things around here that might present an occasion where a gun is required? You, however, are a *tourist!*" she screeched, her nerves breaking.

She wasn't going to be placated. His instinct that Scorpion would show up might have been on target, Jack thought, but everything had rapidly gone downhill from there. *Why had he pulled the damned gun?* He had never considered *not* drawing it, he realized. It had been instinctive, a fierce, automatic urge to protect her. But he had done it too fast, too soon, and he knew that had much less to do with what Scorpion might have done when she opened that door than the way he was starting to feel about this woman.

His gut rolled.

Carly took a deep, shaky breath. "You knew he was coming and you *wanted* him to know what we were doing in this room," she accused as her brain began to clear, as she finally got her bearings again. "That's why you stepped around the door like that."

Jack shook his head. "No. I just didn't think."

"Didn't think about *what?*"

"That I might be embarrassing you."

Her jaw dropped.

Jack realized too late that he should have known that that part wouldn't bother her. She wasn't coy enough to simper and blush because someone had caught her giving in to a purely personal hunger. What tripped her up, what had her hot as a hornet again, was that she thought he had set her up in the first place. He wondered how many women that would have occurred to. Was she that bitter, or that astute?

"I didn't set the stage for that guy," he said shortly.

Her heart chugged. She thought she could accept anything, forgive anything, but his using her.

She nodded and swallowed carefully. "Okay, then. Start talking."

He made a sudden decision to trust her...a very little bit. He wasn't sure he had a choice any longer. It wouldn't be the first time he'd been forced to confide in a pawn, although these days he felt a little like hedging his bets. Still, sometimes it was necessary to take people into his limited confidence when he wasn't working under deep cover. Sometimes it was necessary if he was going to make them do what he needed them to do, if he needed them to do something that would never have occurred to them otherwise.

He needed a great deal from her now.

"I'm caught up in the middle of something nasty," he said finally, neutrally.

Carly didn't know what she had expected him to say, but it wasn't that. For a moment, she was only stunned. "Something nasty?" Her voice squeaked just a little.

"That's right."

"What, with your work?" she tried.

"Yeah."

"What do you do?" That was one thing she hadn't learned by rummaging through his possessions, she realized.

"I work for the government."

"Doing what?"

"I can't tell you that."

"You can't..." The color drained from her face. "What, you're like a...*spy* or something?"

"Or something."

Her eyes went huge. "You have got to be kidding." An ex-wife, my foot, she thought.

She was getting angry. Her face was still white, but Jack saw twin spots of livid color appearing on her cheeks. "Listen," he said quietly. "Everything we say in this room has to stay right here. Okay? You can't repeat a word of it to your sister, your brother, even to the IRS."

"The IRS is government, too," she pointed out.

"Doesn't matter."

What superseded the IRS? she thought wildly. They were one step short of God!

"So what are you doing on my ranch?"

"My job."

She crossed to him very carefully. Suddenly she was so angry it made her blood feel hot. The color on her cheeks spread fast to the rest of her face.

"Let's get one thing straight here, Jack. I don't give a damn who you are or who you work for. This is *my* land, *my* ride, *my* life and *my* livelihood. This is my *world*. And whether I like it or not, I'm responsible for the welfare of the five other guests in this house right now, not to mention my family. So I suggest you start talking and tell me *what the hell is happening here,* because I don't care if you're the President! I have the right to know!" she finished breathlessly.

Jack shook his head. "No," he said calmly, "you don't."

For a minute he thought she might actually strike him. In spite of her green eyes, in that moment she was pure Spanish fire. Instead, she curled her hands very slowly, very carefully, into fists at her sides. She was breathing hard. Her breasts rose and fell, making her T-shirt shift and tremble nicely.

"Listen to me, cowgirl," he went on carefully, keeping his eyes off them. "Civilians have very few rights in situations like this. I've only told you what I have so far because I have no choice. I'm sorry," he said more softly. "I genuinely am. I don't like doing this to you. In fact, I'm doing everything I can to keep you out of it, though you may or may not believe that."

She stared at him mutely and distrustfully. Jack rubbed at a headache behind his eyes. He'd always found it so easy to keep emotion out of his work. He'd genuinely come to believe that he didn't *have* much emotion in his heart to begin with. So why was he finding this so difficult now?

"We've got to leave here tomorrow," he went on, making his voice cold, "and you've got to forget we ever had this conversation. You've got to do it because you're a civilian, and as such, you have a legal responsibility not to interfere with my work."

"I don't believe this," she breathed. Then her eyes snapped with fire again. "I could really learn to hate you."

"I pray to God that we all live long enough for you to enjoy doing it."

She blanched once more. "*Live?* Long enough? Are you in that kind of danger?"

No, cowgirl, you are if your hubby gets his hands on you. If Jack knew one thing by now, it was that she was not going to want to go anywhere with Brett Peterson ever again, and when Scorpion found that out, there would be hell to pay. Which was just another reason to keep him away from her, to get them off this ranch and into Kansas, so Scorpion *had* to leave without her or lose all opportunity to easily do so.

"Not if I can help it," Jack answered quietly, absently, thinking.

Carly paced away from him, going back to the window. He could see in the candlelight that she was shivering hard. Still, she was handling this remarkably well. It was a conversation very few people would ever have in their lifetime.

He thought, sourly, that this was one way to keep himself from touching her again. She wouldn't come near him now.

"Just answer one more question," she said tightly.

He made a sound that might have been agreement. She plunged on.

"Are you any good at what you do?"

"So they say."

"Who says?"

Jack almost grinned. She was good, he thought. But he was better.

"My co-workers."

She gave him a frustrated glance. "The generator. Was that part of this somehow? I thought you looked at me funny last night." Suddenly, something else occurred to her. "Did *you* blow it up?" He'd known right away what the buzzing sound was, she remembered, and he'd finished with his horse long before the others. He'd had plenty of time.

"That's two questions," Jack pointed out.

"Did you blow up my generator?"

"No."

Her shoulders seemed to slump. "Why me? Why *my* ranch? There have to be five hundred dude operations sprinkled over the West!"

"It's just your lucky week, I guess." At her incredulous expression, he said again, quietly, "I'm sorry," and thought that perhaps they were the only completely true words he'd said all night.

His compassion made it a hundred times worse, she thought. She couldn't believe she had actually started getting all worked up and needy inside over some . . . some kind of gun-wielding desperado who was *maybe* on the right side of the law. She couldn't believe she was standing here feeling sort of sorry for him. He looked so miserable, but it was *her* nice, boring life that was being torn apart!

She gave a choked sound, then she thought of something else. "This has something to do with Brad, doesn't it?" Brad, she thought, with all the price tags still on his clothing. *Had* she seen aspirin in his bag? Suddenly it seemed vital that she remember.

But Jack was shaking his head. "No. I thought someone else was coming." He lied easily, out of habit. The words burned like acid in his mouth.

It didn't matter. It couldn't matter now. He had already lost her . . . and *that* brought emotion, the most amazing, poignant regret.

Carly blinked. He could almost see her mind working behind those beautiful green eyes. *Tread carefully,* he thought. He realized again that she was one smart lady. She wouldn't be easy to use.

"Who then?" she asked finally.

"Huh?"

"Who did you think was coming, if not Brad?"

"It doesn't matter. I thought it was someone else."

"Someone here? Someone on my ranch?"

He couldn't answer that. He stayed quiet, watching her. She began pacing again.

"So you're saying that that was just a . . . a false alarm of some sort."

"Yeah."

"Jumpy, aren't you?"

"You would be, too."

"Under what circumstances?"

One corner of his mouth almost twitched into a smile again. "Good try, cowgirl, but I'll take the Fifth on that one."

Her jaw hardened. "And touching me had nothing to do with it?"

Jack let out a harsh burst of breath. So they were back to that again. But at least it was one question he could easily answer.

"Touching you was a gut reaction that's more or less been nagging me ever since I saw you."

She looked surprised again, then uncharacteristically flustered. She touched a hand to her hair in a purely feminine gesture that drove arousal through him all over again. This time he clamped down on it.

"This scares the hell out of me," she said quietly.

He wondered if she was talking about what had happened between them, or what was lurking out there in her hallways. He figured it could be either one, or both.

"You can be scared, cowgirl," he said finally, "just don't be scared of me. I really am the good guy."

Carly gave a halfhearted shrug. "We're not going to pick up where we left off."

"No," Jack said. Now, abruptly sane again, with his head clear, he knew it was impossible. Not because of Scorpion necessarily—he supposed he'd cleared that hurdle in his own mind. And it wasn't because he had so little to give. She was a big girl and she was doing a good job of figuring that out on her own.

It was because of the lies.

He wouldn't make love to her under false pretenses. It would have been one thing if he had not let her into his confidence at all. Those had been lies of omission. But now . . . now everything had changed. Now he owed her some measure of honor. He was vaguely surprised to find that he had some pretty strong scruples after all.

Carly went to the sofa and sat with meticulous care. "You're still not going to let me go upstairs to my room, though, either, are you?"

"No," Jack said again.

Something in her eyes flared, some spark of her old self. "I can't stay here with you all night. I won't. Holly—the other guests—"

"We'll worry about all that at dawn, before they get up," he interrupted.

He had an answer for everything. She finally nodded and lay down with a heavy sigh. He noticed that she didn't put her back to him.

Chapter 8

Somehow, impossibly, Carly slept. But when she woke just before the rooster, she was relatively sure that Jack hadn't.

He was still standing by the window, where he'd been when she'd finally dozed off. She watched him without moving for a moment, not wanting to let him know she was doing it. She wanted just one candid, unguarded glimpse of him, she realized. She wanted some inkling as to who he was, *what* he was, outside of the careful, almost rehearsed explanations he had given her last night.

Lies. She knew instinctively that that was what they were. Bald ones.

"How long before you can get us out of here?" he asked suddenly.

Carly jolted and sat up. "How did you know I was awake?"

Jack finally looked around at her. He wore a small smile. "I heard your eyes open."

Carly gave an unladylike snort that carried at least a tinge of despair. The events of last night crashed in on her again with all their full weight.

"Oh, God," she whispered.

"It's five-thirty," Jack went on with a curious lack of emotion. "How soon before we can get this show on the road?"

Carly looked at him. "I don't remember agreeing to leave today."

"You don't have a choice."

He couldn't spend another night in this parlor with her and hold himself back from touching her again, Jack thought, or at the very least, from wanting to until he couldn't think clearly. He'd realized that at about three o'clock this morning. He had to keep emotion and distraction out of this. It had always been easy enough before, but it was not easy now, not with this woman, so he would work on it.

"*Assuming* I was going to leave today, I'd need a minimum of six hours to get ready," Carly was saying tightly. "And that's *after* everyone wakes up and has breakfast."

"No dice. Six hours is way too much."

"Too bad. It's a hypothetical situation anyway. I'm not leaving."

She stood and stretched. He couldn't help noticing the slide of her muscles beneath her skin. Her shorts left entirely too much of her legs within sight.

Carly saw the way he was watching her and she brought her arms down fast. The hunger in his gaze was finally replaced by something flinty and hard. She wasn't sure which expression was worse.

"Am I correct in assuming that you can make me?" she asked finally.

Jack hesitated. "Not quickly enough for it to matter. By the time I pulled all the necessary strings, tomorrow would be here and you'd be willing to go anyway. I'm not going to force you at gunpoint, if that's what you're asking." Not unless it was a case of ultimate, last resort, anyway, he thought bitterly. Then he would be obligated to whether he wanted to or not.

Carly's brows went up. "And you're telling me so?"

He left the window and came toward her, fast and aggressively. Carly took an instinctive, wary step backward, and she thought she saw him wince.

"Look, I'm telling you as much as I can, without endangering you or me or anyone else. You've got to know that." *You've got to believe it.*

He didn't know why it should be so important. She was just one cog in a great big wheel, he reminded himself, and the wheel was—hopefully—making its final turn here. She was a *pawn*. It shouldn't matter what she believed. This would be over soon, and with any luck, both she and Scorpion would be memories. It shouldn't matter what she believed, but it did.

"So what happens if I refuse?" Carly asked.

"Nothing. Not immediately. But I can pretty much guarantee you that some other calamity will befall your house or your land or your herd sometime during the next twenty-four hours."

Carly stiffened. "Is that a threat? Because—"

"No!" he snapped, suddenly frustrated and angry. "I'm just telling you the way it is here. And if something else happens, then I'm going to have to explain it to some pretty powerful men in Washington. I'm going to have to tell them what the hell I was still doing at Seventy Four Draw under the circumstances, allowing it to happen. I'd be hard-pressed to keep your name out of it. They know me too well to believe I'd simply drop the ball on something like this."

Because none of them, he thought, *none* of them was as wary of his lost nerve as he had become.

"So what happens when these powerful men get ticked off at me?"

"You're obstructing justice, Carly."

She spun away from him. "I don't believe this," she muttered yet again.

Not many people in her position would, he thought. He watched her grapple with it once more, stretching her mind to accept that the unimaginable was really happening to her. And she didn't even know the half of it, he thought.

She let out a long breath but she wouldn't look at him. "I can't leave until my men get the herd together," she muttered.

"So go tell them to do it."

"The steers are all penned together, but the cows... the cows I want to take are scattered all over the ranch. It'll take time to find them all. They're tagged, but—"

"Carly—"

She went on desperately, as though trying to restore order to her world, as though trying to make all the little things matter again. "And there's the cook wagon, of course," she rushed on. "I can't leave until Theresa and I pack it."

"You're babbling, Carly."

She ignored him. "And I *definitely* can't leave until I put you folks on horses for another six hours. That's part of my brother's agreement with the insurance company. I have to give twenty hours of instruction before I can take any of you anywhere."

Ah, Jack thought. That explained why she had been working them so relentlessly, with barely a break. He wished she had told him sooner. His backside might not feel quite so much like a piece of plywood right now.

"If anyone gets hurt," he said quietly, "the government will take care of it. Uncle Sam's your insurance company now. He'll cover any losses you incur."

Carly's eyes narrowed and her expression twisted. "Why aren't I comforted?" Because, she thought, she no longer trusted her government worth a hill of beans. Especially not now.

This was what those precious, scraped-together tax dollars were going toward, she thought wildly, and fought the urge to laugh. She knew it would be a wild, hysterical sound.

"What am I supposed to tell everyone?" she managed finally. "Don't you think they're going to wonder why I'm bolting out of here a day early?"

Scorpion certainly would, Jack thought. He considered the problem.

"Tell them you've heard some bad weather is heading our way over the weekend," he said finally.

"And how exactly was I supposed to hear this without a generator, with no electricity or radio or television?"

One of Jack's brows went up. He thought that if she ever got tired of ranching, he'd have a job for her in Washington.

"You heard it before the generator went out."

She looked at him incredulously. "And I'm just mentioning it *now?*"

He got exasperated. "Damn it, it's the only thing I can think of. Tell them you want to be up in the Kansas flatlands before the storm hits."

"I guess that makes sense," she admitted grudgingly. As much as anything did right now, at any rate.

"So are you going to do this gracefully, or do I have to start pulling strings?"

"Go ahead and pull. Like you said, by tomorrow I'll be ready to leave anyway."

Jack's eyes widened. Comparatively speaking, she was starting to make his stubborn old horse look like a pushover.

"For God's sake, Carly!" he exploded. "Will you please use your head here? What's so bad about leaving today? What's the big deal?"

The big deal, she thought, was the principle of the thing. She felt as though if she did this, if she went along with him, then everything was going to spiral right out of her control. And that terrified her. Because she had always been in control. *Always.* Until Jack Fain had walked into her life. Briefly, with an inward cringe, she remembered what she had been fully prepared to do with him last night.

Well, he had been right about one thing—he was going to be gone in a week, this would all be over, and she would still have a ranch to sustain and the IRS to contend with. She *had* to keep her grip on things. She had the weird suspicion that if she didn't, she might never remember how to handle things on her own again.

"The sooner you get your herd into Fort Dodge the sooner you get paid for it, right?" Jack tried.

"Wrong," she snapped. "They're going to *auction.* And the auction is Wednesday night. I could be there right now, but I still wouldn't get paid for them until Thursday." Except, she thought, if she left this morning, that was one less day that Theresa would have to dance around the electricity problem.

"I'd think you'd want to give yourself plenty of time on this ride," Jack said evenly, "just to be on the safe side, what with the tourists and all. What if you don't get there in time for the auction?''

Then we're bankrupt. ''Oh, hell,'' she groaned, giving up. ''Why not? How much worse can this get?''

He thought it was probably better not to tell her that. ''Is that a yes?'' he asked cautiously.

''It's a sort of,'' she grumbled. ''I'll still need at least…probably four hours.'' She started for the door again.

''Where are you going now?'' he demanded.

Carly spun back to him. ''To take one last, real shower,'' she snapped. ''You might consider it, too. Do I have your permission, or do you want to stand guard over me in the bathroom, too? Just what is it that you think I'm going to do if you let me out of your sight?''

Not you, cowgirl, your hubby. He didn't answer.

Carly jerked the door open and went up the stairs two at a time. When she got her hands on Michael, she thought, this I-told-you-so was going to be a humdinger. She had been opposed to this tourist business from the start, if only because all the work of it would fall on her shoulders. Now she fully intended that her brother was going to be hearing about this until the cows came home.

Assuming she was ever allowed to tell him.

Three hours later, Carly came downstairs into the kitchen and let her duffel bag slide off her shoulder to the floor. Her sister was at the sink, finishing the last of the breakfast dishes, and she was clearly upset.

''I still don't understand why you're doing this,'' Theresa protested. Her hands moved faster. *Splash, swipe, rinse.*

''I've told you. There's a storm coming. Why take chances?''

"But you *are* taking chances!" Theresa cried, spinning about to face her. "What about that insurance?"

Carly knew she was talking about the policy on the guests now, not the one on the house. "I'm just taking the safest of two gambles," she answered. "I'd rather run the risk that no one falls off their horse than gamble that we won't run head-on into a twister if we leave too late. Everyone's riding pretty well. The storm's more of a sure bet."

Carly went to the refrigerator to get a last glass of orange juice. She drank deeply, her stomach heaving hollowly as the juice hit it. She hadn't been able to eat breakfast.

Damn you, Jack. She hated lying to her own sister.

She slid the empty glass into the suds in the sink just as footsteps came thumping down the back stairs. Carly looked that way and her heart skipped a beat. Holly lugged her tent through the door and deposited it on the kitchen floor.

"Does this mean you're going with us?" Carly asked, almost afraid to hope. She had finally decided not to force her, since Theresa would be staying behind now. But there had been a vague, almost imperceptible change in Holly lately.

Lately...since Jack Fain had turned up on the scene. Carly's heart thumped again.

She knew she had to tell her, here and now, right away, that nothing was or ever would be happening in that arena. Especially not now. Not after last night. And she couldn't do it, she realized helplessly, couldn't bring herself to shatter Holly's new enthusiasm and warmth. She wanted her to go with them too badly.

Later, she thought, *when we're on the trail, I'll tell her the truth. I'll do it when my thoughts aren't so scattered and I can break it to her gently.* At least, she thought, she would tell her as much as Jack would let her.

"I'm really glad you changed your mind," she said softly, aloud.

Holly grinned and began dragging her tent to the door. "Well, maybe it'll be worth it."

Carly followed her. She considered eliminating the extra weight of a tent that they wouldn't really need. Holly could sleep in hers. Then she fought off the urge to strip her of that little bit of independence.

Let her grow up. She was going with them. That was enough.

"You can go ahead and put that in the cook wagon," she called out after her. "All the supplies are already loaded."

"Okay."

There were more footsteps on the back stairs. Carly went to that door and pulled it open, looking up. It was Jack.

"We have a problem," he said shortly, stepping into the kitchen, looking pointedly at Theresa's back.

Carly glanced that way, too, but she was not about to make this any easier for him. "What might that be?" she asked sweetly, staying where she was.

Jack glowered and spoke in an undertone. "Holly thinks she's going with us."

"She is."

"I don't think that's a good idea."

He glared at Theresa again. Carly looked that way, too. Her sister was watching them avidly now, still washing dishes but looking their way without apology, straining to overhear their conversation.

Carly heard a noise behind her and realized that Holly had come back into the kitchen as well.

Something, a pulse or a nerve, ticked dangerously at Jack's jaw. He grabbed her elbow and propelled her into the hallway.

"Easy, cowboy." Carly wrenched away from him. His fingers had been digging into her just a little bit more than she thought the situation warranted. He was certainly tense. And she was still angry enough not to give him an inch.

"You're hell-bent and determined not to help this come off smoothly, aren't you?" he snarled.

Carly crossed her arms over her chest. "That's right."

"Why can't you just cooperate?"

"I am," she snapped, "more than I care to. I said I'd go today. I didn't say I liked it."

He put his face close to hers. "I don't give a damn whether you like it or not. I'm trying to keep people alive here. Don't you get that yet? And now one of those people is your daughter. I don't want to have to worry about a kid on top of everything else!" It struck him then that whether he wanted to be involved in their lives or not, he wouldn't be able to stand it if anything happened to wipe last night's smile off the kid's face, if something ever stopped her from imitating her mother just so.

Carly blanched. "I want her to go," she said stubbornly. "I...we need this time together."

"She can't go."

"Why not?"

"Come on, cowgirl, think about it. Use your head."

"Use my head?" she cried. "Just what would you like me to think about, Jack? I don't have any idea what's going on here! What kind of danger are we in? Tell me that, and I'll make up my *own* mind what's best for Holly, what's best for all of us."

"Would you keep your voice down?" He had been crazy, out of his mind, to trust her. She might be honest, she might be true-blue, but when she got a bee in her bonnet, she was uncontrollable, he thought angrily. And there was just no room in this mess for a wild card.

"She could get hurt," he bit out.

"*How?* By *who?*"

"I can't tell you that."

The hallway seemed to fade and shift around her. Something cold replaced her blood. What he hadn't said was clear as a bell. The danger was someone on her ride.

Brad, she thought again. It *had* to be Brad, with all his price tags, even on his underwear, and those weird smiles.

"Then maybe we all ought to stay right here at Seventy Four Draw where we're safe," she said shakily.

"We're not safe here, either," Jack grated. "And I don't want a kid involved. I want her left behind, separate and safe and apart from all this. You've got to stop fighting me and trust me, cowgirl."

Carly watched him, a headache starting behind her eyes. "I don't suppose it's occurred to you that you haven't given me anything worth putting my trust in?"

"Yes," he answered, surprising both of them. "It has. All I can tell you is that I'm trying my damnedest to keep you and your family safe."

"I want Holly to be with me. Given . . . given what's happening here, whatever it is, I just want her to be where I can see her. And . . . we need this trip together, Jack. You don't . . . you just can't understand." And there was no way she could tell him how she so desperately needed to start mending some of the personal fences that the ranch had torn down on her.

He was going to have to work around this, Jack realized with a sinking feeling. She wasn't going to relent. And he was afraid that if he forced her, he'd lose her cooperation entirely.

"Okay. All right," he said finally. He took a deep, steadying breath. He didn't like it. He *hated* it. But, once again, she was pretty much leaving him no choice.

"Did you tell everyone about the storm?" he asked shortly, finally.

Carly relaxed a little, too, knowing a victory when she saw it. But she still eyed him warily. "Yes. Theresa doesn't believe me. If I'd heard something about a storm, she knows I would have mentioned it right away. But I think *she* thinks I'm just frantic enough about money to want to play it completely safe."

"Good." He started to move into the kitchen again, then he paused to say something that had never had a place in any of his jobs before. Not with a pawn.

"Thanks."

Chapter 9

It took them more than five hours to leave, but by noon the house and the outbuildings of Seventy Four Draw were nothing more than a smudge on the horizon behind them. Scorpion rode just behind the cattle, and Jack hung back even farther. He could feel the assassin's awareness of him now, reaching for him like invisible tentacles. Jack figured that as far as Scorpion was concerned, there had been two very unpleasant developments of late. His lady was apparently taking up with one of the guests, and she had suddenly decided to set off a day early.

Either occurrence would have been a small problem in and of itself. Together they were a clear indication that something was off-kilter. Jack wasn't alarmed. It was time to stir things up a little. He wanted Scorpion to become agitated. Now that they were finally off the ranch, he wanted him to leave.

Without Carly.

Jack's gaze slid to her. She was engrossed in moving the cattle. She was everywhere, first riding wide to bring back a stray, then leaning low off the side of her saddle to check the bell on the lead cow. He enjoyed watching her. She was competent, and she was in her element. She moved with the horse as though it were an extension of her own body, fluidly, easily. It was like watching a dance.

Her eyes moved steadily and relentlessly between the animals and the guests and the cowboys, then back again. When she finally seemed to settle down, Jack rode to join her.

"Aren't we heading east?" The sun was high above them now, but it had come from the horizon ahead.

Carly shot him a narrow look. She was still mad, he realized.

"So you can tell direction. Did they teach you that in spy school?"

His lips quirked. "Well, they pay me to be observant."

"Who?"

Jack let himself smile fully. "And being so observant," he went on without answering, "I would have to say that we're not riding north into Kansas at the moment. Are you trying to pull a fast one, cowgirl?"

"Thank you so much for your confidence." Carly looked ahead, her jaw tightening. "Nate Progress's place is north of my ranch," she said finally. "And Nate and my father didn't get along worth a hill of beans. If I tried to cross his land, he'd probably demand half my herd for a tariff. On the other hand, I have a friendly arrangement with my nearest neighbor to the east. I lease a small portion of his spread every summer so that I can graze and camp there on my way to auction. So we'll loop around to the east and stop on Rawley's acres tonight, then we can head straight north across BLM land from there."

"BLM?" Jack repeated. "Bureau of Land Management?"

"Yeah. You know, one of those *government* things."

Jack gave a bark of laughter. "Touché, cowgirl."

She didn't hear him, or pretended not to. She spurred her horse and went deliberately to ride with Plank.

Jack let her go because Scorpion was drifting. His horse began wandering off to the left of the herd, and Jack watched him, scowling. He wondered again where the money was. He'd kept a close eye on the assassin all morning, and he hadn't seen a sign of it. No way would Scorpion have left it behind, not even leaving on such short notice as they had, though Jack had been hoping that that would trip him up a bit, make him sloppy.

He sighed roughly. The money didn't particularly matter. No one had asked him to recover it. But he didn't like uncertainty. He wanted to know.

His gaze went to Carly again, and then Scorpion moved.

Whatever had drawn the man's attention over there to the left must have proved innocuous. What was it? The wagon was far behind them and off to the right....

The wagon.

In that moment, Jack knew where the money was. From the left side of the herd, Scorpion could keep an eye on it from an unobtrusive vantage point.

A guy named Mazie Montoro was driving the cook wagon. He wasn't one of Carly's regular men. She'd said he was a part-timer, a drifter. And now he was a drifter whose days were dangerously numbered.

Jack put his heels to his mount and cantered to catch up with Carly again. "Question," he said when he reached her.

Her eyes slid sideways. "Now there's a surprise."

"Will Mazie sleep in the wagon?"

She looked at him fully and scowled. He knew she was trying to glean something from his off-the-wall question.

"Why on earth would he want to do that?" she asked finally.

"I don't know. That's why I'm asking."

"There's not enough room in there."

"Oh. Good." So if Scorpion took his money at night, Jack thought, then the cowboy was reasonably safe.

"Is it?" Carly asked sharply. "Why?"

He didn't answer. "Do me a favor, cowgirl."

"You mean another one?"

He grinned fleetingly. "Yeah. Can you keep Mazie as far away from the wagon as possible?"

"So how's he supposed to drive it?" she asked incredulously.

"I mean later, when we camp."

Her jaw hardened. "You know, accomplices tend to be much more effective when they know what they're doing and why."

"Yeah," he said softly, "and sometimes they die."

She flinched. That ought to shut her up, he thought.

"I'll see what I can do," she said flatly. Then she swerved, suddenly cutting off the bell cow. "Whoa!"

The herd rumbled on for a few hundred yards before most of them stopped. Then some steers began splitting off, wandering. Jack looked ahead, wondering what she had seen.

The ground sloped downward. There was no real grass to speak of, at least not grass as he had ever known it. Spare shoots of green tufted out of earth that was baked orange by the sun. Spiderweb fissures crisscrossed the land. But down below the rim of the rise, Jack thought he saw the tips of trees.

Carly rode back among the other guests. "We're at a draw," she called out, explaining. "Actually, it's the one the ranch is named for. It's sort of a side gap off a river or stream, where the water drains. Anyway, here's your chance to play cowpoke. I'm going to need all your help. The herd's going to stray badly when we hit the water and the grass at the bottom of this hill, and I'll need you all to flank them. Come on, move up here. You've got to ride outside the herd."

They all came eagerly, even Scorpion.

"Your horses know what to do, and they'll do it," Carly went on. "They're all trained cutting ponies. That means that if they see a steer splitting off, they're going to move after it and cut it back. They'll jump around and swerve a lot to do it, so just grab hold of your saddle horn and *stay on.* The ground gets real boggy the closer we get to the bottom of the draw, so it's going to be a rough ride."

"What about the wagon?" Scorpion called out.

Carly's eyes moved to the man sharply. Jack felt his heart sink hard and fast.

"What about it?" she asked edgily.

"If the ground's boggy, can it get through?"

She hesitated too obviously. "We'll let Mazie worry about that. How about if you just concentrate on staying on your horse?"

Scorpion watched her. His eyes seemed to try to probe into her mind, weighing her reaction to a question that should have been innocuous. Jack cursed himself for mentioning the wagon in the first place. He cursed Scorpion for coming right out and asking about it. None of his recriminations mattered. The bottom line was that Carly Castagne might be remarkably good at a lot of things, but hiding her thoughts wasn't one of them.

She finally started the cattle moving again, and they lowed in anticipation as the ground began sloping downward. They smelled the grass and the water. More tufts of wiry green began to punch up from the earth as they descended the rise. Then, true to her warning, the steers and the cows began to stray. Jack felt his own mount lurch beneath him, spinning right. Its trot was bone-jarring as the ground got softer and its hooves began to suck up mud with each step. He stayed on and the horse leaped to the left, almost unseating him, going after another wayward cow.

He managed to look around at the others. Myra was doing remarkably well, grinning from ear to ear. Leigh looked terrified. Her knuckles were white where she gripped her saddle horn. Winston squeezed his legs around his mount a little too hard in his panic, and the horse lunged forward a little, nearly unseating him for the second time in as many days. Reggie's spine was ramrod straight, and his eyes were narrowed in concentration. Even Scorpion's attention was pretty much focused on staying on his horse.

Jack looked for Carly. She was behind the herd now with Plank and Gofer and they were hooting and shouting, waving their hats at the cattle, driving them on. As he watched, she tossed her hat to Holly, who had lost hers. The girl began waving it, laughing, smiling widely enough to blind the sun. Something happened again in the area of Jack's heart.

The animals plunged into the narrow stream, lowing and bellowing. Even as the last of them passed through and started up the ground on the other side, Mazie began the crossing in the wagon.

It lurched and creaked. Mud clung to its wheels. The team strained, and metal whined and clanked. The cowboy was experienced and determined. He cracked a whip over the horses' backs and they labored on, dragging their load through the water. But the man knew something was wrong, and so did Carly and the other cowboys.

They rode back to the wagon, scowling. "I didn't pack it *that* heavy," Carly muttered.

"Well, the brutes are old," Plank volunteered.

"You best not be saying I am," the grizzled, toothless Mazie warned.

Carly said nothing, only frowned hard at the wheels.

Fifteen million dollars, Jack thought. It was a hell of a lot of paper, any way you looked at it. *Come on, cowgirl, let it go.*

With a last, great popping sound, the wagon lunged up the bank again. Mazie bounced and his hat went flying. He brought the team to a stop when they reached relatively hard ground, then he climbed down heavily and plodded back to get the hat.

"All right," Carly shouted. "Let's keep moving."

She rode into the herd and mud spattered everywhere as the cattle churned forward again. Scorpion was left behind to bring up the rear, still hovering relatively close to the wagon.

Jack's breath came back to him harshly and suddenly. He realized that he had been holding it.

He realized, too, that he was going to have a lot of explaining to do sooner or later. Unless he badly missed his guess, Carly Castagne was not going to let that little episode go by without comment.

Within the hour, the caravan stopped above a convoluted twist of land where three chasms came together. Though none of the ruts was especially deep, the knot they formed made for a treacherous series of ridges and gullies.

Carly sat astride, staring down at the spot, her teeth worrying her lower lip. Jack went to join her.

"What's the matter?"

She glanced at him. "It's gotten worse since the last time I came this way."

"How long ago was that?"

"Is that another spy question?"

Jack stiffened and looked around. The others were all milling about, close enough to overhear them.

"Careful, cowgirl, or you're going to get somebody hurt," he said in an undertone.

Her color faded fast. "Oh. Sorry."

"No harm done." *This time.*

She continued to look shaken. "I don't think I can do this. I can't…I'm not cut out for all this subterfuge, especially when I don't know what it is that I'm supposed to be hiding," she whispered.

No, he thought, she wouldn't be. She was a woman who said what was on her mind when it was on it. "Can't you just forget about it?" he asked. "Put it out of your mind?"

She looked at him incredulously.

"You more or less have to, Carly. You've got to stop *reacting*."

"To what?"

"To anything that seems suspicious to you. Maybe it is, and maybe it isn't, but it's not your concern. Put it out of your mind." Scorpion was watching them closely. Jack changed the subject. "So what are you going to do about that glitch?" He nodded down at the forked gullies again.

Carly hesitated. If he was changing the subject, then there was probably a good reason for it and she fought the urge to look around as he had done. Maybe he was right. Maybe it was better not to think too much. Thinking only made her crazy because there was really nothing she could do but go blindly along with him anyway.

"We're going to have to get through it right here," she said finally. "I don't think it's going to get much better to the north or south. I could spend half a day running us back and forth, looking for a safer way to get through, but I'd probably only end up losing time."

"You're a day ahead of schedule," he pointed out helpfully.

She shot him a withering look. "Don't remind me."

"You should thank me."

"I could choke you."

"Still mad?"

"And confused. And about scared out of my pants."

"Now *there's* an image with possibilities."

She didn't smile.

Jack sobered. His heart moved in a way he was entirely unfamiliar with. "I really am sorry," he heard himself say yet again.

"Are you?" She thought about it. It was all she would get from him, she knew. She swung down off her horse.

"Now what?" he asked.

"I guess this is as good a place as any to stop for dinner. I'm starving."

She wasn't so scared that it interfered with her appetite, Jack noted dryly.

He dismounted as well and his legs nearly gave out. One minute they were where they were supposed to be, beneath him, and in the next, air filled them—hollow, *achy* air, and it seemed that he had left them somewhere behind him. He looked to see Carly smirking at him.

"Problem, cowboy?"

"Maybe I'm too old for this."

"And maybe you're riding wrong." She hesitated, picking her words carefully, looking around at the others in spite of herself. She was learning. "Too bad we couldn't have gotten in a few more hours of lessons," she added carefully.

"Yeah. Too bad."

"If we had, you might have learned that you should be resting your weight more on the insides of your thighs. You should be keeping your seat with your knees. Then your cute little tush wouldn't hurt."

He grinned. "You think it's cute?"

Carly almost stumbled. She couldn't believe him. Someone was trying to kill him—at least she thought that that was what was going on—and here he was worried about his backside and what she thought of it.

Then she realized that something must be decidedly wrong with her, too, because her ride had been infiltrated by something beyond her imagination and she gave in to an uncontrollable urge to laugh.

"I do like you, Jack," she managed finally. He was incorrigible, irreverent . . . strong. Or at least he had nerves of steel.

"Good. So answer my question."

"It'll do."

"Feel free to inspect the merchandise."

This time she did stumble. They had led their horses back to the wagon—*what is it with the wagon? Don't think about it. Don't think*—and she tied her mare without looking at him. "No need to," she answered. "I'm not buying."

"Well, it's not actually for sale. But I'd consider a short-term lease."

Her eyes finally shot back to his. They were wide, so green, and awareness flared in them again, then she just looked scared.

"Thanks all the same," she said quietly, "but I think I'll quit while I'm ahead. I could get in too deeply with you after all, Jack. And you were right. I don't want that. I don't want to take any more chances, especially not with a man who won't tell me exactly why he's running around toting a gun."

Jack felt something kick inside him. It wasn't entirely panic, even though that kind of words, coming from any woman, had always terrified him before. There was so much inherent responsibility in them. They required a great deal in return. He had nothing, nothing at all, to give back to anyone, and he had accepted that a long time ago.

But her words kept ringing in his head. *I could get in too deeply. I don't want to take any more chances.*

Jack looked deliberately out at the tangled, barren land. It was much like his heart, he thought. Yet somehow, incredibly, a few things *did* manage to grow out there.

He looked at Scorpion again.

"You know what, cowgirl?" he murmured. "I think sometimes chances happen whether we're real willing to take them or not."

They got through the tangle of culverts with only one minor mishap. Leigh's horse balked and she went neatly over its head. In and of itself, it wasn't much of a problem, but for a good hour afterward the blonde refused to get back on her horse. Carly was disgusted and Jack was amused. Carly threatened her with bodily harm and Gofer oozed sympathy, and together they finally convinced her to continue with the ride.

They set off again, the wagon pitching wildly on its way through the snarl. They rode until twilight began bruising the sky, then they rode a little farther in darkness. Finally, Carly reined in, studying the landscape. Jack stopped beside her, thinking it looked thoroughly inhospitable.

"I guess we should call it a day," she murmured.

"*Here?* You want to camp here?"

She looked over at him. "What's wrong with here? It's a good spot."

"If you're a cow."

Between and beneath the tough shoots of grass, the ground still looked cracked and hard and parched. Jack tried again. "I don't suppose that if we go any farther, we'll find something more conducive to cushioning a sleeping bag?"

"Wimp."

"Well, I like my creature comforts."

"Then you should have gone to Acapulco, hot or not." Then she remembered that this wasn't a vacation for him after all. Her throat tightened and she breathed carefully past the lump.

"Actually," she went on, "this is the land I told you about earlier. Rawley Cummings's. I lease it. I'd have liked to have gotten a little closer to his house, but thanks to Leigh, this will have to do."

"Too bad," Jack agreed, and it was heartfelt. A house would have had a bathroom, a shower, padded chairs.

"I've got to ride over there and let him know we're here," she went on.

Jack stiffened. "Where?"

"What do you mean, *where?* To his *house.*"

Night was falling hard, Jack thought, and with it, Scorpion would have a hundred opportunities to leave. He had a strong need to keep Carly in sight so that he was sure the assassin would be leaving without her. He didn't want to be worrying about her while he went after the bastard.

Carly saw the reaction on his face. "All right," she said wearily, "what is it now?"

Jack continued to scowl. "If you went, how long would you be gone?"

Her spine snapped straight. "I *am* going, and Rawley's house is about six miles from here. My mare's tired, but I should be able to make it in an hour. So say three before I get back."

"*Three?* You're going to spend an *hour* over there? What for?"

"I told you. Rawley's a friend."

What kind of friend?

The question leaped into his mind, stunning him. It had never consciously occurred to him that she could be involved with someone else, that there could be a current man in her life, a man besides the one Scorpion had once been. She had said she was a woman alone, and he had taken that at face value. Now he realized that it was a stretch to assume that there hadn't been anyone else for her in eleven long years.

A strange little beast began to crawl around in his gut, similar to the one that had nailed him when she'd flashed that smile at Scorpion the other day. He felt, irrationally, that she was his, as much as, if not more than, she was Scorpion's. *He* had been the one carrying her picture around these past many years.

And then there was the matter of last night.

He wanted to grab her and demand to know what the hell she thought she had been doing with him if there was someone else in the picture. "I'm going with you," he said instead.

Carly's jaw dropped. "You're not invited."

"I am now."

"No," she said tightly, "you're not." Then she took a deep, steadying breath. "What is your problem, Jack? What do you think I'm going to do if you let me out of your sight for a few hours? I want to get these cattle into Fort Dodge without any further complications. I'm not going to do anything that's going to cost me time. So go ahead and play cops and robbers if that's what turns you on, but *I've* got a living to make here and I owe Rawley the professional courtesy of letting him know that I'm making use of my lease tonight!"

She started to turn away. Jack cleared his throat carefully. "I just don't think you should be riding across twelve miles of pitch-darkness by yourself tonight."

"I ride these same miles four times every summer." But something inside her squirmed nervously. All of a sudden, twelve miles of night shadows sounded decidedly unnerving.

She groaned, feeling something hot spring to her eyes, and that was ridiculous. Ever since this man had set foot on her ranch, her emotions had been unruly and wild, and she *hated* that, hated it more than anything, because her emotions had always toed the line before.

"Leave me alone, Jack," she said quietly, her voice breaking. "Just . . . leave me alone, will you, please?"

She trotted away. Jack hesitated, then he followed her.

If he thought about it rationally, he knew he could safeguard against Scorpion getting to her from either end. He could watch over her, or he could keep his eye on the assassin. And it made a lot more sense to watch over Scorpion, he realized, so that he could interfere at the very first sign of any move. Jack knew he couldn't really tag along with Carly, no matter how much he wondered who the hell Rawley Cummings was.

"All right, how about this?" he suggested neutrally. "Can you take someone else with you? Plank or Gofer or Mazie?"

She reined in suddenly. "Damn it, Jack! *Why?*"

He didn't answer.

"Scratch what I said earlier about liking you," she muttered. "I'm starting to hate you."

"I know. Please take Plank. And Holly, too, while you're at it." As long as one of them was gone, he decided, it was easiest to get both mother and daughter out of the immediate picture, to keep them together. And safe. Yeah, that would definitely make him feel better.

Carly glared at him, then she looked doggedly out to the horizon. Put that way, how could she say no? Her throat started to hurt again.

"You'll have to help Gofer keep an eye on the herd," she said finally. "They tend to stray."

"I'll do the best I can."

"Reggie might be able to help you. But leave Winston out of it. He's as likely as not to send them bolting into Kansas without us." She laughed nervously. "As for Brad . . ." She trailed off, shaking her head noncommittally.

Jack nodded. She was stalling. They both seemed to realize it at the same time. She took up her reins again.

"Listen, don't stop for anything, okay?" he said suddenly.

She frowned. "Like what?"

"Like the sound of a calf in distress, or a call for help, anything that would ordinarily get you to stop."

She closed her eyes hard. "You're scaring me, Jack."

"Good." Scorpion would have to kill him to be able to go after her, he thought, but that sort of thing had happened before, to other agents.

Carly gave him a long, worried, last look, then she rode off to get Plank and Holly. This time Jack let her go.

A few minutes later, the three of them headed off into the darkness at a steady canter. Jack watched her go with a very bad feeling, but he had done all he could think of to keep this turn of events from blowing things sky-high.

Chapter 10

Rawley was waiting on his porch for Carly. It was five days before auction time up at Dodge, and she always stopped in when she was making use of her lease. He leaned forward in his wheelchair, watching them approach.

Carly swung down from her mare, tied her to the fence post and jogged up the steps. Plank called out that he was going over to the bunkhouse to try to scare up a game of cards. Holly wanted to tag along. Carly seemed to hesitate before she let her daughter go.

Carly's hug was tight and long.

"Keep it up and you're gonna choke me. You want a drink?"

Carly finally straightened. "I'd love one."

"Come on in."

She held the screen door for him and followed him into his kitchen. He was a good-looking man. He had the Cummings Welsh-bred appeal with black hair and startling blue eyes. She had gone through school with him and he had been her friend for as long as she could remember. He'd been the first boy she'd ever kissed, and then he had taken a hellacious fall off a cantankerous stallion a week later. Sometime after that, they'd grown up and apart.

Still, his reputation with the ladies hadn't suffered after his accident, at least not anywhere near as much as she would have expected. Probably because he was such a good, uncomplicated man. Why *couldn't* she have fallen for him? Carly wondered suddenly, wildly. Why was she interested in someone like Jack Fain?

"What's with Plank?" Rawley took a bottle of bourbon from beneath the sink.

Carly's hand faltered as she reached over his head into a cabinet for glasses. *Not your brother, not your sister, not the IRS.* She had to assume that Rawley Cummings fell into that category somewhere.

She clenched her jaw against answering. She knew he'd find it odd that she showed up with Plank when she normally stopped by alone. But she just couldn't tell him the real reason.

Rawley's eyes narrowed, then widened. "Oh, man!" he burst out. "Did they go over to your place? They did, didn't they?"

"Did who go to my place?" She took the bottle from him and poured for both of them. Her knuckles looked funny, she noticed absently. White and bony.

"The guys with that rogue plane over at the airport."

"I don't have a clue as to what you're talking about." But Carly's heart constricted and her hands went suddenly clumsy. She spilled the bourbon and found a dishcloth to wipe it up, then she tossed back her shot, closing her eyes, shuddering a little as its warmth tried to thaw the block of ice that her stomach had become.

"Hell of a way to savor fine liquor," Rawley commented.

Carly picked the bottle up again to examine the label. "Right," she said dryly. She put it down again with a sharp *thunk*.

"So what's wrong with you tonight?" Rawley went on.

"Nothing. I'm fine."

"Do you know something about that plane?"

"No!" She almost shouted it, then she carefully got a grip on herself again.

"Still not much for TV, huh?" Rawley asked.

"When do I have the time?"

"Have you even listened to the radio lately?"

I don't want to hear this.

He was trying to tell her something, and Carly knew instinctively that she didn't want to know what it was, because it was just going to make everything worse. She didn't want him to tell her because if there was a plane somewhere where it wasn't supposed to be, as innocuous as that might sound on the surface, it almost *had* to have something to do with Jack Fain, and whatever crazy thing it was that was happening with her ride. And maybe Jack was right. Maybe she just didn't need to know.

She shook her head and paced to the window. "Nope," she answered, her voice strident. "The generator blew two nights ago. No electricity. And we set out late this morning, so I've pretty much been on the trail all day." *Please, please, shut up and don't tell me any more.*

"What's happening, Rawley?" she heard herself whisper.

Rawley sipped his own bourbon. "Some plane came in down at the airport in Oklahoma City on Monday. It was all over the news because it didn't file a flight plan and it almost went nose first into a commercial jet. Then it turned out that a bunch of federal agents were waiting for it. Clyde Messenguer—you know, that guy from KLTP News—was catching a flight out at the same time, and he caught wind of the whole business. I guess he did some digging and found out that the guy in the plane was wanted for some pretty nasty business. Gotta be, I guess, if the feds are involved. Clyde tried to follow the dude himself and he got as far as our neck of the woods, then a bunch of Very Important Suits caught him and warned him off. So we don't know what happened after that. Everybody I've talked to lately has been panicked. The Bucking B even cancelled their trip to auction."

Carly brightened a little at that. It might drive the price up on her own steers. Then Rawley kept talking.

"Bobby—over at the B—didn't want to take the chance of crossing his herd over two hundred miles of empty land if there's a manhunt going on."

"A...manhunt?" Carly repeated. She dragged a chair out from the kitchen table. She sat in it carefully, her legs feeling wobbly. And Jack hadn't thought she needed to know this?

"So what you're saying here is that there's some felon on the loose, hiding out somewhere on the panhandle, and the government is chasing him?" she asked Rawley. "And at any given moment this guy is liable to come jumping out from behind a clump of mesquite, shooting away?" *Holly*. No wonder Jack hadn't wanted to bring Holly! Why hadn't he just *told* her? Oh, God, she had to get back to her daughter, couldn't let her out of her sight now! But even as she jumped to her feet, Rawley answered her.

"Hey, don't yell at me. Messenguer's good, he's won all those awards and all, but I guess he's not God. Like I said, the federal authorities are involved somehow, and when they say back off, you back off. Messenguer didn't have a chance to tell us anything more."

The federal authorities. Jack had said that he was government. And as for her suspicions of Brad . . .

Oh, God, she thought again. *He* was the . . . the felon. Oh, my God.

Suddenly, white, hot fury exploded in her head. Why *hadn't* Jack seen fit to tell her any of this? She had a sudden, wild scenario of how it might play out.

How's everything, Brad? Having fun?

No, not really. Bang, bang, you're dead. Oh, and while I'm at it, let me kill your daughter.

Carly gave a thin, high-pitched laugh.

"Are you going to lose it or something?" Rawley asked warily. "Are you having problems? Well, hell, you must be. I've known you for more than thirty years, and you've never brought a bodyguard for the ride to my house before."

Carly nodded, shook her head, nodded again. "I don't know."

Should she tell him? She didn't know what to do! She didn't know what to *think!* She hurried into the hallway. The only emotion that seemed to come through loud and clear now was a sense of betrayal, and it had to do with Jack. It was gathering fiercely right in the pit of her stomach.

"Where are you going?" Rawley called after her. "Do you want me to call the sheriff?"

She didn't answer. First she was going to be sick, she thought. Then she'd go back to camp and find out what was going on. *Everything*. The *truth*.

She wasn't sure what she'd thought was happening, but it wasn't this. She'd trusted Jack—at least enough to reason that if they were in terrible danger, he would have told her.

But he hadn't. He *hadn't.*

Carly sank down onto the tiled floor of the bathroom and leaned her forehead against the cool porcelain. One thing was certain. She couldn't keep riding into Kansas under the circumstances.

Except then she'd have to give the money back to her guests. She'd be right back to square one with the IRS. *Think*, she told herself, *think*. But everything she thought was bad.

She wouldn't even have the revenues from the auction if she didn't get the herd into Dodge! Forget the tourists, she thought desperately. She could think of some way to pay them back later. It would be months before any of them got around to suing her anyway. But if she didn't get the herd in, the Draw would literally be bankrupt by Wednesday.

Carly groaned aloud, feeling worse by the moment.

When she returned to the kitchen, she felt shaky and defeated. She looked at Rawley and blinked. There was a duffel bag beside his wheelchair. His .44 revolver was in his lap. Josh Carpenter, his foreman, was standing on his other side, and Plank and Holly hovered behind Josh.

"Mom?" Holly asked nervously. "What's going on? I'm scared."

Carly moved instinctively to put an arm around her daughter.

"We're going with you," Rawley said. "You can't turn around and go home. You need the money too badly. Can't see any other reason why you'd let Michael talk you into taking a bunch of tourists to Kansas, unless you're almost broke."

Carly swallowed carefully. *Almost* was an understatement.

"We're going to get those steers of yours into Dodge," Rawley went on. "If you don't want to call in the law, then I guess we'll just have to handle it the way we've always done around these parts since the days of the pioneers."

"By ourselves," agreed Josh, nodding.

Carly was tempted, but then she shook her head. "I can't do it," she said quietly. "I can't ride four more days not knowing if there's a gun aimed at the back of my head or who's aiming it." She shuddered, and dragged in a deep breath. She heard Holly cry out softly, and she tightened her hold on her. "I think I've just finally come up against something here that I can't climb over or move by sheer force of will. This is . . . big."

Rawley's face reddened with anger. "You're not a quitter, Carlotta. And you've been through more than most anybody I know, except maybe me. You just need a little help this time." He started rolling his chair toward the door. "Me and Josh and Mr. Magnum here are gonna be right behind you, watching the back of your head every step of the way."

Carly sat down hard in the kitchen chair again. Josh helped Rawley get through the door. Plank and Holly hesitated uncertainly in the kitchen, watching her.

"Well, you coming?" Plank asked after a moment.

"I guess so," she said softly, rubbing her eyes.

"What's going on, Mom?" Holly asked again. Her own eyes shone, and her lower lip trembled. "Is it Mr. Fain?"

Carly bit back on what she really wanted to say. Holly didn't need any more disillusionment where men were concerned.

"No," she said softly. "Jack's actually the good guy." She stood up again before she could choke on how badly she had wanted to believe that herself, and tried to ignore Holly's beatific smile.

Two more people? She had brought two more people back with her, and one of them was an *invalid?*

Jack watched Carly return to camp, unsure if he was stunned, furious or overwhelmed. A sense of things unraveling hit him hard. He felt as if this whole situation was a ball of twine, spinning fast, faster, faster still.

Everyone was sitting at the fire, a reasonable distance from the wagon. That was the last thing that had gone right as far as Jack was concerned. He remained seated while Carly and her entourage approached. She wouldn't look at him.

He watched her make her way to the wagon. The second newcomer helped the lame man out of his special saddle. He carried him to the fire and helped him to sit there.

"This is Rawley," Carly called out without looking at any of them. Her voice sounded strange, flat. "And that there is Josh, giving him a hand. They're going to Dodge with us. I'm going down to the creek to wash."

Rawley? Rawley Cummings was in a wheelchair? Jack spared the man a glance, then he put his eyes back on Carly.

"I saved you a steak," Gofer called out to her.

"I don't want it."

"You don't . . ." Gofer's jaw dropped. Jack rubbed his forehead. Now there was a *serious* indication that something was amiss. Carly had never turned down food in the several days he had known her.

Her duffel bag was stashed inside the wagon. Carly tossed her hat inside, found the bag and slung it over her shoulder. She had a plan now, the only one left after she had thrown out half a dozen others on the ride back to camp. Unfortunately, a great deal of her plan depended upon just how much Jack Fain genuinely wanted her.

He'd backed off last night, but he had sort of mentioned it again today, and she would gamble that with a little provocation he could be enticed again. She would gamble that he had told her at least one truth last night—that he really hadn't just been setting a scene when he'd touched her.

She checked to see where Holly was—settling down beside the fire near Rawley. That was the next best thing to Carly staying in the camp herself, she thought. Holly was as safe as she could be under the circumstances. Carly knew Rawley would protect her with his own life. And in the meantime, she had a few things to take care of.

She headed off toward the water. The creek was down on the other side of a rise. When she reached the highest point of land, she deliberately paused and pulled the braid out of her hair as she had done that night at the barn. Could he see her? The moon was finally coming up, so she was pretty sure it was possible.

She bent over, swishing her hands through her hair, then she straightened again, tossing it back. Grimly she began unbuttoning her shirt.

She guessed she really ought to give it a little bump and grind, but the truth of the matter was that she wouldn't know where to start, and she didn't have the heart for it right now anyway. She finally started down the other side of the rise again, remembering at the last moment to grab her bag. Her hands were shaking.

When she got out of sight at the creek, she dug her revolver out of the bag. She sat down on the far side of the bank to wait. Jack came no more than five minutes later.

"Stop," she said quietly. "I'm armed and I can be considered truly dangerous."

He went still. She had kind of thought that might get his attention.

"I suggest you start talking and tell me the truth this time," she went on, "because more lies are going to burn me royally, and then I won't be responsible for my actions."

"What happened at Rawley's?" he countered.

Carly ignored his question. "You're too easy, cowboy." Her throat hurt abominably. "I guess if I had actually taken my shirt off, you would have gotten down here before I could blink."

"That had nothing to do with it," he said carefully.

"You blew out the generator, didn't you? You didn't want me to catch the news. Is that why you didn't want me to go to Rawley's, either, because I might hear something?"

As aggravated as he was, he felt another jolt of respect for her. She was quick. But in this case, she was also wrong.

At least now he understood what had happened.

Something must have leaked, Jack thought, and Paul hadn't been able to get word to him without blowing his limited cover. And Scorpion hadn't blown out the generator to prevent them leaving on time. He had very nearly gotten snagged in Oklahoma City before Jack had come in, and he had done it so that no one at the Draw would hear the news before he was ready for them to hear it.

Jack swore richly.

"And that tells me exactly nothing," Carly said harshly.

"*I* didn't blow out your generator. I've told you that already."

"Well, what you've told me so far hasn't exactly been the sterling truth, now, has it?"

"Yes, it has." He hesitated. "I just haven't told you everything."

"So start filling in the holes."

He didn't answer. Carly felt tears of frustration burn at her eyes. No, she was *not* going to cry again. She was going to get answers. This time, she was finally going to get some honest answers.

"Can I come down there without getting shot?" Jack asked carefully.

Carly hesitated, understanding what he didn't say aloud. If he talked from up there on the rise, then the bad guy—*Brad, it had to be Brad*—might overhear him.

"All right," she said finally.

Jack came down to the creek. He stepped over the narrow trickle of water and stopped a judicious distance away from her. He sat and watched her from the corner of his eye.

"So what happened?" he asked. "Your friend Rawley heard the news?"

Carly shook her head hard and fast. "No way, Jack. I'm asking the questions this time, and I've got a whole lot at stake here. So start explaining everything you left out last night. It seems there's a good bit more to this story."

For a wild minute, he couldn't even remember what he had told her so far. His instincts were crazy now, knotted. Half of him knew he was taking an unforgivable risk leaving Scorpion back in the camp. What if he changed his mind about Carly and just took off now? The other half knew that what was happening here was just as important. Carly could screw everything up if she were so inclined. It was purely a professional consideration to work her through this, and he nearly convinced himself of that until he looked into her eyes.

The accusation there was like a kick in the gut. He had used people before. Easily. Usually it was the only way to get things done. But he couldn't handle this woman looking at him that way, as though he had just kicked an injured puppy.

"Is Brad a criminal?" she asked very softly. Jack had said that it was a false alarm when the man had come to the parlor last night, but then Brad had asked her about the wagon this afternoon. Of course, she thought, that could just be a coincidence. What did she know about cops and robbers and feds and fugitives after all?

She groaned softly. And she knew what Jack was going to say before he said it.

"I can't tell you that."

She raised the gun and pulled the trigger. The shot went over their heads and behind them. The report was loud and jarring.

"What the hell are you doing?" he shouted.

"I told you," she grated. "I'm burned."

"Well, I'm not the one you should be burned at!"

"I didn't shoot you, either, did I? That was just a warning."

"Give me that thing."

Carly reared back, holding the gun out of his reach. "Not on your life, cowboy."

The others came running to the top of the rise. Winston tripped all over himself, and Jack thought suddenly that Reggie approached like a man he wouldn't mind having back him up in a fight.

Scorpion, however, led the pack. He was still with them, then. Jack was relieved, though not surprised. There was really little chance that the man could get to his money and get away right now, with everyone awake. He could start killing people off to do it, but that wasn't his style, not unless he was panicked. He was usually neater, more coldly concise than that.

Jack's ears were ringing with the gunshot. Carly Castagne was easily the most unpredictable, complicated, crazy, impulsive woman he'd ever met.

"What's going on down there?" Gofer yelled.

"Snake," Carly called back calmly. "Nothing I can't handle."

Jack shot her a look. "Cute, cowgirl."

"Don't push your luck. I've still got the gun."

"You're sure?" came Plank's voice.

"Absolutely," Carly called back.

Jack remained quiet, waiting for his pulse to settle again and his ears to clear. The others went back to the camp.

Scorpion went last, with a lingering, narrow-eyed look at them. Carly didn't seem to notice.

"That was the stupidest thing you've ever done," Jack finally snapped.

"You haven't known me long enough to say that. Personally, I think it was pretty stupid of me to take your twelve hundred dollars."

Jack ignored that. "It's a miracle he didn't come down here shooting first, asking questions later. I've got him just nervous enough that he's jumpy."

"Who?" Carly demanded. "Is it Brad? Don't make me shoot again, Jack."

Jack was relatively sure that if she tried it, he could be compelled to kill her himself. "Just shut up and listen, will you? I'll tell you as much as I can."

Carly didn't like the sound of that, but she waited. Her bravado was turning out to be little more than skin deep after all.

"I'm chasing a guy we call Scorpion."

"Scorpion," she breathed.

"Code name," he explained absently, raking a hand through his hair.

"Oh. Sure. Of course." *Dear God.*

In spite of everything, until that moment, she hadn't fully accepted that this was all really happening. She hadn't fully realized just how completely out of her control this ride was.

The fugitive had a code name.

She started shaking.

"*If* I told you, if I came right out and told you which guest he was, then you would look at him differently," Jack went on, whispering. "If he came up behind you and asked you for a cup of coffee, you'd come out of your skin." She opened her mouth to argue and he cut her off. "You wouldn't be able to help it, Carly. You're human and you haven't been playing this game for as many years as I have, and even *I'd* have a hard time staying put if he startled me."

Carly finally nodded, conceding the point.

There was a tiny, clicking sound. Jack paused and frowned, listening to it. It was her teeth. They were chattering together.

"You've as good as told me that I'm right," she whispered. "It's Brad."

"I haven't said anything of the sort," he said tightly. "I only said it was one of them."

"I'm not stupid."

No, she definitely was not. "Can I come closer?"

Carly nodded spasmodically. She finally put the gun down on the ground on her other side. Jack closed the distance between them and drew her slowly, cautiously into his arms.

Her trembling rocked through him. He tucked her head against his shoulder, wondering if she would let him do it, and he wasn't sure if he was relieved or appalled when she did—she was that scared.

Finally, she was scared. Maybe now she'd have some sense and cooperate.

"Come on, cowgirl, don't fall apart on me now."

"I can't . . . I'm not . . ."

"Sure you are." He didn't know what she had been about to say, but he thought it would be a good idea to argue with her. She was perilously close to going into shock. He could feel it in her rigidity, in the ice of her skin.

"Don't think about it, Carly. For God's sake, just put it out of your mind. Worry about your cattle. Let me sweat it out about Scorpion. That's what I'm here for."

She trusted him, she realized. It was an instinct, something in her heart, not in her head. Her head told her never *ever* to trust a man. They died, they ran, they were about as useful as a bucket full of holes. Her head told her that Jack Fain was even more transient and elusive than most, a man *used* to living with lies, a man who preferred it.

He walked in shadows, and, she imagined, he'd broken quite a few laws of his own in the name of a larger justice. He had that feeling about him. He was an honest-to-God, modern-day desperado, who might wear a white hat but who still carried a gun at his calf. And she needed him to keep holding her right now. She needed it because no matter what her head told her, it was the only way her heart felt safe.

And in the end, that scared her most of all.

Chapter 11

They sat in silence for a long time.

"Sorry about the gun," Carly muttered finally.

Jack's arm tightened briefly around her. "You're just used to taking care of yourself."

"Yes. But I wouldn't really have shot you."

She looked up and saw his mouth curl halfway to a smile. "If I thought for a minute that it was a possibility, you wouldn't have possession of the damned thing now."

She sighed. He felt the release of breath relax her entire body. Talking seemed to have a calming effect on her, so he kept it up.

"Do you remember when that senator was killed in Dallas?" He felt her shrug. "There was a big to-do about some oil leases. This guy was standing in the way of them. It was a deal that would have funneled multimillions into some very greedy pockets, and the guys who owned those pockets hired Scorpion to get rid of the senator. They put an end to his interference so the deal could go through."

Carly stiffened in his arms again, but it was a different kind of tension now. It was sharpening interest.

"That Dallas hit started it," he went on. "It was so clean, so cold, and Scorpion pretty much vanished into thin air afterward. There's a portion of our population who appreciate talent like that. So someone hired him to take out an English prime minister next. There was a summit meeting in Istanbul. It would have opened a free trade agreement with several countries, and that would have siphoned off some substantial business from certain American companies. The prime minister was a big proponent of the plan, so Scorpion took him out.

"He got a lot of work after that. His hits started taking on the same…flavor. My superiors thought the best way to catch him—to even thwart some of his efforts—was to put one man on him, one man who could devote his full attention to him. Since I'd picked up the Dallas job, they gave Scorpion to me."

On some distant level, Jack heard himself and was amazed. He never talked like this. He honestly didn't have any friends, at least no one who was not part of the agency. There had been Zoe once, but he'd traveled so much, moved around so much, that he'd managed to avoid putting down those treacherous things called roots. He sure as hell had never spoken of his work to her. That had been one of his many ways of keeping her at a distance, he realized now.

He thought that if Zoe could have heard him now, she would have been stunned. And infuriated.

"Scorpion is a paid assassin, Carly," he heard himself go on. "He's a for-hire terrorist. And *that's* why I'm not telling you too much. Because you're no match for someone like him, cowgirl."

"I . . . oh." She shuddered.

"He's killed for the Red Army Faction and God knows how many Palestinian organizations. And those are just the hits that I know about for certain. There are others we suspect he was involved in and just can't prove." He paused, shaking his head. "There have been times when I've followed him . . . to Belgium, to Iran, and lost him once I got there. Someone important would die, and then I'd *know* it was him, but I couldn't prove it. A lot of times I've just sort of guessed where he would show up. There'd be something politically important going on, some world leader would receive a death threat, or he'd take a stand that could tick off some powerful people, so I'd go there and keep my eyes and ears open, and at least half the time he'd *still* get the hit in." *Like in São Paulo*, Jack thought. "Anyway, my point is that guys like Scorpion don't easily get caught. The best I've been able to do over the years is identify some of

his marks ahead of time and whisk them out of harm's way
before he could move on them."

"So who's his mark in Oklahoma? What's he doing here?"

Jack's heart stalled.

He should have seen the question coming, knowing her. And
now that it had, there was no way he could answer it. Not
without opening the door to a hundred other questions.

Her weight leaned sweetly and warmly against his ribs, and
Jack knew suddenly that it was not enough to keep Scorpion
from making contact with her. He knew in that moment that
he was *never* going to let her know who Scorpion was. If he
could manage it, if he could pull it off, this woman would never
have to know what her ex-husband, her daughter's father, had
become.

If she had been a mark, he would have whisked her out of
harm's way. Instead, he would whisk her out of the way of the
truth, her own past, would let her go on living being none the
wiser. If it was another lie, then he could live with it.

"You're thinking about this too much, cowgirl," he said
quietly, after a moment.

"Just tell me that much and I'll let it go."

"No, you won't."

"I'll try," she amended.

Jack chose his words carefully. "I don't think he's here to hit
anyone."

Carly looked up at him silently, waiting.

"I've learned a lot about him over the years. And there was
something about his latest hit that made me think that he was
going to retire. And if he was going to call it a day, then I
thought he'd pass by here on his way."

"Pass by *here?* From Belgium to Iran to *Oklahoma?*"

The hairs on Jack's nape stirred with wariness. *Careful,* he
thought. "We picked up his plane on radar," he went on without answering. "That substantiated my hunch."

"Does he know you're after him?"

"Let it go, Carly."

"Has he seen you before?"

"No. Not exactly. He's seen a man he knows as Gemini. We
rarely enter the field looking like ourselves. Usually our cover's pretty deep." *And why on God's earth was he telling her*

this? Because, he realized, the compulsion was as deep as any one of Gemini's disguises.

Carly suddenly understood enough to feel cold inside anyway. "How long have you been on this guy? How long has he *known* you've been on him?"

Jack hesitated, wishing to God that he'd never opened his mouth. "A long time."

"Years?"

"Yeah."

"How many years?"

"I think you've gone a long way beyond one question, cowgirl."

Carly ignored that. "More than five?"

"Yeah," he said reluctantly.

"More than *ten?*"

"Close enough. Let it *go,* Carly."

She did fall silent. For a moment.

"So what are you planning to do with him?" she went on suddenly.

"*Do* with him?" He leaned away from her to look at her warily.

"How are you going to get rid of him now that you've caught up with him?" she asked. Her voice was getting wild again. "Are you just going to walk up to him and . . . and blow him away?"

He'd thought of it. Oh, how he'd thought of it. "Can't."

"Why not? Why can't you just get rid of him, Jack?"

"Because if I shoot and I miss, and he shoots and he *doesn't* miss, then I've left a whole lot of innocent people at the mercy of one very angry assassin," he bit out. That was the biggest reason. "Worst-case scenario number two is that when bullets started flying, someone could get hit."

"Oh," she answered. Her voice had gotten small.

Suddenly, Carly felt sick again. It was clear now, the unspeakable danger they were in, that *he* was in. Scorpion was an assassin, not just a fugitive. He was a terrorist, not just someone who'd robbed a liquor store and shot an old lady out of panic. And she knew—God help her, she knew—it had to be Brad, no matter what Jack had said. Or what he hadn't said.

"So," he went on finally, "will you please send Rawley and Josh home now?"

"No."

"*No?* Why not?"

"Rawley won the Ellis County shoot-out three years running."

Jack nearly choked. *The Ellis County shoot-out?* "Damn it, hasn't anything I've just told you made a dent?"

"If it's all the same to you, I want as many good people as possible armed and guarding my back right now," she said stiffly.

"Your good people aren't in the same league as mine, sweetheart. Stay out of it."

"Well, that may be, but they're all I can muster."

Jack felt his headache building again. "The fewer people who have guns around here, the better off we are. Can't you just trust me?"

"Honestly? No. I have to take care of myself."

He grabbed her arm. "Not this time," he said quietly. "This time you have someone to watch over you."

She looked into his eyes and felt again the irrational terror she'd felt that morning, when he'd talked her into leaving a day early. If she got used to leaning on him, to letting him take over, she might never be strong enough to duke it out on her own again.

And *then* where would the Draw be?

Jack watched her for a moment and thought he understood. She was not a woman who would turn over the reins easily, and he had a hunch that forcing her to do so now would be as traumatic as letting her know who Scorpion really was. He couldn't stay and take care of her forever, and he couldn't strip her self-sufficiency away. He needed to let her feel that she still had some control here, even as he knew that she had precious little.

"You're not going to let anything happen to anyone anyway," Carly went on tremulously.

"No. I'm going to wait for him to leave this little tea party, then I'm going to go after him."

"Will he do that? Will he just . . . leave?" Her voice escalated again, trembling as the implications of that sank in on her.

"Let's hope so." Jack stood up abruptly and pulled on her arm. "Come on," he said shortly. "We have to go back."

But she needed time to think about this. At any given moment, Jack could take off after his...his *terrorist,* and he would be gone. Maybe even dead.

"Carly," he said quietly, "I have to go back to the others."

"I know," she whispered. "Do you think . . . I mean, will he just start shooting people for no reason?" *Holly,* she thought. *Tell me Holly is safe enough, more than safe enough, with Rawley, the way I thought.*

"No," Jack said, watching her face. "I don't think so. Not unless he's threatened."

She breathed carefully. "No one up there is going to threaten him."

"If I thought that, I would never have come down here in the first place." No, all the danger was right here at this creek, Jack thought. He was double sure of it when she finally stood up and moved closer to him.

She touched her palms to his chest and slid them up over his shirt slowly as though to be able to reassure herself later, when this was over, that he had really been here, had really existed, that he hadn't been a mirage. There was something almost tentative, even self-conscious about her touch. That alone undid him because he knew what she was thinking.

"I'm going to be fine, cowgirl," he said hoarsely. "I really am going to shoot him first."

But his words were hollow. He realized that he wasn't entirely sure he believed them himself, not anymore, not with his instincts scattered to the wind. He told himself that it was because he *didn't* believe himself that he let himself kiss her again.

It was as good an excuse as any.

In truth, he didn't think it was humanly possible for him to step away from her, while her hands trembled and reached for him, while she looked up at him with those hot, green eyes, her lips slightly parted, her breath soft and fast. He lowered his mouth to hers slowly, with a groan, as though drawn to her by the force of a steady, strong magnet.

He had told himself last night that touching her again would be the worst thing he could do to her. He'd thought she believed that, too. But there were fewer lies between them now, he thought, and there was only one that really mattered anyway.

Suddenly, he wanted to hold her, to protect her, as he had never wanted anything before in his life. And he wanted more than that. He wanted to lose himself in her, just in case Brad *did* shoot him first. He wanted to be warm inside her. He wanted to be...just a man, without responsibility for what suddenly felt like the whole world on his shoulders.

He dragged her the rest of the way to him, crushing his mouth to hers even harder.

Her hands got somehow trapped between them as she began fumbling with his buttons. Jack made a frustrated sound in his throat and struggled out of one sleeve without breaking the contact of their mouths. He swept his tongue past her teeth and tugged the other sleeve off, then he put his free hand to the back of her head, into all that long, glorious hair, holding her mouth still for his assault so he could taste her again.

He hooked his thumb over the edge of her bra and pulled it down, his hand covering her bare breast. As soon as he touched her she was leaning hungrily into him again, her mouth hot. She was the one who changed the angle of their kiss this time, wanting more, so much more.

When she slid her lips to his shoulder, when she laved her tongue over the rigid muscle there, Jack found his voice again. It was raw.

"We're crossing a line here." And it was going to make the rest of his job so damned complicated and dangerous.

"I know." She did, and it made her voice breathless. "I don't care." And she didn't, and that was frightening even as it felt so, so right.

Jack knew *he* would care later. Almost certainly, he would. He had always known a little panic at letting women get this close before, even as his body had demanded such release. And this woman was so much more than any other. He knew instinctively that whatever happened next would not be just sex, at least not as he had always kept it. His hand found her chin and he pulled her face up, forcing her to look at him. He lost himself in her eyes—eyes that had captivated him for so much longer than she knew. Guilt ravaged him at that, but it wasn't strong enough to stop him. It wasn't as strong as what he had come to feel for her in a few treacherous, precious days.

His mouth came back to hers and worked on it without hesitation or apology. His hands slid up over her ribs, closing over her breasts again, one covered, one not, and the sensation of his calluses against her skin left her reeling. Last night had been sudden, reckless, and every touch had been one of discovery. Last night, she had been fighting with herself. But this was heat and desperation, defiance and need.

He needed to see her this time, really see her, all of her. There could be no fumbling this time, no pushing clothing just far enough out of the way. That would be unfair to both of them. He eased away from her a little, though his blood pounded with urgency, though he was hard to the point of pain.

Carly was confused when he broke their kiss, then she understood. As he set her away from him, he caught the thin, stretchy fabric of her bra again and this time he tore it away completely, snapping the center clasp. She gasped and fought the urge to cover herself. She brought her chin up as though defying him not to like what he saw.

She started trembling and her eyes burned again, because he looked at her as if he had just discovered gold.

Jack felt a strange ache fill his throat at the way the moonlight spilled over her skin. Her breasts were small, her nipples dark and hardening under his gaze. He pushed the straps off her shoulders and her bra fell away.

"Take your jeans off," he said hoarsely. "I need to see you."

She felt vulnerable. She felt scared and self-conscious and exquisitely alive. She hesitated.

"Please," he added.

Just as when he had asked her to take Plank to Rawley's, the simple word broke something inside her. Carly sat down quickly to pull her boots off, but it took her a moment too long. He lowered himself on top of her, pushing her back into the sand, tugging at her belt.

She sought his mouth again, and he found hers. She forgot what she was doing, and how she had meant to do it. Her hands flew desperately, sliding over his skin, her fingers tangling with the soft mat of golden-brown hair on his chest. Then they skimmed over a puckered ridge of scar tissue just below his waist.

Jack stiffened and waited for her reaction. Women had always avoided his nicks and wounds and scars. Carly snatched her hand back and he wasn't surprised.

Then she understood what it was that she had felt.

"He shot you," she breathed. "That came from him, didn't it?"

Jack didn't answer, but she could see the truth on his face. It made her even more desperate to feel him inside her before everything could go wrong.

She touched the bullet scar again, sliding her palm over it, then she began pulling at his jeans. Jack felt his breath catch oddly. He hadn't known relief could be so sweet. He didn't know if relief was purely what he felt. There was satisfaction and a fierce kind of exhilaration all tangled up with it, that she really was woman enough, strong enough, loving enough to move past the ugliness and try to find the man inside.

And maybe, he thought, maybe she would find that something remained of his heart after all.

He dragged her jeans down her hips. He lowered himself more fully on top of her, feeling her nipples graze against his chest. He wanted to get his own jeans off and realized with a scraping, amazed laugh that he didn't want to take the time. Not while she was quivering beneath him. He didn't want to take his attention from her. Not while her mouth was so hot, sliding over his neck, his shoulder, coming back to seek out his own again. He wanted to feel everything, feel her, all of her.

He eased down to take one of her nipples gently between his teeth. Carly arched her back at the wet heat of his mouth, her hands diving into his hair to hold his head against her. *More.* He traced his tongue to the other side, laving that nipple, too. *Not enough.* Finally, in desperation, he used his hands, cupping her breasts together, sliding his mouth back and forth.

Carly cried out. They rolled together until somehow she was above him, straddling him, and then she finally remembered that she had been trying to get his jeans off. She tugged and pulled at his clothing until he was naked, but then she found his gun.

She gasped unconsciously. He unstrapped it as fast as he could while his mouth searched her neck, beneath her hair, and he made her forget it again. His hard-gentle hands moved up her thighs and she moaned. His fingers slid between her legs and she cried out.

"Now," she managed. "I can't...I don't..."

"I know."

Later there would be time for finesse, for protracted pleasure—if he ever allowed himself a later. He groaned, knowing he would never be able to keep his hands off her, not now that he had given in to the need once. But now there was her skin and the sand, both still warm from the sun, and later was a long time away. He rolled again, pinning her beneath him. Though he'd wanted to explore more of her first, he couldn't have denied her plea if Scorpion had held a gun to his head.

Scorpion. Dear God, what if he came over the rise *now?* Nothing like a little insane jealousy to get things rolling, he thought, and had another wild urge to laugh. But then Carly wrapped her legs around him, ensnaring him, and he could no longer think about the man, about anything at all.

Carly gasped at the sudden fullness of him, her body tightening first in shock at the invasion, then going liquid, melting. He went still for a moment, kissing her again, more gently this time. He covered her mouth, swallowing her breath even as it exploded from her. Then he finally moved inside her, slowly at first, as though savoring the moment, as though there would never be another one like it, and there *was* something reverent about it, something almost too good to be true. He plunged harder, faster. Carly felt an exquisite tension, building, tightening, wanted it to last and knew there was no time because Scorpion was back in the camp, waiting for him.

And Holly, too. Oh, God, there was Holly—

But Holly's safe with Rawley and this is mine, she thought wildly. *Finally, this is mine.*

Jack caught her hips and held her still and thrust inside her until the tension in her exploded. Then she could no longer think of anything at all. Release rained through her in colors like a sunset, the red of heat and the purple of twilight. *Don't stop, don't let this end.* But of course there was nothing she could do about it any longer and her breath caught as she felt him stiffen above her.

This time he said her name, her full name, and it was so sweet that she couldn't remember anymore why she had ever hated it.

"Carlotta . . ."

Chapter 12

Jack finally braced his weight on his elbows to look down into her face. He brushed his mouth over her cheek. Carly smiled, but then her own mouth trembled. Reality came back, cruel and cold.

"You have to go back," she said quietly.

"Yeah. I do."

She turned her head to the side so she wouldn't have to watch him leaving her. It felt too fast, too soon.

Jack heard himself explaining though he hadn't intended to, listened to himself and wondered again why he felt compelled to make her understand. Maybe it was as simple as the fact that, try as he might, he couldn't ever remember sex being like that before...that *genuine*. He felt as if he owed her something more than a kiss goodbye.

And he needed her to understand.

"If we don't go back up there, I'm afraid Scorpion's going to start wondering what we're up to." He didn't add that he probably already had, and he would be none too pleased about it. "He doesn't want anything odd, anything different, to happen right now," Jack went on carefully. "If it does, then he *could* get antsy and dangerous."

Her eyes finally slid back to him. "You don't ever turn it off, do you?"

"What?"

"That predator in your brain."

He eased off her without comment.

She was being unreasonable. Carly knew that. She'd known what he was when she'd let herself make love with him. *Let* herself? The lure of him was more than she could withstand any longer. Either way, now was a fine time to start feeling put out by it, she realized.

Jack sat in the creek-bed sand, watching pensively as she washed and dressed again. Once he scrubbed a hand over his jaw. More than once his gaze went to the rim above them. He wasn't sure if it was good or bad that Brad hadn't appeared there yet to find out what was going on. He knew that Carly was still disgruntled, and he was stunned that he had left the man out of his sight for this long.

When she was ready, she picked up her bag with one hand and her gun with the other.

"I really wish you'd give me that," Jack muttered.

"I'll just feel better if I have it within reach," she said tightly.

"It won't do you any good. You can't possibly be fast enough with it to make any difference."

He was trying to scare her into cooperation, but it didn't work this time. Her jaw became hard.

"Then, too, there are all those things I warned you about when I was tossing firecrackers your way," she pointed out stubbornly. She laid the gun neatly on top of her clothing inside the bag. She didn't zip it. "There could be snakes, or a cow could go down. I couldn't just leave an animal lying there, dying slowly, so—"

"You're babbling again, Carly."

No, she thought, no, she was just trying to make her world normal again. Trying desperately. And if she had to babble to do it, well, then, she'd babble.

"I'd carry this gun with or without your Scorpion, Jack," she went on. "I'm just glad I have it, and believe me, I'm ready to use it."

Something about the way she said it alerted him. "Don't tell me. You're the Ellis County shoot-out champ from four years ago, before Rawley."

"Five. But who's counting?"

Jack thought about it. "Did Rawley compete that year?"

She looked pained. "No. But I'll get him this year. I've been practicing since the snow melted."

A corner of Jack's mouth lifted. God bless Rawley, he thought, if the man had the audacity to edge her again.

Then something wrapped itself tightly around his windpipe. He didn't know when the next shoot-out was, but he found himself praying that both she and Rawley would be alive by then to lock horns, to worry about such inane concerns. He found himself praying fiercely, thinking about God again when he hadn't done so for years before this trip... maybe since he was ten years old and he had prayed and prayed, and no one had ever answered.

He finally dressed as well and they started back up the slope. At the last minute he took her hand.

Carly was surprised, then she thought she understood. He was trying to send his Scorpion—*which one?*—some kind of signal.

She thought about pulling away from him, but she couldn't fight any of this any longer, and she was finally coming to realize it.

"Where'd you put your tent?" she asked tightly.

"I didn't."

She opened her mouth, then she snapped it shut again. She understood that, too. He wanted to be outside, aware of every little thing that went on in the camp tonight. This Scorpion character was definitely one of them, she thought again.

Fear slid through her coldly. This time it stole the breath right out of her, and she was glad Jack still held her hand.

Carly couldn't sleep, and the camp never really did, either. She didn't know if that was good, bad or merely nerve-racking.

She stayed outside, too. The idea of being trapped inside her tent brought a hard, heavy weight to her chest, though she had never really been claustrophobic before. She lay in her sleeping bag beside the fire, her gun tucked inside with her, though she had not let Jack know that.

Well past midnight, she heard the first footsteps. It was enough to make her scramble out of her sleeping bag and perch on one of the supply boxes, her gun in her lap. But it was only Leigh, creeping through the darkness to one of the other tents. Carly wasn't sure whom the blonde was meeting. Too many of the group had retired while she had still been down at the creek with Jack. She could only pray, for Leigh's sake, that it wasn't the man Jack called Scorpion.

A little while later, Myra scurried back from a nearby culvert. *That* surprised her, though she supposed it shouldn't. The teacher had sat beside the fire with Rawley until late, and they had been talking quietly and laughing with each other. Rawley had a custom-made, all-terrain wheelchair and he could get around just fine. Carly wondered if it had just taken him to a tryst with Myra.

There was nothing more invigorating to the libido than a little dust and fresh air, Carly reflected, finally relaxing enough to rest her chin in her hand. The very nature of these trips always lent a feeling of disassociation and unreality. The eleven of them—thirteen now with Josh and Rawley—were isolated in a place that always felt like nowhere, no matter how many times she crossed it. The whole world seemed to be made of rocky red soil and immeasurable sky. It was hard to remember that there was a real world out there, a place just past the horizon where real life would have to be resumed with real people who weren't caught in this space in time.

Carly grimaced. That being the case, she supposed it made it easier to accept what had happened between her and Jack.

She felt no regret, no remorse, she realized. Right or wrong, she had succumbed to the mood of the ride, and she had grabbed what she could for herself, had given to him what she was able. Oddly enough, she knew she still didn't trust him exactly, yet she trusted in his kindness, and in his heart. He genuinely thought that he was doing the best for her—for all of them—that he could. And right now, in the middle of nowhere, she supposed that was enough.

If there were heavier implications to any of it—such as why she had succumbed to wanting *him* after so many years alone—then she would deal with them after he was gone. And she would survive his leaving, too, she told herself, assuming he wasn't killed. Unlike the guests, she had a full appreciation of how suddenly and brutally the end of the trail could come.

When they got to Fort Dodge, if Jack was still alive and it came time to say goodbye, she'd be ready.

She wondered if being on the trail also made it easier to accept that there was a cold-blooded killer in their midst. Probably, she reasoned. Everything was so unreal out here anyway, what was a little interference from an assassin?

A high-pitched laugh escaped her at the thought.

"Can't sleep?"

Carly jumped, then shook her head. She couldn't see Jack. He was just a disembodied voice in the night.

"I'm going to feel like hell tomorrow," she answered just as softly.

"You'll get by," his voice said.

"Probably."

He finally left his sleeping bag on the other side of the barely smoldering fire. He stood up and came to the crate to sit beside her. If he noticed the gun, he didn't comment on it.

For a long time he just studied her face in the moonlight. "What's the matter?" she asked warily.

Jack shook his head. He already knew that she didn't handle compliments well. She was suspicious of them, as though the person giving one might want too much from her in return. What would she do if he told her that she wasn't actually pretty—that her mouth was a little too wide for that, her eyes a little too arresting—but that he had just realized again how beautiful she was?

Her hair was down, the way he liked it. With her eyes so worried and haunted, and the last of the firelight flickering across her face, he found it hard to pull his own eyes away from her.

"Which tent is Holly in?" he asked suddenly, because, impossibly, he wanted her again, as strongly as if he had never had the pleasure just a few short hours ago. He already knew the answer, but he had to divert himself.

Carly looked around the camp. "The last one over there to the right, next to Rawley's." She hesitated. Her voice cracked. "Please don't hurt her, Jack. She thinks you're...great."

His heart spasmed. What did she think he was? Some kind of animal? A cold-blooded killer himself?

"And you know better," he answered shortly.

Carly hesitated. "I know that she doesn't need to know who—*what*—you really are."

Sometimes Jack wondered if he really knew himself.

"She asked me if I had kids," he said finally. "She seemed to think I was too old *not* to have any."

Carly surprised herself by laughing softly. "She says what's on her mind."

"Like mother, like daughter."

"So how come you *don't* have kids?" she asked suddenly. "Didn't you and Zoe get that far? Do you like them?" She already knew it made him relatively frantic when one was involved in a . . . what would he call this? A case? A job?

"I don't think I ever really thought about it before," he muttered.

"So think now."

"I don't want to."

"You don't want to think, or you don't want to like them?"

"The former."

"Oh, come on. What else is there to do while we sit here waiting for dawn?" She waved a hand at the timeless, immense sky.

Jack scowled and shrugged and finally answered her. "Kids are okay." He hated to see them die, he thought.

"Well, now *there's* an earth-shaking revelation of your inner feelings. Do you want any?"

"I'm forty-three years old, Carly. It's kind of late to be thinking about it."

"On second thought, you'd better not have any," she decided.

He eyed her warily. "Why?"

"Because they make you love them. You can't hide from them. You can't *not* give them your whole heart, all your energy, even when it hurts and tears you apart." She thought of the problems she'd been having with Holly lately and frowned.

"Well, I don't have time for that whole scene anyway," he said tightly. She was doing it to him again, he realized. She was digging...or trying to, trying to get deeper than he wanted her to get. He wasn't going to get sucked into arguing with her this time, and ultimately saying things he didn't mean to say.

"If you finally get your bad guy," she whispered, "you'd be sort of retired, right? I mean, he's essentially been your whole job."

Sometimes her insight amazed him. "Yeah," he answered warily.

"So maybe you'd have time for kids then."

"I will." What was he saying? "I would, if I wanted to. I don't want to." He stood up again suddenly. "Go to sleep, cowgirl."

Carly hesitated. "Are you going to stay awake now?"

"I never slept in the first place," he whispered back to her. And he felt like he hadn't slept. God, was he beginning to feel the strain of this job. No wonder his emotions were running all over the board, wild.

He was getting too old for this, he thought again.

Carly pushed to her feet as well, but then she only put her gun back in her bag and wandered off to the edge of the camp, her arms crossed protectively over her chest. Jack swore and followed her.

"To *sleep,* Carly. I can't protect you if you're all the way out here."

"Is it me you're protecting?"

He looked at her oddly. He felt his heart thump. "You and nine others," he said carefully. "Well, eleven, now. Come on. Let's go back."

"What I mean is, if you kill this Scorpion guy, if you don't have to chase him all over the place anymore, then you'll have all kinds of time on your hands," she said suddenly. "Have you thought of that, Jack? You said you've been on this guy's tail for more than ten years."

"No, I didn't."

"Yes, you did. And that's almost like a *marriage.*"

Something inside him clenched hard and painfully. "Not quite. We've never shared a bathroom."

"He must be like a part of you by now," she went on doggedly.

Jack flinched noticeably. He looked sharply back at the camp, but that was just an excuse not to meet her gaze. They were far enough away that no one could hear them, and she was talking quietly.

"Cancer can be a part of you, too," he said grimly, finally, "but only a fool would hesitate to have it cut out."

"But I guess you'd still miss the part that you lost."

"And then you'd get used to it being gone."

Carly shrugged, but she didn't look convinced. Jack felt himself getting irritated.

"Damn it, cowgirl! What's your point here?"

"As long as you've had this guy to chase, you've had an excuse not to settle down and get comfy with anyone. You were the one who said your marriage didn't work because you were never home."

"When did we decide I had a thing about not settling down?"

"Last night."

"No. *You* decided."

"Well, it's just the way you are, Jack. It shows. Like how you weren't really loving me last night. You were listening to what was going on outside in the hallway."

"That's garbage."

"It's true."

"You don't know a thing about me or my feelings, cowgirl. You don't know what I was thinking." He realized, surprised, that he was getting genuinely angry. He felt cornered again, like when she had started this business last night.

"Well, I know that you didn't hang on to Zoe," she went on. "Because you travel a lot, you said. And you travel looking for Scorpion." She changed tacks suddenly. "So where are your parents? Do you have any family?"

Jack jolted. "What does that have to do with anything?"

Carly found herself thinking of that picture she'd seen in his wallet. "Well, do you?"

"My father walked out on me—on me and my mother," he corrected carefully, "when I was ten. Apparently Mom couldn't handle single parenthood, so she dropped me off at the nearest orphanage. No brothers or sisters. Now, are you satisfied?"

Carly's heart kicked hard. It had been his father's picture he'd kept. There'd been no trace of his mother in his wallet. But then, when his mother had taken off, she'd been all he had left. That would be very hard to forgive.

Something inside her bled for him. "See?" she said softly.

"No." His voice was hard. "I don't."

"Scorpion is all you've got, Jack. He's the only person in the whole world you've let yourself get close to."

"What are you? A damned *shrink?*" he demanded angrily. "I'm still close to Zoe. I mean, if I see her, I say hello. We live in the same city. We parted amicably. We're ... friends."

"Yeah, I can tell. That's why you just made love with me."

"That was sex, cowgirl. Great sex, but it was still just sex, and love didn't have a damned thing to do with it."

She flinched.

He didn't know why he needed to hurt her ... or maybe he did. Maybe something inside him was just frantic for her to shut up, to stop psychoanalyzing him, stop making him examine, think, feel, because if he looked too closely, he would just see too damned many holes in his life.

"I rest my case," Carly managed after a moment.

"You don't have a case, damn it!" His temper burst all over again, and he didn't know why he felt so defensive. "I don't *know* you well enough to love you. No man could love you inside a few days!" *But what about a few years?* an inner voice taunted him. Could a man fall in love with a picture, especially when the image had turned out to be so much like the real thing? He had always thought that he saw hearth and home in her eyes. And he had, he realized. He had. She was that kind of woman.

"So what about Scorpion?" she persisted.

"What *about* him?" he growled.

"You've certainly known him longer than a few days. Do you love *him?*"

He looked at her, dumbfounded. "He's a *man,* for God's sake!"

"Love doesn't have to be sexual, Jack. You can love a father, a brother, a best buddy."

"You're crazy, do you know that?"

"Well, I just see what I see."

Jack took a deep, careful breath. "Okay. Let's assume for the sake of argument that there's something ... personal between Scorpion and me, after all these years. That doesn't mean the man doesn't deserve to die."

"Well, now you're getting into the whole moralistic issue of capital punishment," she pointed out.

"Oh, for God's sake!" he exploded.

Carly thought maybe she'd pushed him too far. "Okay, okay. Calm down. We'll assume that he *does* deserve to die, just for the sake of argument. You're still going to be lonely, Jack, when he's gone."

Jack turned away from her. "On second thought, stay out here by yourself if you want to. It's your life."

She didn't really expect him to go back to the camp, to leave her alone, but he did. Carly hugged herself. She guessed she must really have struck a nerve.

And she knew suddenly that everything she had said was true. She thought of his parents, and she could have wept for the boy he had been. *How could a mother do something like that?* She could understand a father leaving—oh, she could understand that very well. But how could his own mother have yanked the last of the rug out from under him that way?

She finally followed him, slowly, feeling a chill despite the warmth of the June night. She crawled back into her sleeping bag and hugged it close around her. For the first time she wondered what would happen to all of them if it turned out that Jack *couldn't* shoot Scorpion, whoever he was. What would happen if he found that he couldn't actually pull the trigger to cut out the cancer? Because whether he'd admit it or not, she thought it might be a very real possibility. She thought maybe this Scorpion was the only person Jack had ever let get under his skin.

Then she had another jarring thought. How could Jack possibly believe that Scorpion didn't know who he was? It seemed perfectly clear to her, to someone outside looking in. After all this time, after so many years, the assassin would almost have to recognize him, would have to know his walk, his grin, his *scent*. Those things didn't change with disguises. She was suddenly very, very sure that she herself was going to be remembering those things long after Jack Fain was gone.

So Scorpion had to know, too, she reasoned.

Carly groaned softly. Maybe Scorpion saw the possibility that Jack couldn't really shoot him.

Maybe he was gambling on it.

Chapter 13

While Carly and the cowboys made breakfast, Jack managed to snag one of the loose threads that had been bothering him. After he rolled up his sleeping bag, he sauntered over to the cook wagon.

"Can I help with anything?"

Plank handed him a coffeepot. "Beans are already ground," he answered. "They're in the third crate inside the wagon, right hand side."

Jack went to the wagon. He found the crate easily. He dug the scoop into the cask, then he promptly spilled the grounds.

Plank looked over and made a sound of amazement when he saw him bend down to pick up the mess. "We ain't serving it after it's been in the dirt!"

"Just cleaning up after myself."

"The coyotes won't mind."

Jack straightened. He had seen what he'd needed to see, what he had more or less expected to find.

He'd known the money was in the wagon. Now he knew where. The bottom was all fresh, new plywood. He had long since stopped wondering how Scorpion managed such things. He wasn't amazed that the assassin had located the materials and found the time to construct the false bottom. All that mattered was that now he had some idea how the man was going to have to go about getting his money before he could leave. That simplified things immensely.

Jack filled the coffeepot and took it back to the fire, then he looked around. The door flap of Scorpion's tent tugged back and the man stepped outside.

For the briefest of moments, the assassin seemed to watch Jack. Then fury blazed in his eyes unconcealed.

A strange chill spread through Jack. He fought the immediate and urgent impulse to go for his gun, then, there, and caution be damned. He didn't like that look. That look seemed even deeper, hotter, than what losing his lady to another might have warranted. But then Scorpion turned away toward the creek.

Soon now, Jack thought again, still feeling the adrenaline. Very soon.

And if he could just get his mind and his hormones off the cowgirl, he might even be ready for it.

Carly was finally forced by circumstance to acknowledge the other men in the group. All three of them—Reggie and Winston and Brad—were seated on the opposite side of the fire from where she stood.

After a brief hesitation, she determined to ignore them. She refused to allow this whole nightmare to affect her appetite any longer. She had already missed dinner because of this mess, so she moved closer to the fire to pile her plate with eggs, sausages and potatoes.

She sat down, her eyes doggedly on her food. As her stomach gradually filled, she realized that she felt more rested and replete than she had any right to. She wondered how Jack was holding up. She wondered if he had slept last night at all.

Her gaze wandered over to him and her eyes widened. She felt as though she was walking on glass, and he was leaning lazily against the wagon as though he hadn't a care in the world. One elbow was hooked back to rest upon the wooden side. He sipped coffee from the cup in his other hand and when he saw her looking at him, he raised a brow at her with a private smile.

Something both warm and cold trembled through her. She found herself wishing fiercely that they didn't have to worry about cattle and killers, that they could somehow greet the day the way they had greeted the moon last night. And she was thoroughly irritated that he could handle this whole situation so calmly.

She stood, no longer interested in finishing her eggs. Winston stepped around the fire to meet her.

"This isn't as hard as I thought it would be," he told her happily. He stuck his hands into his pockets and rolled back on his heels as if he really thought he was a cowboy.

Carly took a deep breath and dredged for her manners. "You get used to it after a few days," she agreed politely. "Your body parts stop hurting."

He nodded. "You're sure having fun," he went on.

Her heart skipped. She looked at him more closely. Was he *leering* at her? Fat, nervous, innocuous Winston?

He was.

Her first instinct was to snap at him that she wasn't up for grabs. Her second was to get defensive, to protest that anything she had done with Jack had come straight from the bottom of her heart. Then that same heart stalled.

Why should this man even care what she was doing? Why, unless *he* had some interest in Jack, some professional interest. Oh, God, she thought, was she wrong? Was Scorpion *not* Brad?

No, she thought, no. This was all just wearing on her. She was getting paranoid and crazy.

"We'll leave in fifteen minutes," she said tersely, turning away from Winston to include everyone. "Come on, Plank, ride with me for a few quick miles. Let's make sure none of the herd has strayed too far."

"I've got my new bull over on my southernmost corner," Rawley called out.

Carly nodded. "Then we'll ride in that direction first."

"Why?" Myra asked.

"Because he either caught the scent of the cows, or they picked up on him," Rawley explained. "Ten to one, he's gotten together with a few of them overnight."

"How interesting," Myra breathed, as though he had just imparted the most fascinating information in the world.

Carly looked at her and raised a brow.

Rawley watched Carly.

Jack followed the man's gaze carefully, weighing it, trying to see what it might reveal about their friendship.

She finally rode off with Plank. Jack stood away from the wagon, watching her go.

"Want any?" He turned around to see Holly behind him, holding out one of the frying pans.

"No, thanks." If he ate, he knew it would make him unbearably sleepy, and he couldn't afford that. "Coffee's fine."

His eyes stayed on Carly. Holly followed his gaze.

"She always gets grouchy when she's working," she told him helpfully. "It's not anything you did, I bet."

Jack looked at the girl again. He needed badly to tell her that she was barking up the wrong tree—at least he was beginning to think she was barking, trying her damnedest to throw him and her mother together. But what, really did he know about kids? He fished for a way to explain to her that what was happening between him and Carly wasn't . . . wasn't . . .

What the hell *was* it? he wondered, the air going out of him.

It's not a forever kind of thing, he told himself. He'd nail Scorpion and go to Florida. She'd go on to Dodge, or wherever the hell it was that they were heading in this no-man's-land. They'd have some pretty dynamite memories, and that would be that.

Holly was still watching him.

"What?" he demanded.

She grinned. "Nothing. Sure you don't want any eggs?"

"No. And maybe you ought to think about why your mom always gets grouchy while she's working," he added sharply.

Holly's face fell. She started to turn away. Jack felt cruel.

"Listen, all I'm saying is, if that's the case, maybe she doesn't *want* to be working. Did you ever think of that? Maybe she'd rather be doing something else. Maybe she'd rather be with you. And maybe if she had some help to get the work done faster, she'd be happier."

Holly looked back at him. Her expression said she didn't know whether she wanted to be rebellious or sad.

"You think?" she asked after a moment.

"Yeah, I think."

"She ought to get a foreman," Holly grumbled. "Aunt Tee keeps telling her that."

Jack almost mentioned that he doubted if the IRS left enough money for one. Then he thought better of it. Maybe Carly didn't want the kid to know how bad their financial situation was. Theresa sure didn't seem to have the full picture. It certainly wasn't his place to fill either one of them in.

"Yeah," he agreed instead. "Probably."

"Maybe she could hire you."

Jack hesitated. Where had *that* twist come from? This kid had a quicksilver mind like her mother's. "I already have a job."

"Doing what?"

He thought fast. "I'm a policeman." Close enough. "Look, your mom's coming back now." *Why was he getting involved with these people's lives?* It had only been a few relatively innocent questions and comments, but damned if it didn't feel like more than that.

He glanced at Holly again, then at Carly, and he doubted if he'd been so glad to see anybody in a very long time. Like mother, like daughter, he thought again. They both had a way of taking conversation right to the heart of the matter, making a man think . . . too much.

"I think," Holly went on quietly, "that more than just about *anything,* I wish we were normal."

Jack's heart thumped. Oh, yeah, he could remember thinking that once upon a time. "It's easy to think that normal is what the other guy has, that you're the only person in the world who hurts the way you do," he heard himself say.

Holly's eyes widened. "Yeah," she breathed.

Then, Jack thought, he'd ended up at the orphanage and found ten or twenty other kids in his same exact shoes. "It's not always true," he went on, though he admitted that knowing that didn't always help.

"Everybody I know has a mom and a dad and brothers and sisters. And they go to work in dresses and stuff, and they never smell like *steers.*"

Jack's mouth quirked. He realized that he was enjoying this. "And maybe they wish they did."

"Smell like steers?" She laughed. "I bet not."

"You know, I know a lot of people who hate wearing high heels and ties. I sure couldn't stand it on a daily basis. The thing is, practically everybody can find something they don't like about their lives. You've sort of got to play up what you *do* like, Holly.'' And that, he thought, was something he had learned how to do. ''Sometimes the bad parts are just things you can't fix. If there's nothing you can do about them, you can't let them eat at you.''

Carly was watching them closely. Suddenly he felt self-conscious.

''Anyway, just think about it,'' he finished shortly, moving to tack his horse.

''You, on the other hand,'' he muttered to the gelding, ''are ugly as sin, stubborn as hell, and I can't think of a thing you can do about it.''

The split-eared horse glared at him. Jack felt much better for having insulted him.

It took a little more than fifteen minutes to get on the trail again, but within half an hour dust plumed and the earth seemed to rumble as they drove on. The wagon pitched and rolled along behind them, and Scorpion took up his place again at the left rear side of the herd. Jack fell in behind him and watched him.

By eleven o'clock, Carly started to feel herself unraveling.

It didn't matter that Jack had a pretty valid point and that she was trying her hardest not to think about what was happening, or which one was Scorpion, she thought. It didn't matter because she was growing increasingly terrified of *all* the men the longer this went on.

They had just crossed over a narrow stream, barely enough to get the horses' fetlocks wet, when Brad rode up beside her. She had her eyes on the herd and didn't notice him coming until he spoke.

''Carly?''

Her heart hurtled into her throat and her skin went to ice. She jumped and looked over at him even as she cursed herself for her reaction.

''Is this the deepest water we'll have to cross?'' he asked. ''This and that draw thing that we came through yesterday?''

Carly's throat closed. She couldn't find her voice. *Talk. Answer him, damn it. Act normal.*

Jack came up on her other side. ''Problem?'' he asked.

Carly felt her breath rush out of her, hitching halfway.

"I just wondered if we'd have to cross any deep water," Brad explained. "I can't swim."

"Do we?" Jack asked Carly.

It was on the tip of her tongue to snap that he knew they did. He had already asked her that before they had even left the Draw. Then she caught herself. She breathed again carefully and nodded.

"We'll hit the North Canadian River first," she managed.

"How soon?" Jack asked.

Carly swallowed. "Soon."

"Today?" Brad asked. "I can't swim," he repeated.

Good. Maybe you'll drown. But what if she was wrong? What if it wasn't him? Was he Scorpion just because he asked about rivers? It was a natural question if he really couldn't swim. She remembered suddenly that Holly's father had floated like a block of cement, too. He'd been terrified of even the bathtub and would only take showers. A river like the North Canadian had generally unhinged him, which just went to show that more sane and self-confident men than Brad had been scared by such a challenge.

"I...we'll reach it any time now," she managed finally. "Probably in about an hour."

"How am I going to get over?" Brad asked.

"We'll stick you in the wagon." *The one you were so worried about yesterday.* She bit back on the words and glanced at Jack. If he didn't like the arrangement, then the hell with him. If he wouldn't tell her what the problem was with the wagon, then he could hardly expect her to work around it.

Jack looked unperturbed. Oh, God, maybe it *wasn't* Brad, she thought again. Surely Jack would show some reaction over her putting him in the wagon if it was.

Carly spurred her mare, irritated, and trotted away from both of them. Jack caught up with her again a few minutes later. "You're doing fine, cowgirl."

"No," she said tightly. "I'm not."

"Were you telling the truth?" he asked. "Will we hit that river within the hour?"

"Barring calamity."

"Then I promise I'll try to get this over with before we hit the next river after this."

Carly's gaze flew to him. Jack had to look away. There was so much hope in her eyes, a plea, a certain desperation that was so unlike Carly it tore at something inside him. *Make it end,* her eyes said. *Please make this craziness end.*

She finally looked doggedly ahead again. Jack cleared his throat.

"In the meantime," he said carefully, "I'll need your help."

"Do tell," she answered, her teeth gritted.

He wanted to smile and couldn't quite manage it. "You can't put Brad in the wagon with Mazie Montoro."

And there it was.

Her eyes came around to him again, sharp and stricken. "The wagon again, huh?" she asked finally, her voice cracking with the strain.

"Forget it." He couldn't stand the look on her face. He'd work around the problem. Somehow. "Forget I said anything."

"Right," she muttered sarcastically. Then, after a moment, she added, "If Mazie is in danger, then I have to do something about it, Jack."

Jack grimaced. "Yeah. I guess you're right." The reason this whole damned thing had gone on as long as it had was his preoccupation with getting anyone else hurt.

Damn it.

Carly made a sound of distress. Jack flinched and watched her visibly get a grip on herself, and he was amazed by her all over again. This, he thought, was one very tough lady.

"So what do you want me to do?" she asked finally.

Jack thought about it. "Tell him that you've changed your mind, that you've thought about it and you've realized the wagon's already too heavy as it is."

"So if he doesn't ride in it, what am I supposed to do with him?"

Jack smiled in a look so cold, it made her heart stop. She realized, suddenly, that she didn't know him at all. He had touched her, had made love with her, but she simply did not know any man who could smile like that.

"I guess we'll just have to let him try to get over on his horse," Jack said. The more he thought about it, the better he liked it. He doubted if the bit about not swimming was true anyway. More than likely, it was a ploy to stay close to the money. So they would separate him from his wagon, and send it across the river without him.

"Sometime in all this, you're going to have to mention that the Cimarron is even harder to get over than the North Canadian," he went on, thinking aloud.

"It's not."

"It is now."

Carly forced herself to nod.

Scorpion wouldn't risk making such a crossing a second time, Jack thought. He'd finally have to go, before they got to it.

When they came up on the North Canadian forty-five minutes later, Jack kept a close eye on the assassin. The sight of the muddy, yellow water and its steep banks seemed to get no appreciable rise out of him. The river would hardly ruin the money, Jack thought. It would still spend. But it was going to be a hell of a job drying out fifteen million dollars. Then again, Jack thought, *he'd* certainly be willing to tackle such a chore for so much cash. If he had to. If there was a very valid reason for keeping it in that wagon a little while longer.

A reason like not wanting to leave, not wanting to panic and bolt, without the woman he had come to get.

Jack removed his hat, squeezed his eyes shut and rubbed them. They felt dry and grainy from the dust and from far too little sleep. And Scorpion, good old Scorpion, was still hanging loose.

He finally looked up again to see Carly hesitating at the bank. He rode to her.

"Well?" he asked.

She shot him a frustrated look. "I was about to ask you the same thing. What do I do now?"

"Talk to Brad."

She blanched.

Jack swore quietly. *Just a pawn, she's just a pawn.*

No, he thought, she had stopped being that days ago, even before he had touched her.

He didn't want to ask her to get anywhere near the man, he realized. It was professionally dangerous, as well as personally appalling. "Here's what I want you to do," he said softly. "Wait a few minutes after I ride away from you. Then just call out to him, tell him what you've decided about the wagon.

Don't make a big deal of it. You don't have to go over to him to talk to him. I'll take it from there."

Carly nodded, her face still pale.

"Are you okay?" he went on.

"Okay," she repeated, whispering.

"So how *are* we supposed to get over this thing?" He motioned to the river.

"I need to find a place where the bank's not this steep." She pulled her braid forward over her shoulder and played with it nervously. "The catch is that it can't be steep on either side."

"You've been this way before," he pointed out. "Don't you remember where you crossed last time?"

"It doesn't matter. It changes. Every time, it changes."

Jack waited, one brow raised in a question. He wanted her to talk about it. He wanted to snag her attention with the logistics of the ride so that she would calm down.

It worked. Her gaze finally cleared again.

"My father used to say that a river is just like a woman," she mused, half-smiling. "Contrary, sometimes even bitchy, giving you a fit if you look the other way even for a moment."

"I know one like that."

Her grin flashed a little wider for a second. "You can't go anywhere without having to cross one sooner or later," she went on, "and once you do, once you experience the thrill, you'll keep going back for more. It's scary, but it really is an adrenaline high."

"Yeah," Jack said. "That's the one."

Carly's heart hitched and she looked at him. She found herself hoping yet again, fiercely, that this would be over soon. Before she knew it, she would look up and see Jack walking back into the camp, calmly blowing on a smoking gun, and Brad would just be . . . gone. Would it happen that way, or had she seen too many old movies? She found herself hoping that if it did happen, if it could only happen, then maybe she would see him again somehow. Maybe the end of the trail didn't have to be Fort Dodge after all.

And *that* was a startling, treacherous hope. She knew better. All men left, sooner or later, one way or another.

Her jaw hardened and she looked deliberately back at the river. She tossed her braid back over her shoulder. "There's no time like the present, I guess."

Jack watched her go. At the very least, she didn't seem to be overly concerned about Scorpion now. He wondered what she *had* been thinking about. Whatever it had been, it had changed her face for a moment, making it go soft, yearning, in a way that stroked something deep inside him, something he wasn't even sure he could name.

He left the river as well, riding back behind the herd. His air went out of him slowly. He realized his breath had snagged somewhere in his mid-chest.

He felt a fierce rush of pride when her voice rose over the other commotion. It was remarkably steady. He watched Scorpion digest the news that he would be crossing on a horse, and that he'd better get used to it, because the next river was even worse.

Now the man was starting to look uncomfortable.

Suddenly, Jack didn't feel tired anymore.

Chapter 14

They rode nearly a mile to the east before Carly found a place to cross the river. There was some tree cover on the opposite bank, but only a few scrubby bushes on the close side where the cattle and the guests waited.

A look of utter horror began dawning on Brad's face. Maybe he really couldn't swim, Jack thought.

"I can't do it!" he protested, his voice grainy with nerves.

Carly didn't even look at him. "Sure you can," she snapped. "You float. Your horse floats. You'll just buoy up a little more than he does. Your legs will try to drift out. You've got to concentrate on keeping yourself centered above him. Hold onto his mane, and hold on *tight* when he gets his footing again. It'll be a bumpy ride for a few seconds there."

"But I *can't* float!" Brad protested.

"Then just let your horse do it and hang on to him," Carly said flatly.

She circled around the herd, coming up on its rear. Brad glared at her with a look of such utter fury that Jack felt his skin crawl. He looked quickly around at the others to see if anyone else noticed. They were all too preoccupied with their own concerns about the crossing. He breathed again and only then did he realize that his hand was like a claw on his thigh, ready to go for his gun again.

Easy, he cautioned himself. *Easy does it.*

He looked for Holly. She rode up beside him.

"Scared?" she asked.

"Who? Me? Never."

She giggled. It made his heart move.

Carly started waving her hat again and hooting at the cattle to urge them down toward the bottom of the bank. The cowboys took up their places to keep the animals from bolting back toward solid ground. The other guests all more or less waited for Carly to shout more orders at them. Finally she did, pausing now and then to interject comments at the cowboys and the cattle.

"Come on, everybody! Move!" A cow tried to turn around, heading back toward her. "Oh, no, you don't, Mama. Not that way." She turned her again. "Josh, watch out there, that calf's going to run for his life. Let's *go,* Leigh, or I swear I'll smack your mare's rump so hard you'll fly over. Okay, I want you all to follow the cattle. Enter the water right after the last of them are in. The *last* of them. Got it? After that, all you've got to do is stay on. Your horse will do the rest. Just hang on, no matter what. If there's a problem, the men and I will take care of it. Holly, are you okay?"

"Sure. Do you want me to ride up ahead with you? Maybe you'll need some help."

Carly opened her mouth and closed it again. What was this? Holly hadn't offered help in more than a year, since she had decided she resented Carly and everything connected with her.

"Sure," she said finally, bemusedly. "Come on. You can keep an eye on this calf here. He's a little small to be handling this. You know what to do if he starts getting swept away."

"Swept *away?*" Leigh bleated.

Holly rode forward to join her. The first cattle had reached the bottom of the bank and they bawled and churned there. Jack watched them with a feeling of misgiving. He found himself trying to figure out just how many pounds of beef were down there, crashing into one another, trying to get back up the bank while three hundred more steers crowded in behind them.

"Okay," Carly called out. "Let's do it!"

Let's not, Jack thought dourly.

Then he glanced at Scorpion. The man's face was almost literally white now. Perfect, Jack thought. He wouldn't bolt now—there was no way he could get to his money—but there was no way he'd risk this again at the Cimarron, either.

The first cattle entered the water. Carly was halfway across now, standing up in her stirrups despite the efforts of the water to disengage her from her horse. Jack was impressed. He imagined that that was pretty hard to do. Then again, she had quite a pair of legs on her. He already knew that when they decided they were going to wrap themselves around something, they didn't budge.

He grinned to himself, then, impossibly, he wanted her again—then, there, immediately. His body reacted with a surge of readiness and heat. He dragged his eyes away from her.

Josh and Gofer and Plank had taken up positions behind her and on either side of the herd. Rawley rode complacently in the back. Apparently this wasn't going to be a problem for him, either. In spite of himself, Jack felt his gaze going back to Carly. She was grinning, but then he saw her expression falter.

Something was wrong.

Instinctively, his eyes went back to Scorpion. No trouble there, not yet. The man was too scared to make any move at the moment. Jack looked back at the water. Carly's horse was struggling a little now. She'd sat down again because the animal's hind end kept getting swept around.

Finally, Jack understood what was wrong. The current had to be stronger than she had anticipated. He watched her for some signal that she would stop the guests from trying to cross, but she never looked up. Her eyes were narrowed in concentration as the herd started drifting too, and she and the cowboys fought to hold them.

Only Jack remained on high ground. Leigh was already in the water and Myra had waded in close behind her. The men were right on their tails.

Jack threw a last look at Carly, then another at the wagon just now entering the river. He didn't want to let that out of his sight, so it was now or never. He gave a heartfelt sigh and urged his horse into the water with the others.

He gritted his teeth at the cold shock. The tide swept him and his horse sideways. A cow bobbed past him, lowing in panic.

Carly was beginning to feel a little panic of her own.

She hauled on her left rein and thumped her right leg against her mare, trying to keep her swimming into the current. She had to block the steers that were drifting. How could the water be this strong? She had tested it before bringing the cows in and it hadn't pulled at her this fiercely. Except maybe she hadn't been paying enough attention. Maybe half her thoughts had really been on where Jack would go after Dodge—if he even made it to Dodge—and maybe the other half of them had been on Scorpion, and why Jack seemed to think he wouldn't cross *two* rivers.

Either way, it was too late now. One by one, the cattle were tugged past her, some bumping into her mare, others merely bobbing by. A moan of dismay caught at her throat. It was drowned out by a screaming, metallic sound.

The wagon.

She looked that way helplessly. It overturned, spilling out poor Mazie. The horses that had been pulling it were struggling on toward the opposite shore. The hitch had snapped, but at least the animals were free of the encumbrance. Their harnesses and reins trailed wildly behind them in the current.

Brad looked apoplectic.

Jack looked ecstatic.

The wagon surged wildly past her. It got lodged against the far bank in a snarl of bared tree roots, but even as she watched, it was tugged loose again and went dancing wildly down the river.

Carly finally gave up on the cattle. She leaned over her mare's neck, urging her on, and finally she felt the animal's straining rhythm change to a jarring gait as her hooves found purchase in the river sand on the far bank. The mare heaved herself up onto solid ground, and Carly slid from her back even before the horse stopped to tremble and shake off water.

One by one, the others struggled to the shore. Holly came triumphantly with her calf in tow. She had roped it. Carly hugged her shakily. Brad—Scorpion, she thought wildly—had made it, and she stepped back quickly, instinctively, dragging Holly with her, to give him a wide berth as he came ashore. Jack was right behind him, and when he noticed her reflex, he gave a little shake of his head.

Don't react, she remembered. Oh, God, how could she *not?*

Carly took a deep breath and went to help a trembling, stricken Leigh off her horse. Rawley reached dry ground and gave a loud, hooting whistle, exhilarated.

That was when Carly realized that Brad had disappeared. Cattle streamed up the bank all around them, lowing and confused. She caught her breath and looked around, and saw Brad trotting back toward them from farther down the bank.

"The wagon's safe!" he called out. "Just around that bend, the river narrows. It's sort of stuck in there, between the banks. It can't go any farther."

The damned wagon again!

Carly felt her legs give out. She sat hard where she stood, her adrenaline draining out of her so suddenly she felt hollow. The cowboys went to try to bring the wagon back, Scorpion tagging along to show them where it was. The cattle would have to be collected again, she thought. At least half the herd had been swept down the river. Those who survived could find hard ground up to a mile from here. She wondered dismally how many she would lose.

The wagon hitch would have to be repaired, too. Everything inside would have to be sorted through. They would save what could be dried out, and toss what had been rendered useless by the water. She had packed it so that anything perishable would ride high, but the way it had been bobbing and tumbling, she knew that wouldn't have saved much.

They would be going no farther today.

The guests seemed to know it without being told, because they began to gather their soggy gear and set their tents up to dry. Carly felt movement beside her and looked over at a pair of very wet legs. Jack.

"You okay, cowgirl?" he asked quietly.

"Right . . . as rain." Her voice broke. She was still shaking. At least no one had been hurt.

Jack sat down. Now she noticed that he was grinning widely.

"What's wrong with you?" she cried. "That was nearly a disaster!"

"I know." Jack looked up at the sky. "I'm beginning to think there might be a God after all." He couldn't have asked for a better crossing if he'd put a request in straight to heaven, what with the wagon breaking and nearly being dashed away. Soon, very soon now, Scorpion was going to have to leave.

"How far to the Cimarron?" he asked suddenly.

"About sixty miles," she answered shakily, getting used to the quick way his mind seemed to change tracks.

He wished it was less, but it would have to do. "Make sure you mention that within everyone's hearing," he directed. "I want him to go to the wagon tonight."

Carly stiffened. Her eyes flared. "What in the world is in that wagon?"

He hesitated again.

"Oh, for God's sake, Jack! It's a little late to be playing games, and I'm warning you—I can't take much more!"

She probably couldn't, he thought, and playing games with her would just stress her out more. He'd asked an awful lot of her so far.

There was no sense in shielding her from this particular angle. It might even help, he thought. She'd know what Scorpion would have to do to leave—or at least what little he would be *able* to do, because Jack wasn't going to let him get near Carly to see to the other loose end he'd have to tie up.

He hesitated, then went with it. "I told you that something about his latest job tipped me off that he was retiring," he said finally, quietly.

Carly nodded tensely.

"He turned on the people who'd hired him and stole fifteen million dollars from them."

Carly's expression didn't change. "And you think he's got it with him?"

"I know he does."

Her expression finally changed. Her eyes widened slowly, understanding dawning there. "In my *wagon?*"

"Keep your voice down."

"*There's fifteen million dollars hidden in my wagon?*" she demanded in a whispery screech.

He looked at her warily. "More or less. Could be fourteen, could be sixteen."

"Where?" she demanded, her heart slamming. "That's impossible. I packed it myself! I didn't see—"

"Underneath," Jack said. "False bottom."

Her jaw dropped. "How'd he do that? When?"

"I have no idea, but it's there."

"I got into this mess for a few *thousand,* and I end up carting around fifteen *million?*" Her mind was staggering, stumbling, reeling. She couldn't imagine that much money. "In cash?" She couldn't comprehend it being essentially in her possession.

"Yeah," Jack said reluctantly.

Suddenly she shoved at him. "Four days ago, I had cows. I had tourists. I had a tax problem. And then you came along and..." Her throat closed. She choked. "Take it all and go away, Jack. Take your money and your killer and just...go... just leave me alone!"

She tried to shoot to her feet and couldn't quite manage it because the bank was slippery. He caught her and pulled her down again. She landed with a small gasp. He had known that it was bound to happen sooner or later, that the shock and the disbelief of all this would wear off, and when it did, emotion would set in. But he wasn't ready for it now, because what she'd just said made guilt come alive inside him all over again.

He tried to tell himself that if he hadn't taken on this last chase, then Paul Manning would just have sent someone else. That this was Scorpion's fault, Brett's fault, whoever the man was in his own mind. He had come here, leading the agency behind him.

Still, another agent wouldn't necessarily have made love with Carly Castagne. Maybe another man wouldn't have gotten...involved.

He was involved. It was a shock with reverberations that shimmied clear down to his toes. It was the first time in a very long time, probably since Zoe. It left him itchy and warm, panicked and wild and amazed. It kept his breath short.

Carly straightened and dragged a hand over her cheek. He wasn't sure, but he thought he saw a tear shining there.

"Well," she said finally, taking a deep breath. "I guess that explains why you don't think he'll be eager to cross the Cimarron."

"Right." He hesitated. His voice was hoarse. "It's also why you've got to keep everyone away from that wagon. He's going to have to make contact with it before he moves on."

Carly pressed her fingers to her temples. "I still don't understand this," she murmured. "Why *Oklahoma?*"

Jack waved a careful hand around at all the nothingness of the land. "What better place to disappear into thin air?"

"Wyoming and someone else's dude ride would have done just as nicely," she snapped.

Jack got to his feet and pulled her up with him. This next part was going to be tricky, he thought.

"I need you to stay in your tent tonight," he said finally. "You can't sleep outside."

"Where will you be?"

"Inside with you."

He watched her feet hesitate, then move again. "Why?" she asked with decisive care.

It was a reasonable question, he thought. "Because."

She looked at him. "Because of Scorpion?"

He didn't answer. Something in her belly shifted. There was more, she realized. He still hadn't told her everything yet.

"I just want to know that you're safe until he takes off," he went on finally. "And that could very well happen tonight if you let it out that we'll hit the Cimarron tomorrow."

"We won't! It'll probably be early on Sunday morning."

"He doesn't need to know that."

Carly shook her head. He would stay in her tent, then. Something squeezed inside her. She blew out her breath. "Holly's just about going to love this."

"Speaking of Holly, I want to put her tent right behind ours, sort of bracketed between us and Rawley." Rawley was the closest thing to backup he could manage, Jack realized. Maybe it was a good thing Carly had brought him along after all.

Carly's face leached of color again. "Is *Holly* in some specific danger?"

Not unless Scorpion takes a good look at her. So far, he was still pretty much ignoring the kid—and Jack had been watching closely for any signs that he wasn't. The assassin seemed to be going to inordinate lengths to keep a distance from Carly as well, at least after that first day when flirting with her had failed. His reserve had surprised Jack, but then he'd understood. If the bastard wasn't going to be able to sweep her off her feet a second time, then he would have to tell her who he was. And *that* would bring an explosive reaction, enough of one that he probably didn't want to risk it until this charade was nearly over and he was ready to go. By the same token, he wouldn't want her to recognize him before then, either.

"I don't think so," he said finally, slowly, in answer to her question. "It's just a precaution. Until—"

"Until he takes the damned money and leaves," Carly finished for him bitterly. "And then you're going to take off after him." In spite of herself, no matter that she'd told herself she could handle it, she wondered if that would be the last she'd ever see of Jack Fain, and her heart hurt.

They had almost reached the others. The cowboys had managed to haul the wagon back. Scorpion was with them, hovering over them, watching the repairs.

"Start complaining about how you've lost half a day," Jack said abruptly. "We need a first-class Carly-style foul temper here because you're behind schedule. I want him to think that's all we were discussing."

Carly thought again of fifteen million dollars in her poor, old wagon.

"A foul temper," she muttered, "is something I ought to be able to manage just fine right about now."

They got through dinner without trouble. If the others felt the undercurrents of tension, if it occurred to any of them that Brad seemed unusually quiet, they didn't comment on it. Carly figured that Myra and Rawley, Leigh and Gofer, were just absorbed enough in each other not to notice. And Leigh, at least, was getting on Carly's nerves.

Jack was sprawled by the fire on his side, his head propped on one hand near her thigh. She leaned over to whisper to him.

"Look at her."

"Who?"

"Leigh."

"What's the matter with her?"

"I can't believe the way she's falling all over that poor cowboy!"

Jack looked. *Poor* cowboy? Gofer definitely did not look distressed.

"It's her vacation, cowgirl. Let her be."

Still, Carly scowled. "I'd just rather that she *vacation* in her tent where we wouldn't have to watch this."

"No doubt she'll do it there, too. Look, it's a natural reaction," he said finally. "That was a real scary ride this afternoon. Leigh looked her own mortality right in the eye, and now she's grabbing onto life with a gusto."

Carly fell quiet again. "Did you ever do that?" she asked after a while. "Look your own mortality in the eye?"

"Many times." Unconsciously, he touched his newest scar.

"Did you . . . did you react like that, like she is?"

Jack hesitated. There was no sense in lying to her. He wondered why it had even occurred to him. "Sometimes."

Carly ran her tongue along her lower lip. He noticed that she wouldn't look at him.

"Did that have anything to do with what happened between us last night?" She knew that it had, a little bit, at least on her part. She had definitely thought about him dying.

She would have done what she did anyway, she realized. The only thing was, she might not have done it so spontaneously, so soon. Then again, with Jack Fain, she got the strong impression she didn't have a whole lot of time, with or without his Scorpion.

Jack fought a smile. This time he didn't falter, didn't need to think about it. "No. My mortality was nowhere in evidence last night."

"Yet. I guess you've got to be thinking about it."

Jack shrugged. "Knowing it's out there somewhere around one of the next bends isn't enough to get that kind of rise out of me anymore."

"So to speak."

He grinned fast. "Last night was all you, cowgirl."

She was appalled and frightened at how pleased she was. She got to her feet and called out to the others.

"Instead of tiptoeing around camp tonight—" she looked pointedly at Myra and Leigh "—I think we should all try to get some sleep. I want to leave extra early tomorrow to make up for some of this lost time."

There were a few mild grumbles but most of them looked done in by the events of the afternoon. And they didn't even know the half of it, Carly thought. Plank was already asleep, flat on his back, with his head propped on his saddle. His hands were clasped together at his waist, and one of the cowboys had stuck a wild river flower in there.

"Uh, what about him?" Reggie asked. "Shouldn't we try to get him to his tent?"

"He's slept in odder places," Carly murmured.

"Yeah," Holly joined in. "Remember that trip when he got drunk and fell off into the river, and you got mad, Mom, and just left him there and drove on? And he slept there, right in the water, and caught up with us the next day."

"With his fingers all wrinkly and a leech in his underwear," Gofer supplied.

Plank grunted in his sleep as though he heard them and remembered, and everyone laughed. *How could everything seem so normal?* Carly wondered wildly.

Reggie finally shrugged and went into his tent. The others began standing and stretching. Holly dropped to her knees and crawled into her own small tarpaulin, but she gave a sly look back in the direction of Jack and Carly.

After a moment, it was just Carly and Jack, Plank and Scorpion, and Plank remained unconscious. Jack didn't move from where he lay beside the fire. Scorpion stood watching them. Carly's nerves stretched out until they felt like live wires.

"Uh...good night," she managed finally, hoarsely. She turned for her tent, looking at Jack as she did. He'd said he was going to stay with her tonight, but he didn't move. True, they'd agreed that he'd wait until after Holly went to bed before he came to her tent. But Holly had gone now, so why didn't he do something?

"Sleeping alone tonight, cowgirl?" he finally asked, but his voice seemed too deliberate, at least to her, and she finally understood. He wanted Scorpion to know that he'd be with her.

She fought him out of sheer contrariness. Or maybe, she thought, maybe it was just disappointment that he was so purely the predator after all. "I'm...uh, pretty tired."

"Bet I could fix that."

"Talk's cheap," she shot back angrily.

Something flared in his eyes, and suddenly she was positive that it had nothing to do with Scorpion after all. Her heart thundered.

Scorpion looked back and forth between them, sharply, and, she thought, angrily.

Angrily?

Then Jack finally got to his feet, one of his brows raised, and she forgot about it.

"Let's find out," he drawled.

Chapter 15

Carly ducked into her tent. She was trembling again. She told herself it was because this was the first time all day she had been out of the assassin's sight. It was purely relief.

A heartbeat later, the tent door snapped behind her and Jack came in. She whirled about to face him.

"Is Holly going to be all right?" she demanded.

"I asked Rawley to help keep an eye and an ear on her tonight."

"Is that good enough?"

"I'll be listening, too."

She turned away from him. "You wanted Brad to know you'd be in here, didn't you?"

"Yeah."

Her jaw tensed. "Well, does he? Does he know?"

"I think so. He went to his tent first. Sometimes you just can't be sure, Carly," Jack said quietly. "There are no absolutes in this game."

A game. Was it all just a game to him? She flinched and searched his face.

"How can you stand it?" she asked finally, quietly.

He looked away from her. "That's what makes it interesting. It's all one big gamble."

"A gamble? With your *life?*"

He closed the distance between them, gathering her close as he had wanted to do for hours now. The rigidity of her muscles relaxed a little. She groaned softly and wrapped her arms around his neck. He felt so solid, so strong, so good, she thought.

"Maybe I'm as bad as Leigh," she whispered. "Maybe I'm just trying to grab hold of life, but God, Jack, I need you right now."

"It's okay. I don't care why."

And he didn't, he realized. Maybe his male pride was seriously lacking. Or maybe it was just strong enough that he didn't sweat the small stuff. Either way, if she needed to use him, then he was glad to be used.

He found her mouth and she almost literally melted into him. Everything drained out of her with the touch of his lips on hers. For a moment, she was free of the fear. And his alarm escalated.

It would be so easy to forget Scorpion right now. And so deadly. He had tweaked him on purpose, letting him know he'd be in here with his woman. It had to be killing the bastard, even as twisted as he was and as cold as he could be. It had to be straining all the dispassionate common sense that was keeping him at a distance from her right now. And, Jack hoped, it would be an added incentive, on top of the imminent river, to move tonight, to take her away now or even to leave by himself, to do anything to put an end to the torment.

"Do you have a lantern in here?" he asked against her lips, still thinking.

Carly pulled back. It took her a moment to focus on him again. "What? Why?"

"It'll cast a silhouette. Then we can be sure that he knows I'm in here."

Carly felt something cold slide down through her. When it finally reached her toes, she felt as fragile as handblown glass.

"You want to put on a show for him?" she whispered.

"Nothing so explicit as that." But then Jack realized how his words had sounded. Too late he knew that she thought that he was staging a scene for the assassin's benefit again, that it meant nothing more to him than that.

"You wanted to be sure," he pointed out carefully.

"Get out of here."

He flinched at the lack of venom in her voice, at the hollow hurt. He reached for her arm to try to pull her back to him, then he almost lost his balance in the cramped space when she came too willingly. Her fists began pummeling him as soon as she was close enough to reach him.

"Carly, I didn't mean—" He broke off, grunting as she got in a particularly good shot. Then she reeled back from him.

"Yes, you did!" she cried. "Is that all this has been for you? Was touching me just part of your... your game?"

"Stop it, Carly." He caught her wrists. "Come on, don't talk so loud."

That only inflamed her more. She shouted instead and struggled to pull away from him.

"Tell me, Jack! *Talk* to me!"

Oh, hell, Scorpion was going to love this. "We've already been through this!" he snapped. "No, it was—*isn't*—part of a game!"

She wrenched away from him. "All I wanted was to get my cows to Kansas!" she bit out. "And then...when you...when we...I just wanted you to want me...to honestly *want* me back!" And she had been fool enough to believe that maybe he had.

God, how she hated being a fool! And she had played the role time after time since this man had appeared in her barnyard, doing things she never would have done for or with another man. And she knew again, suddenly and horribly, that for him, involvement went only as deep as a touch.

"Listen to me," he said quietly. "I've been hunting, chasing, playing this game for a lot longer than I've known you. It's second nature. It has nothing to do with you. It's *in* me. I can't turn it off. I don't know how to anymore, and even if I did, this is too important. But that doesn't mean I want you less! One doesn't have anything to do with the other!"

But it did, she thought desperately, because even while he had been kissing her, he had been thinking about Brad, playing him, setting him up again. Because even while he was touching her, there was a part of him she *couldn't* touch, that part of him that hid behind his excuses.

"That's why you do it, isn't it?" she asked hollowly, realizing it suddenly like a light bulb going on in her head.

"Do what?" He was instantly wary, recognizing that tone in her voice. She was going to start digging at him again.

"It's like, which came first, the chicken or the egg? Which was it, Jack?"

"I don't know what you're talking about."

He didn't need this now, he thought. He needed to touch her, to lose himself in her. Maybe *that* was why he hadn't minded being used, because his own needs were just as consuming. He didn't want to talk. He could feel the heat of her in the darkness of the tent and he just wanted to steep himself in it, and Scorpion could be damned.

Scorpion could *almost* be damned. He wondered a little crazily how she would feel about making love with his gun still strapped to his calf.

But she was relentless, and she wasn't thinking about making love. When he made a move toward her again she took a half step back.

He finally lit the lantern himself. In the new, dim light, he saw that her eyes blazed.

"You don't actually use your Scorpion as an excuse so you don't have to stay in one place and settle down," she accused, her voice lower so no one but Jack could hear her. "You chose your job in the first place because it won't let you settle down."

Jack's jaw clenched. "Wrong, cowgirl. I didn't choose my work. It chose me."

She blinked. She hadn't expected that. "What do you mean?"

"You don't decide to go into the...the agency I'm a part of. They recruit you, out of college, the armed forces, wherever you happen to be when you snag their attention."

Her skin paled. In the light from the lantern, it looked translucent. He wanted his words back and couldn't take them.

"The agency?" she repeated carefully. "What agency? The CIA?" She'd just assumed that he was with the FBI, she realized. But he wouldn't call that an agency. That was a *bureau*.

"No," he said shortly.

She thought fast. "Secret Service?"

"No."

"Even if I guessed, you'd lie, wouldn't you?"

"No," he said yet again. "I won't lie, because you won't ever guess." He raked a hand through his hair. "Carly, there are so many more branches of the government than the public knows about. There are organizations that only the *President* knows of. There are teams that only investigate other teams.''

"And what . . . what exactly are you?'' she whispered.

Without making a conscious decision, he decided to tell her. His head was pounding hard with tension, yet he knew he had to make her understand as Zoe never had. This woman wouldn't be content with half truths, wouldn't take comfort in them, and he had a sudden need for her to *know* the truth, or at least as much of it as he was allowed to tell her.

He would examine why later. For now, if she was going to condemn him, then it was damned well going to be for something he was guilty of. And if she wasn't, if she was going to accept him . . . well, then, she was going to know exactly what it was that she was accepting.

He refused to acknowledge why he wanted her to do so so badly, why it even mattered since he was going to be gone in a few days anyway.

"We chase Scorpion and guys like him," he said flatly. "And when we catch them, sometimes we kill them. If we have to. If the opportunity presents itself. We do all the nasty stuff that the CIA and the FBI can't get away with, stuff that would raise a hue and a cry among the American people if they ever got wind of it. We cross over gray areas that would have bleeding hearts and liberals up in arms. We pretty much do the same things the bad guys do, but we do it for the right reasons."

She took a little stumbling step away from him. It was no more or less than he had expected, yet the impact of it felt like a fist in his gut.

"Why?" she asked, her voice seeming to hitch over the single syllable.

"Because if the bleeding hearts had their way, guys like Scorpion would be ruling the world. Because while the liberals are preaching up on their soapboxes, whole countries are dying, are being deliberately killed off. Because it's nice to talk about love and peace and flower power, but the fact of the matter is that the sixties are a long way behind us, and that stuff didn't work then, either. Guns and killing and hatred are still what make the world go round, and more guns and more killing are needed to combat that. You need to meet guys like

Scorpion on their own terms. They can't be stopped any other way. They don't respect anything else. They *laugh* at the CIA."

"Is that why you joined this...the agency?" she asked hoarsely. "Because you believe all that?" That was the important thing, she thought, not her own moral judgments. *She* didn't have to go around shooting people to even the score. The important thing was how *he* dealt with it...and if he did it easily.

Jack's eyes narrowed. "For the most part. Some instances are more painless than others."

"Just because they recruited you, it didn't mean you had to stay with them. Did it?"

He could have told her that he hadn't known exactly what he was getting into until it was too late. He truly hadn't. He'd been flattered at first, proud. *Somebody* had wanted him. Then he'd understood what was expected of him, the kind of amazing leeway he had, how very few laws he had to salute to. He'd understood...and he'd stayed.

Because she was right, he realized. As long as he was with the agency, there was no possibility of laying down roots. If he'd really wanted out, if he'd really wanted to go to Florida, there would have been no way Paul could have talked him into this last foray.

That rocked him.

"They need guys like me," he pushed on. "And yeah, I do believe that men like Scorpion have to be stopped in any way it takes. That prime minister and the senator I told you about sure as hell didn't deserve to die."

Carly remembered the picture in his wallet and what he had told her last night. "They need guys without strings, without family and messy attachments?"

Jack stiffened. "Good enough."

"Did they know about your parents? Is that why they picked you?"

She was good, he thought. Astute and sharp...and not afraid to use the edge. "They pulled me out of the Navy. I was a SEAL. They liked what I could do in pressure situations."

"But it couldn't have hurt that your mom and your dad were both gone."

"Damn it, Carly! Leave that alone!"

Her thoughts raced on, sharp and curious. "But you had a wife," she realized.

"Later," he snapped. "I had a wife *later,* not when they took me. I got married after I made the commitment to the agency. They warned me that it wouldn't last and they were right."

Suddenly it occurred to him that they probably *wouldn't* have been right if they had been talking about this woman. It astounded him . . . and it panicked him all over again. It made something prickle his skin and roll in his gut and it made his heart skip a beat.

He needed to put an end to this conversation after all.

"Well, I guess that answers my question," Carly said.

"It does?" He eyed her warily.

"The chicken came first."

She staggered him. He had almost forgotten that part of their conversation.

"I guess you're going to tell me why," he said slowly.

"Sure. You tell yourself you can't settle down, that your job won't let you. *'It's in me. I can't turn it off,'*" she mimicked. "Convenient, isn't it?"

He didn't answer. His heart was pounding.

"I bet you could, cowboy."

"I could what?"

"Turn it off."

She turned away from him and switched off the lantern again, then waited as though defying him to turn it back on. Finally, he felt her moving close to him again in the darkness.

"I bet you could," she repeated quietly, "if you had the guts."

He felt her breath at his jaw, then her teeth closed on his earlobe, and he wondered what an Oklahoma cowgirl thought she was going teach *him* about guts. And then he realized that he didn't want to know. He was too relieved that her temper had fizzled out to care if he was meeting her challenge.

She was in front of him now. He reached out for her in the darkness, and slid his hand beneath her braid to cup the back of her neck. He held her still, plunging his tongue past her teeth, and now Carly kissed him back because she *did* need to feel life. In the end she needed him just the way he was, a predator standing between her and the killer who was lurking out there in the night. She shuddered and met his tongue desperately, groaning and closing her eyes.

She hadn't unrolled her sleeping bag, but it didn't matter. The rocky dirt wasn't as kind as the creek-bed sand, but that didn't matter either. They eased down to the ground together, and if it was inhospitable, if some part of him really did keep listening for Scorpion, then he was too relieved to care and she didn't seem to sense it.

She knelt above him, straddling him, then she lowered herself to touch her mouth to his again. Peace, warmth, all the things he had mocked earlier were there in his kiss, she thought.

She slid down his body, a slow, deliberate friction against every one of his nerve endings. She popped the buttons on his shirt as she went, trailing small, hot kisses along the skin that was exposed. Jack groaned.

She reached his belt buckle and undid it, and pulled his jeans off, then his boots. This time she didn't hesitate when she came to his gun. She unstrapped it from his calf.

Jack struggled back to sanity. "Put it up here, Carly," he said evenly. *Where I can easily get to it.* He didn't add that aloud, but she knew. He waited for her temper again, but her eyes only burned with determination. She gave him the gun.

"I'm going to make you forget, Jack," she breathed. "For just a minute, for just a little while, you're going to be all mine and Scorpion can go to hell." Then she stroked her hands over his hardness, and he was.

Jack plunged his hands into her braid. She hadn't taken it down this time but he dug his fingers into its folds, forcing it loose, until her glorious hair spilled through his hands. Her mouth followed her hands, hot and wet, and it tortured him. His muscles ached with the pain of restraint, but she was right. He didn't think about Scorpion and he didn't think about the agency, and he didn't think about the void that was his life.

Just when he thought he would lose control, she slid back up over him again slowly. Her clothing dragged over his heated skin. Her grin was wicked and satisfied.

He couldn't let *that* challenge go unanswered. "My turn, cowgirl."

He dragged her T-shirt over her head, and worked her jeans down her hips. His hands slid beneath the elastic of her panties, holding her against him for a moment while he caught his breath and tried to take back the upper hand. Then he dived into her mouth, seeking forgetfulness once more.

Where his hands touched, her skin came alive. When his tongue probed, her soul seemed to melt. His touch stroked and heated her, up her thighs, her hips, her ribs, down again, a rough-gentle caress. And she knew then that she was forgetting, too, and it was as good and sweet and necessary as the air she breathed. Something wild and heated exploded in her as soon as his fingers slid beneath the elastic, against her most sensitive flesh, seeking entrance. Her world grew narrow and smaller until it was centered right there inside her. His fingers moved in and out of her, teasing, urging, until she could bear no more and knew she would die if he stopped.

He finally eased her panties down, too, and then she straddled him, fitting herself over him, and a hoarse chuckle broke from his throat as he considered that for a minute there, he had actually thought himself in control.

He found the clasp of her bra and worked it free. He wrapped his arms around her waist and pulled her back down toward him. His mouth sought her breasts, moving over her hard nipples, making her cry out even as he thrust his hips against her, driving himself into oblivion, into her heat.

Carly felt her cry change to a gasp. She dug her nails into his shoulders and held on.

He plunged into her again and again and she moved with him, feeling wild and alive, so fully *alive,* as she had not felt for too, too long. A part of her had been sleeping, she realized, just waiting for this broken, complicated, kind man.

Her climax hit her in a stunning ambush, but he was with her and he *was* all hers now. She felt his own explosion as though he were a part of her. When he groaned it seemed to be with her own voice.

The feeling didn't entirely dissipate when she lowered herself slowly to rest against his chest again. Her breath was short and fast. His hands stayed at her hips and he made no effort to leave her this time. She felt like part of him. In spite of everything, she felt safe, whole . . . and drained.

She couldn't believe the exhaustion that seeped through her muscles. Her limbs felt weighted.

"It's okay," he said quietly, and she realized that somehow he understood. "You don't have to do anything now. You can sleep. I'm here."

Carly wondered if anyone had ever said that to her before. No, she thought, not in recent memory. And she realized that he had been doing it, had been taking over for her, since he had first set foot on her ranch.

She closed her eyes.

Watching over her was the one thing Jack felt sure he could manage right now. It seemed like the rest of his world was suddenly a place of hazy uncertainties, shadows where there had been absolute clarity before. He glanced over at his gun. He wasn't sure what he could give her if he managed to pull them both through this, but suddenly he knew that he wanted to see her again. Somehow, impossibly, she'd managed to find something inside him that wasn't entirely cold and dead after all. And he needed that—oh, God, how he needed that—even more than he needed the self-protection of solitude.

He wasn't sure when the thought of roots had started to make him feel more panicky than actually terrified, but he wondered if maybe he could plant just one small, cautious seed here, and see if the roots held.

"Sweet God," he whispered aloud.

Uncharacteristically, he needed to talk about it. But when he angled his eyes down to look at her, he only let his breath out on an amazed sigh.

Carly was fast asleep.

Chapter 16

Jack finally dozed, a suspended half sleep that he succumbed to out of pure exhaustion. His ears were still listening and his brain was still alert, but when he opened his eyes again, the new sun made the tent walls glow golden.

Carly stirred. He looked over at her and realized that she had been awake for some time.

"That's what I like about you, Jack," she said dryly. "You're so chivalrous."

He managed to grin. When she had rolled off him last night without waking, he'd decided not to disturb her to wrestle her into the sleeping bag he'd finally unrolled. He'd laid it close beside her instead, thinking that she'd eventually get cold and wriggle over into it to join him. She hadn't. After the rigors of the trail, she'd slept the way she ate, the way she dug into his psyche, with single-minded fervor and determination.

"I didn't want to wake you," he said finally, and enjoyed the way she cocked a sardonic brow at him. Then she sat up and stretched.

She was so beautiful, he thought, all strong, fluid muscles beneath smooth skin. His breath snagged and hunger quickened inside him again. He started to reach for her, needing to touch her now as much as he had last night. That urgency hadn't waned yet, and it didn't, until she spoke.

"So what do we do now?"

Jack flinched. "We ride. And we wait. Something will give today. Something will have to."

His response shook her because she heard what he didn't say. Scorpion would probably take his money and go before they reached the Cimarron, and Jack would go, too, stalking him.

She groaned and crawled to him on her hands and knees. He had already reached for his shirt, and she pulled it out of his hands to press herself against him.

"Shhh," he managed. "We've got time."

He didn't know if he was referring to Scorpion or to the spare moments that remained until the rest of the camp awoke. It didn't matter. He caught her hips as she knelt over him. He eased down onto his back again and slid his hands up to her breasts, covering them as he'd wanted to do when she'd first woke and stretched, arching her back and thrusting them toward him. He followed his hands with his mouth, slowly, as though to memorize the taste and feel of her. He traced circles around her nipples with his tongue and then he played with each one until she moaned and writhed above him. Oh, yes, they had time. And maybe it was the last time they'd ever have together.

The thought made him angry. He pulled her down to him almost roughly and held her mouth to his while he plundered it, seeking, needing, aching for the forgetfulness she had given him last night. He cursed fate and his life that this couldn't be all there was, just him and her, alone with the dawn. He wished he had met her in a different time, a different place, so that he could have kept her away from all the ugliness—and then he didn't. Because the way she had wormed her way into his life, the way she had become a part of his innermost thoughts, was so uniquely her, and he realized that he wouldn't change any part of her at all. She was everything he had imagined, and so much more.

His hands moved over her body as though to brand every curve, as though to memorize every lean, lovely line. He cupped her bottom and traced each rib, and he felt her muscles tense beneath her skin. He delighted in it, craved it, then she began to quiver.

It was like a tonic, strengthening him, that she could want him so much when there was a killer somewhere on the other side of the tent door. But then, he thought, that was the way she approached everything—intensely, with integrity and fervor. It was just . . . Carly.

His hands melted her even as they tightened everything inside her, she thought. They finally rolled together, their legs twined, their arms wrapped around each other, clinging, grasping, until they came up hard against the tent wall. Their bodies bulged it outward and Jack tore his mouth from hers. He almost grinned.

"Careful, cowgirl," he managed, "unless you want the whole camp standing out there watching."

"I thought . . . you wanted that."

"No, no."

Then she was on top of him again and she leaned over him so his mouth could close gently over her nipple as his hands swept up the back of her thighs again. His fingers found her hot center and she groaned, shifting her weight on her knees, opening to him, wanting so much more.

There was nothing inside her now but the wanting, the greed for more of him. It didn't matter what they would do when they left this tent. He made her fear go away again. Suddenly she knew that it *wasn't* just sex she needed. Yes, it was vital and it reminded her that she was exquisitely alive, but it was more than that. It was the way he made her feel, as no other man had ever done. He coddled her in his own unique way, even as he expected too much of her. He soothed her even as he heated her, demanded even as he gave.

She needed Jack Fain, and there was nobody else in the world quite like him.

He rolled her over again and his mouth moved lower, brushing over her belly, his tongue dipping into her navel. She felt her muscles contract in anticipation as he moved lower, then his tongue slid along her most sensitive flesh. He probed and laved until she could only dig her nails into his shoulders, her breath coming again and again in short, hard gasps. It was so right, so perfect, so incredible, she thought that she might cry. He never seemed to doubt himself, she thought, or anything he was doing. There was no hesitation in him, just an arrogant confidence and a spirit for giving. And the giving was poignant, shattering, because she knew he truly did not expect that anyone would give him anything back.

When he finally came up over her again, he watched her face with a small half smile. "Turn about," he said quietly, "is fair play." Then, before she could breathe again, without warning, he drove himself into her hard.

Carly gasped then she laughed, a low, throaty sound. She clung to him though she had always been strong, whimpered though she had never been weak. She wanted to wait for him, needed him to stay with her again, but the tension inside her was too much, too ready, too powerful. He stroked within her and nuzzled at her neck, finally taking her mouth again. She stiffened as everything inside her exploded and he finally followed her.

He didn't leave her this time, either.

Jack braced his weight on his elbows and watched her, enjoying the way her face changed until the one expression came that hurt something inside him. Fear came to her eyes again, then hope flared there.

"Maybe he left last night!" she gasped, her eyes going wide as she realized the possibility. "Maybe he already took that damned money and when we go outside, he'll be gone."

"No," Jack said reluctantly.

"How can you be sure?"

"I'm sure."

"How? You slept in here. Anything could have happened out there."

"I didn't sleep. Not really. I would have heard him at the wagon."

Hope plummeted inside her. Still, Carly grappled with it, trying to hold it. "Maybe he was real quiet."

"You can't pry wood loose so quietly that someone listening for it wouldn't hear it," he pointed out grimly. "I only slept outside the first night because I didn't know where in the wagon the money was. I didn't know for sure what he would have to do to get to it. Last night I knew what I was listening for and I didn't hear it. I didn't hear anything at all. It was peaceful out there."

He finally pulled away from her. Carly sat up slowly and looked at the tent door, her throat closing.

"So...we've got to go out there," she said woodenly. She had never truly been afraid of anything in her life, she realized, but this terrified and appalled her. She felt as if she was handing him over to Scorpion, that her short, precious time with him was over and now she had to give him back to the world—to the *agency*—that had claimed him first. And she was helpless to fight back, to do anything about it.

She looked at him again. His face had already changed. A moment ago he had made love to her with more heat than she had ever known, but now he seemed cold again. His eyes were different, hooded, hard, and what little she could see in them chilled her. Carly reached for her jeans and hugged them to her chest.

"Okay," she said, her voice strained. "I guess you'd better get out of here before Holly wakes up."

They were several hours into the day's ride when Jack's demeanor changed again. It struck fear like an icy blade into Carly's heart.

He was taunting Scorpion now, working at it hard, seeming determined to get a rise out of him.

She didn't want to keep track of where the assassin was because she knew it would only make her crazy. But even without consciously looking for the man, even without *wanting* to look for him, she knew where he was at all times because Jack kept dogging Scorpion's horse, alternately staying close to him, then riding unnaturally close to the wagon as though he were studying it.

"You're going to get yourself killed," she whispered when he finally positioned himself beside her again.

"That's what I get paid for, cowgirl."

"To *die?*"

"If that's what it takes," he answered absently, his gaze still on Scorpion.

"So how are you going to spend the money when you're six feet under?"

"Let me worry about that."

"No! I—" But he was gone again, moving ahead of her as Scorpion picked up into a trot.

He was a man she hardly recognized now, the one she had glimpsed briefly that morning, the man who had smiled so thinly yesterday when they'd talked of sending Scorpion over the river on his horse. He was cold, emotionless. But his eyes were hot, with a kind of unforgiving intent she couldn't even imagine.

Jack watched Scorpion as he rode up ahead and grinned through his teeth when the man glanced over his shoulder at him one more time. This would be over and done with soon, he thought again. Today. He'd realized a good many things in the past twenty-four hours, and he was ready now. He *wanted* it to be over...for himself, but especially for Carly and Holly. He realized he could no longer even bear to think what would happen if the man started thinking too much about Holly.

Or maybe he already had.

He'd given no real outward appearance of being interested in Carly, either, but that certainly didn't mean he *wasn't*. It only meant that if Jack had never found that picture, he would have assumed the woman meant nothing to the assassin...just as he was assuming that he wasn't interested in Holly.

Fear like cold steel pierced deeply into Jack's heart. He had assumed all along that the assassin had come back for *Carly*. Sweet God, was he planning on taking *both* of them? It was entirely possible. Hell, it was probable. Even if he hadn't known that Carly was pregnant when he took off—and Jack had been clinging to that—he had to know now.

Jack looked at the girl again. He had protected her, had kept Rawley on her last night, as the merest precaution. Today he would step up his vigilance. Yes, today he would get this bastard to move.

Scorpion stopped trotting. Jack would have passed him if he had kept going. He didn't. He reined in again until Carly caught up with him.

"This is like a game of cat and mouse!" she burst out, just loudly enough that he could hear her.

"Not quite," he answered quietly. "I'd say he and I are more evenly matched than that."

"I can't handle this," Carly said, snagging his attention again.

"Sure you can. You're doing fine. Just keep riding." He was quiet for a moment. "What comes up next on the trail?"

She had to think for a minute. Her brain felt fragmented. "We're about forty miles from the Cimarron now," she said finally. "We still won't reach it before tomorrow." Although she had, at Jack's insistence, told everyone that they'd be there by nightfall. Rawley and the cowboys had looked at her as though wondering if she was going to airlift them there.

"There's nothing between us and the river but hard, dry ground," she finished tightly. *Hard, dry ground and terror,* she amended silently.

They rode on. The sun peaked. It was blisteringly hot, and the cattle became listless and even slower than usual. They trudged on unhappily, as though it had finally dawned on them what was going to happen to them—or at least to most of them—at the end of the trail.

Scorpion did nothing. To Carly's mind, he behaved the same way he had for days now. Her heart alternately stalled and pounded.

They stopped for a quick lunch, and the tension on Jack's face became etched more and more deeply. Carly noticed that he scarcely ate. Then they moved on again until the sun started sinking. It was the kind of day Carly had hoped for before they had set out on the ride, before she'd known how wildly awry this trip would go. It was uneventful, even boring for those of them who had made the trek so many times before.

At dusk, Jack finally rode up beside her again. "How many miles to the river now?" he demanded.

"Nothing's changed, Jack." She was frustrated, near tears. "We're still on target for tomorrow morning. We're about ten miles away now, but I've got to stop. I can't push these cattle any farther without giving them a rest."

Jack scowled. Why the hell hadn't the man *done* anything yet? Was it for sheer lack of opportunity? Was he simply waiting for darkfall?

At least, he prayed to God that that was all it was.

"Okay," he said finally.

"Okay *what?*" Carly demanded.

"Okay, we can stop."

"You keep forgetting, cowboy. This ride is still my show. Of course, we'll stop. I can't auction off dead cows." Then she closed her eyes briefly. "I'm sorry. I'm just . . . tense."

"And handling it like a pro," Jack murmured, wanting badly to touch her.

"I'm rattling apart."

"It doesn't show."

"I just snapped your head off."

"Yeah, but you did that the first day I got here, before you knew any of this was going on."

Carly smiled weakly.

She swung out of her saddle and went about settling the herd, then she and Plank and Gofer began making dinner. The steaks she had packed in dry ice had been ruined by the wagon's side trip down the river, not so much because of the water but because they'd lost the ice. The group had eaten as much of it as they could last night, but Carly had been forced to discard the remainder. Now they made do with potatoes and beans and muffins, the stuff that had been packed in tins and watertight casks.

Myra pointed out helpfully that carbohydrates were energy food. Most of the others looked as though they needed all the energy could get, and they began to retire early. Holly was the first to yawn and set up her tent. Carly let her go reluctantly, needing badly to drag her back and hold her until this nightmare was over.

Jack saw her expression. "You can't, cowgirl," he said in an undertone.

"Can't she at least sleep in my tent?" she pleaded. "Please?"

Jack hesitated, then shook his head.

"But—"

"We can't do anything too obviously skittish or out of the norm," he interrupted. "I want him to leave without ever suspecting that any of us know who he is, that anybody's on to him." Or maybe he wouldn't just leave, Jack thought. Maybe he'd blow this whole damned thing sky-high.

Carly nodded stiffly. She could see where that would make it more possible for Jack to sneak after him and take him by surprise. But that didn't mean she had to like it.

By the time the moon rose, even Scorpion professed to be tired. He went to his tent, and Jack scowled in that direction.

Tonight. It had to be tonight.

"Now what?" Carly asked quietly. Only they and Rawley were left at the fire, and Rawley was watching them with an odd look of understanding and curiosity.

Jack spared the man a glance. He knew Rawley must have a relatively clear idea of what was happening by now. He'd been the one to clue Carly in about the news broadcast, after all. But Jack still wasn't eager to confirm or deny his suspicions. Thankfully, Rawley seemed willing enough to go along with Jack reasonably blindly.

"Can you do the same as last night?" Jack asked him.

Rawley nodded. "You want me to keep an eye on the kid again?"

"An extra eye. I'm going to stay awake and watch her, too."

Carly stiffened. Why was *that* necessary?

"No problem," Rawley said. "There's just one thing."

"What's that?" Jack asked warily.

"When this is all over, I want a bottle of bourbon, and all the sordid details. *Good* bourbon. I want to know exactly what I've been doing and why. Hell, this is the most exciting thing that's happened to me since I fell off that damned stallion."

Jack surprised himself by chuckling. He surprised himself even more by liking the man. "Fair enough."

Rawley rolled his chair away, bumping and winding over the hard ground toward his tent. Jack stood up and gave Carly a hand, pulling her to her feet.

Carly was purely amazed at herself. She was bone-deep exhausted. She was terrified. And she was still hungry, because as far as her body was concerned, carbohydrates just didn't cut it. She had a driving headache from the tension of the day, and she felt grimy with trail dust. Despite all that, she still wanted Jack.

As soon as everyone had gone and they were alone, she discovered that she wanted him just as fiercely as she had last night and this morning. She wanted him to make everything else go away again, and she knew he could, he would.

"Wait," she said suddenly, pulling her hand out of his. "I want to go wash up first."

He looked at her as if she had grown horns. "Wash up? Where?"

"The same place where all those cattle are guzzling."

Jack looked that way. "It's a *mud* hole."

"Nope. It's an underground spring. Come on, I'll show you."

She hurried off, away from the tents. Jack followed her reluctantly, casting a look back over his shoulder. Something rigid and wary invaded his muscles at the thought of leaving

Scorpion and the wagon. It just wasn't possible right now, he thought, not tonight.

His gut rolled. They were already too far away for him to see much in the camp, and he didn't entirely trust his ears to sort through all the night sounds from this distance. Rawley was minimal backup. Following her was an unconscionable risk.

"Carly, I can't..."

Some sound alerted him. He trailed off to look back at her.

She was at the hole, and she had already taken off her shirt and her bra. His breath went out of him as if someone had punched him. It would take a stronger man than he to walk away right now.

"Look. Right here," she said, kneeling.

Jack looked down dumbly. The water seemed to bubble at the spot she motioned to.

"It's clean—well, it's clean enough," she amended. "We make do with what we can find out here." She unbraided her hair, then tied it up in a knot, well off her neck. Jack tried to find his voice as he watched her, and he couldn't do it for the life of him.

It struck him that she looked so very much like she belonged right here, surrounded by stark land and the simplest essentials of nature. She leaned back, spilling water over her chest from her cupped hands, and smiled like a cat being stroked just right. Her back was arched a little so that her breasts were thrust toward him. Her nipples tightened as the water dripped over them.

Jack began moving toward her, shrugging out of his shirt as he moved. When he reached her, he sat down near the mud to tug off his boots. She leaned forward to capture his mouth.

"Come on, cowboy," she said after a moment. "Hurry up."

He thought about Scorpion. "Damned right. How do you feel about quickies?" He tried to convince himself that Scorpion wouldn't do anything until the camp was asleep. After all, he'd already waited this long.

"Give me your other foot," she answered, her voice husky, "and I'll show you."

She grabbed his heel and pried his left boot off. She made a move to throw it aside, then a strange sound caught in her throat as she inadvertently turned it upside down. Something fluttered out.

"You carry *pictures* in your boot? Is this a spy thing?"

"What?" He pulled his eyes away from her breasts, away from the slender column of her throat, to the ground. This time the invisible fist that plowed into him left him without air.

He moved fast, instinctively, to grab the photograph before she could. But he wasn't fast enough, because his moment of understanding had been half a second behind hers, and she was closer to it, kneeling, not off balance as he was. Carly grabbed the photo and wiped it off on her jeans, then she held it close to inspect it in the first of the moonlight.

He saw the exact moment when she realized that she was looking at herself.

Her head spun. Her eyes widened. Her throat closed. Carly knew the photograph. In it, she was standing beside the first horse barn at the Draw, barefoot in a white, gauze dress, her hair long and free except for some baby's breath that held it back on one side. She recognized the dress, and she'd only worn flowers in her hair once in her life.

The picture had been taken on the morning of the day she had married Brett.

She looked up at Jack slowly. *Why did he have this?*

Her blood turned to ice, drenching everything inside her. She knew, instinctively, that this was the last little bit he had been holding out on her. This was the part that she had sensed, the part she had known, somehow, that it was useless to pursue. She could have pestered him until the cows came home, and she knew he never, *ever,* would have told her that he had this picture in his boot. He had never intended to.

In his boot. The simple fact that he had hidden it, that it hadn't been in the wallet she'd peeped through, told her more than she had ever wanted to know.

The photograph fluttered from her nerveless fingers. She turned away.

"Carly. . ." He couldn't bear the look in her eyes, so bleak, so haunted, so. . .betrayed.

"Don't." Her voice snagged hoarsely. She cleared her throat and spoke without looking back at him. "I don't want to know, Jack. I don't want to hear it." She began grabbing her clothing again.

"There's an explanation."

She laughed shrilly. "There always is." Easy, she told herself, hearing her own strident, desperate tone. *Easy.* "You've got explanations and excuses for everything. You won't tell me the truth about this anyway, so spare me another lie. At least give me that much."

She dressed again and headed back for the camp, halfrunning, stumbling in the darkness.

"Carly, wait!" He had to say something—*what?*—to stop her from going. He had to tell her that all that picture meant was that he had loved her for so many more years than she could know. He had loved the image of her, the flash in her eyes, the sweet simplicity of the world she represented, a world he'd never hoped to find. But she had given that world to him. He had found her, and she had laid it right in the palms of his hands.

Tell her. If he told her that, she would come back, maybe she wouldn't run from him. Surely he wouldn't run from this, not when she had accepted him through everything else.

But his head pounded and the words wouldn't come. They were trapped in his throat, trapped by his past and by her future, because *I love you* was so much more than planting a first, tentative seed. It was a whole damned tree, he thought wildly. And he wasn't ready, couldn't bridge that chasm between his own yesterday and what she had offered to him now.

He couldn't tell her, because there really was no way to explain that picture without letting her know that Scorpion was Brett. And he couldn't bring himself to destroy her with the truth, no more than he could betray her with more evasions.

He let her go, feeling a misery and regret so deep it staggered him.

Chapter 17

Carly moved blindly, without direction or intent. When she realized that she had returned to the camp, she panicked.

Jack would find her here. He'd try to talk to her, to explain with more half truths. *More lies.* Her head was filled with too many jagged, conflicting thoughts to let her listen to him, so she kept running through the camp, to the place where her mare was hobbled. She snatched the leathers off her fetlocks and swung up on her back, pulling her around by the mane.

Jack reached the camp just as she galloped off. His stomach rolled with the true nausea of fear. *Not tonight, cowgirl, please don't go off by yourself tonight.*

Blessedly, Scorpion was in his tent and did not seem to know that she had left. Jack looked at the tarpaulin. There was no movement there, no light inside. At least he prayed to God the man was still in there.

His eyes moved tensely along the lines of Rawley's wheelchair tracks. If he went after her himself, Jack knew she'd just outride him, and that could be disastrous. He couldn't leave Scorpion. His heart twisted with fresh pain at what had happened, but there was no time for it now.

She might stop for Rawley, he thought. He went to the man's tent and rattled the door.

"Hey!" Rawley answered.

Jack stuck his head inside. Rawley took his duties seriously. He had been dozing in his chair, with his gun on his lap.

"Carly's in trouble," Jack said tersely. "You've got to go after her."

"Where?" Rawley began wheeling his chair toward the door before he even finished biting out the single word.

"She took her horse. She left camp. She can't be alone right now. I'll watch Holly, you go after her. Stay with her until she's ready to come back."

"Get me up on my horse."

The man's upper body was amazingly strong. It didn't take anywhere near as much effort on Jack's part as he would have anticipated.

"Which way?" Rawley asked when he was astride.

Jack pointed.

"I reckon you're going to be talking for a good long time when this is over. And it better be one hell of a bottle of bourbon." But, true to form, Rawley didn't ask questions now. Jack watched him canter away, then he went slowly back to Carly's tent to wait.

It was going to be a very long night.

Rawley found Carly sitting beside a deep, chiseled gorge. She was at the edge, holding herself very still, staring down into the hole as though the answers she sought were in there somewhere.

Rawley reined in beside her. She acknowledged him with a quick glance, then she turned her attention back to the gorge.

"Leave me alone, Rawley," she said softly, without venom.

"Well, that's just not a good idea right about now."

She stiffened. "Did Jack send you?"

Rawley made an affirmative sound.

"With explanations?"

"Nope. With my gun."

"Oh." She wasn't sure if she was disappointed or relieved. "You know, he's not what he says he is."

"No kidding."

Her throat felt strangled. "You don't understand. It's not...it's not just a killer running around through my ride. That would have been almost easy."

"Everything's easy, Carly. *We* make it hard."

Carly hugged herself and stared down again at the patterns of moonlight on the rocks below her. The gorge was filled with strange, provocative shadows. *Secrets*, she thought. Everywhere, there were secrets. Even if she listened to Jack again, if she accepted whatever explanation he had for that picture, how many more shadows was he concealing?

She blew out her breath helplessly, needing to cry, unwilling to do it. Not for a man. Not again.

"Oh, boy," she managed after a moment. "Can I pick them, or what?"

Rawley shrugged. "He seems like a good man to me."

"You don't know."

"You love him, huh?"

She recoiled as though he had physically struck her. "No."

"Well, okay, so the both of you are a little wary—"

"Wary?" she repeated, emotion finally breaking through in her voice. *"I* gave him the best, truest part of myself!" Rawley gave a sound of derision. "Hell, I've been watching you two for days now, Carly. You've been circling him just the same way he's circling you. You both want each other so bad, and you're playing games with each other, scared to death to take that one last little step to close the gap. So I guess you've just been waiting for this...whatever just happened. You've been waiting for any excuse so you won't have to take that last step, so you can turn tail and run."

She jolted. "No," she answered, strangled. "You're wrong."

But was he? She hadn't been able to fight her physical attraction to him, so had she given in to it because deep down she knew that this was coming, that *something* was coming, that there really wasn't any future for them anyway?

He had accused her once of considering him safe because she knew he wasn't going to stay. *Did* she?

Why did he have her picture?

What could that possibly have to do with Scorpion? Her mind reeled again. No, she thought, no, that was another issue entirely, one she couldn't quite deal with yet, not until she had her own heart straightened out. It was just another secret, and the real problem was that he had so many of them, not the truths they hid.

Not yet. Later, she would deal with the truths. She could only handle one thing at a time.

She felt Rawley's eyes on her and looked up at him defiantly. "Well, so what if I was?"

He was quiet, thoughtful. "Do you want to know what I think?" he asked after a moment.

"Not particularly, but I guess you're going to tell me."

"Yeah, I am. It's long past time. You've got to give up hiding behind your father and Brett, Carly, and what they did to you. Gabe Castagne was a selfish bastard, and Brett was an opportunistic thief, and if you cling to those old scars, you're gonna dry up into a withered, bitter old woman and blow away on this damned Oklahoma wind."

Carly blanched. Hurt shimmered through her. "How can you say that?" she whispered. He was the last person she'd ever expect to take a hurtful swipe at her. They were friends.

"Because it needs to be said. I should have done it a long time ago. All along here, I've been the quiet guy in the background, the nice, polite friend and neighbor, sitting back in my chair, watching all the goings-on over there at the Draw. And I've seen a whole lot, let me tell you."

"Daddy—"

"Was a coldhearted, selfish man," Rawley finished for her. "He sure as hell wasn't worth what you're doing to yourself now, killing yourself to keep his ranch alive, sealing yourself off so no other man has the chance to take another piece of you like he did."

Carly gasped. *She* could resent Gabriel Castagne. She could do it because she had loved him profoundly. How dare Rawley say these things?

She struggled to her feet.

"Come on, Carlotta, wake up and smell the coffee," Rawley went on implacably.

"I've smelled it a lot more clearly than you have all these years! I've *lived* it!"

"Nope. You've got great big blinders on, girl. Now *me,* well, I was one of the few people who ever recognized Gabe Castagne for what he really was. Guess that's why he always gave me a pretty wide berth. Gabe didn't take much notice of me, if you'll remember."

"Don't say this," Carly warned.

"You idolized him, Carly. And he didn't deserve it. You never really saw him, never knew what he was capable of. You think he entrusted the Draw to you. Well, that's hogwash, lady. Gabe didn't want you to run the ranch. He wanted *Michael* to run the ranch. He *settled* for you. He used you because you loved him to death and if he asked you on what turned out to be his deathbed, then at least you'd break your back trying to do it. He settled for you, Carly, because his son wasn't going to do it and he didn't have any other choice if he wanted it to stay in the family."

"Don't say that!" *Why was he saying this?*

"He kept bullying your brother and coercing him for years to come back here to the panhandle, to take over the Draw, after Michael moved to the city. Do you think Mike didn't confide in me how much he hated the old man? Why do you think he never sets foot on that goddamned ranch now, Carly? He hates the place, that's why. It was Gabe's baby, the only one of you that really mattered to him."

"No," she whispered.

"Gabe only settled for you when he figured that he'd run all out of time to try to twist Michael to his will."

"Stop it!"

"I remember when we were all little, and he was teaching you guys to ride. When Mike would get thrown, you'd hoot and whistle. 'Look, Daddy, look, I'm doing it!' And he never looked, Carlotta, because he never gave a tinker's damn whether you could ride or not. You were just a girl who wasn't even much use in the kitchen, and his son couldn't ride. His *son* couldn't ride, and what kind of man didn't ride? The boy was going to learn that damned ranch if Gabe had to burn every book in his room and *beat* the knowledge into him. And that was all that mattered. He never even glanced your way, Carly."

"Shut up!"

"He was a bastard, Carly. A selfish, manipulative bastard. All he ever cared about was his land and his cattle and keeping it all going. Theresa was the perfect little lady, and I guess that was what he planned, but you were a tomboy and Michael was a bookworm, and *that* sure wasn't what he intended from his offspring. Did you know that Michael was accepted at Harvard? I reckon not, because I never told him. He could have been a lawyer, Carly, but Gabe hid his scholarship letter. He hid it and told Michael that if he wanted to leave the Draw and go to college, then he had to pay for it himself. He didn't think the boy could do it, that he'd keep him home. But Michael was a true Castagne—determined and stubborn as a Missouri mule. Maybe all he could scrape up enough money for was Oklahoma City University, but at least he's a fine accountant.''

"You can't know this," Carly breathed.

"Sure I can. I found the scholarship letter after Gabe died. You didn't want to go through his stuff and pack it up, remember? You asked me if I'd mind coming over and taking care of it for you.''

She remembered that. She did.

She didn't want to ask and knew she had to know. "What else?" she asked warily. "Did you find anything else?"

Rawley looked at her evenly. "Isn't that enough?"

"There was something else." He was avoiding her question, and she was sick to death of avoidance and evasions. Even though pain was choking her—somewhere inside her chest it felt like pain upon pain upon pain—she sensed that there was something else Rawley wasn't telling her and she wanted to know what it was. She waited pointedly.

"He paid Brett off," Rawley said finally, tightly.

Her jaw dropped. "Paid . . . Brett? *My* Brett? Holly's father? What *for?*"

"To leave the Draw. To leave you."

"Why?"

"How the hell should I know? I can tell you what I guess. He did it just in case Michael kept earning his tuition. Like I said, you were his ace in the hole, and he had to keep you tucked aside here, just in case Michael really wouldn't come back, in case he needed you in the end.''

"But—"

"Brett wanted you to go to Dallas with him, remember? He had some great job offer there.''

Oh, God, she did remember that now, too.

"He wasn't that excited about it," she tried. "I mean, he was at first, but then he never mentioned it again.''

"Yeah, well, I still have the canceled check that says he was more than happy to take Gabe's money and go to Dallas without you. Gabe made him sign an agreement. That was in his papers, too.''

"An *agreement?* And you've *kept* all this? Why?"

For the first time Rawley looked uncomfortable. "In case it ever seemed like the right time to tell you guys about all this, and you didn't want to believe me." He glanced back in the direction of the camp. "It sure seems like the right time now."

"Why? What difference can it possibly make?" she cried. "Dad's *dead!*"

"Not hardly," Rawley scoffed. "His kind of ghost just hangs on and on. He's still here, and he's working you into the ground. And I guess I'm just tired of watching it. I can't stand to watch you crumble up and blow away on the wind. It didn't matter so much before, but now, well, I just hate to watch you throw a good man away."

She shook her head frantically. It didn't make sense. She didn't *want* it to make sense.

"Why couldn't he just have paid Brett to stay here? You make it sound like he *wanted* to ruin my life."

"To tell you the truth, I don't think he cared about your life one way or the other."

She flinched. "But a son-in-law could work as well as a son if he didn't . . . if he didn't . . ." *Want me to run the ranch.* She couldn't bring herself to say it aloud.

"My guess is that he would have had to match whatever Brett would have gotten paid in Dallas. And maybe that would have put a strain on his beloved Draw."

"I can't . . ." Carly trailed off and turned away shakily. She felt dizzy, shell-shocked, like the dazed survivor of a war. Everything was gone.

Everything.

Rawley had stripped away all the simple truths she'd lived by and had always taken for granted. He'd robbed her of everything she'd always clung to in order to pull herself through one more day. She felt naked, befuddled, lost.

She couldn't deal with this. Not now.

"I need . . ." she began again, but then she didn't know how to finish.

"What?" Rawley asked quietly. "Tell me and I'll get it for you. Unless you want help hiding again. That I won't do."

I need to talk to Jack. She needed him to make it all go away, to make everything right again. But Jack was gone. She pressed her fingers to her temples. He was as gone as if he had already followed Scorpion, because he had betrayed her, too.

There were only two ways that picture could have come to be in his boot, she realized. Maybe he had snooped through her drawers at the ranch, maybe he had found it during his days there, but Carly didn't think so. She thought maybe he'd had it with him all along.

Either case was a violation of her privacy and her trust. He knew a whole lot more about her than he had ever let on. She had accepted and lived with his not telling her everything about his case, about this Scorpion business. But that was his work, and this was personal.

This was *her* picture.

So she would lean on herself again. Somehow. She had always done it before, and she would remember how to do it again now.

"I'm going to bed," she managed finally.

She pulled herself up on her mare again and headed back for the camp. After a moment, she heard Rawley's hoofbeats behind her.

She wanted to hate him for what he had said, for what he had done, and couldn't quite manage it. Because she knew he was right? She realized that she hadn't actually laid eyes on Michael for six months now, since the last time she'd taken Holly to the pediatrician in the city and had stopped to visit him. It was true. He *never* came out to the Draw. She knew that he hadn't gotten along with their father, but she supposed she'd always shied away from examining why too closely. She'd certainly never discussed it with him.

She reached the camp and tethered her mare again. She looked around briefly. Jack was nowhere in sight. Maybe he had already taken off after his bad guy.

Suddenly, she was too exhausted to care.

Tomorrow, she would care. She knew that. She thought maybe she would care for a long, long time. But right now, she was tired and her heart hurt. She was going to assume that he was in her tent, waiting for her. He would have a long wait.

She crawled into Holly's tent and sat down inside, hugging her knees to her chest, staring grimly at her sleeping daughter.

Betrayal was a whole lot harder to swallow than loss, she discovered. Why couldn't Gabriel Castagne have just settled for dying on her?

Chapter 18

Carly slept deeply and dreamlessly. No doubt it was an escape, she thought when she woke up groggily just before dawn. Then she had the strange sensation that someone was watching her.

Her heart began to race. She sat up fast, and found Holly studying her.

"What?" she mumbled. "Was I snoring?"

Holly shook her head. "How come you're not with Mr. Fain?"

Carly's heart skipped a beat. She wasn't sure she could handle *this* imminent discussion without coffee.

Then she remembered everything that had happened last night, and she realized that she probably wasn't going to be able to handle it today, or this week, or even this month. She had the feeling she wasn't going to be able to handle much of anything for a very long time.

"Why should I be with him?" she asked carefully.

Holly skipped around that. "Well, you're not even in your own tent. What's going on?"

Carly rubbed her eyes, fishing through cobwebs of sleep for an answer.

"You've been with him every night," Holly went on. "Even that one when you slept outside. Even then, you guys left the camp to talk."

So much for their subterfuge. And Carly knew, suddenly, that she couldn't lie to her anymore. She thought of all the countless, heartbreaking lies that had been told to *her,* and all those she had perpetrated upon herself.

No, she thought. No more. She wasn't protecting Holly by not being honest with her, she realized. She had only been alienating her. Still, there was just so much she wanted her daughter to know about Jack Fain.

Carly chose her words with care. "There's…uh, some kind of an escaped convict that the government's looking for. They think he's hiding out somewhere on the panhandle. So Jack's looking for him, and he's watching out for us."

"Yeah, I know."

Her heart skipped in surprise. "You do?"

"He told me."

"He did?"

"Well, he said he was a cop. And he's got that look on his face all the time, like he's worried about something."

"Well, that's the only reason he was…uh, staying with me." And *that* was a half truth she could live with, Carly decided.

"But you like him. I know you do, Mom." Her face said *please tell me you do.*

Carly took a deep breath. Her heart spasmed painfully.

"Do you remember that time when I let you save the wild horse up in Wyoming?" she asked. There had been an auction, and Holly had been avid to buy one of the mustangs. She'd been six. It had been for a good cause, so Carly had relented. The herd had been starving because there were too many of them in a small area. The government had wanted to disperse a portion of them, so they had rounded up a few and put them up for "adoption."

Holly nodded slowly, remembering. "I sure loved Buck."

"I know you did. And Buck loved you." And even after they had gelded him and had gentled him, even after he'd nibble a carrot right out of Holly's mouth if she held it between her teeth, the mustang would allow no one—*no one*—on his back. He'd proved impossible to break. He still grazed on the back acres, but he ran free, essentially useless as a ranch horse. They only caught a glimpse of him now and then.

"Loving him wasn't enough," Carly pointed out quietly.

Holly chewed her lip. Carly thought she might cry, and if she did, she wouldn't be able to stand it.

"So it's like that with you guys?" she asked finally.

"Yes. I'm sorry, honey."

"Even if you loved him, he wouldn't be good for anything?"

Carly bit down hard on her tongue in an effort not to laugh. She thought that if she started, she might end up crying, too. "Exactly."

"We'll see." Her chin came up.

"Huh?"

"That's what you always say—*we'll see.* So I'll just wait and see. We're still a couple of days from Kansas, right? A lot could happen between now and then."

If only she knew. "Sure," Carly agreed vaguely. "Anyway, I've got to go check on the herd." She knelt and moved toward the tent door.

"Hey, Mom."

"Hey, what?"

"Thanks for telling me."

Carly's heart moved hard. She had done the right thing, and there was a certain gratification in that, her only spot of gratification in a very big nightmare.

"You're welcome," she said softly.

"And I'm not scared of that robber or whoever," Holly went on. "Mr. Fain'll get him."

"I hope so. Listen, just don't . . . don't talk to anyone else about it, okay? It's supposed to be a secret."

She got outside and stood on legs that felt unsteady. Jack was standing right outside her own tent, looking back at her.

Her heart lurched, then thudded miserably. *Don't look at me that way!* There was such naked regret in his face, such a need to set things right. And that was impossible. She knew suddenly that what Rawley had told her hadn't quite had the effect on her that he'd planned. She couldn't imagine herself ever trusting a man again.

Especially not this one.

She crossed to Jack, not wanting to, unable to do anything else. He waited for her to say something, and she cleared her throat.

"I just want you to know I meant what I said. I don't want to hear your explanation, Jack. Not this time. I don't want one unless you're going to tell me the truth this time, the *whole* truth. Can you understand? I can't keep playing this game with you. Either tell me everything, or stop tormenting me with bits and pieces." He looked back at her silently, his face grim.

"You're not going to do it, are you?" she asked wretchedly. "You're not going to tell me it all."

"Carly, I can't."

She felt as though he had struck her. She wanted to hurt him back. "Then just . . . go to hell."

She spun away from him, hurt pounding through her with each beat of her heart. He didn't trust her. She couldn't trust him. So that was that.

I did fall in love with him, she thought as tears began burning her eyes. *That's the only way this could hurt so badly.* But then she fought the truth. No, she definitely did not love him, she told herself out of sheer self-preservation. What was it he had said the other night? I don't know you well enough to love you. Well, there you have it, she thought. She knew so little about him. He only showed her those parts of himself he wanted her to see. He was a man full of lies, full of shadows.

Jack let her go, feeling something inside him crack. But it was better this way, he told himself. He had to concentrate on Scorpion now. Scorpion was all that could matter today.

He finally followed her to the fire that Plank had built. He held back a good distance, staying out of her way as she helped to get breakfast together, then she rode out to collect the herd. He was amazed that he'd actually thought once that he knew what it was to feel hollow.

Everything good, everything precious, had been within his grasp. Now it was gone, and there was nothing he could do to fix that, nothing at all.

They were less than three miles from the river when Carly noticed the storm clouds. It looked like a major front coming in and everything inside her plummeted.

She didn't need this now! There was Scorpion and Jack to deal with, and everything Rawley had told her last night. Her heart was tied in knots, and even though she had lost a handful of steers at the North Canadian, she still had 355 animals to contend with, not to mention the horses and the guests. She couldn't take much more.

She felt herself getting hysterical. It took a physical effort to keep herself in control.

"What's the matter?"

She flinched at Jack's voice and looked over as he came up beside her. Just treat him civilly, professionally, she told herself. No matter what else lay between them—a chasm now— there was still the matter of Scorpion, so he had a right to know.

"Scratch what I said about nothing but dry land standing between us and the Cimarron," she said expressionlessly.

He started to ask her what she meant, then he noticed the clouds as well. And in that moment he knew exactly what Scorpion had been waiting for.

The assassin had believed Carly about the storm she had blamed for their early departure. Or at least Scorpion hadn't discounted that possibility. And he was going to use it.

Suddenly Jack knew something else. He knew why Scorpion had not tried harder to get Carly alone in all the days that had just passed. It hadn't been necessary. He *wasn't* going to try to win her heart all over again—that had been clear after the first couple of days. But Jack realized now that he wasn't even going to reveal himself and ask her to run away with him. Not at the last moment. Not at all—not until they were already gone.

He was simply going to take her whether Carly Castagne was willing to go with him or not.

Jack's heart stalled. Things kept clicking into place. *Why did he need the storm?* Because he must know that Jack Fain was Gemini, and he hadn't left yet, couldn't leave, until he'd left no trace of his passing behind. He would have to kill Jack first, and the confusion of a storm was the perfect opportunity.

The business about Saturday *had* been more or less a red herring, convenient if it worked out, but not crucial if it didn't. More than anything, Jack thought, the fire with the generator had probably been to draw Carly away from him, out of the parlor.

His heart started up again. It roared. "Over my dead body," Jack breathed aloud. None of it would happen unless it was over his dead body.

"What?" Carly whispered back.

"Just hold on, cowgirl. All hell's about to break loose."

What was more, Jack realized, Scorpion wasn't going to remove the money from the wagon. He was planning on taking the whole damned thing with him.

Carly finally halted the ride when the wind started to blow hard enough to flatten the spare tufts of grass. It moaned like a man dying, snatching her voice right out of her throat when she reined in to talk to Jack.

"I can't take a chance on going any farther!" she shouted. "We have to find low ground!"

Jack flicked his gaze to the assassin, then back to her. "You mean like one of these chasms?"

Carly nodded. "There's one straight ahead about a quarter of a mile. I remember it from the last trip. It's big enough to protect everything."

"You want to drive the herd and everything else down inside?"

"That's the idea."

Jack didn't like it. If they were all trapped in a relatively enclosed area, making it impossible for the others to scatter and let Scorpion do his thing, then this was going to go down a whole lot worse. "No," he said flatly.

Carly's jaw dropped. "What?"

"I said no. And don't give me that business about this being your ride. This is too important. We have to stay on high ground."

She stared at him, aghast. She had been holding herself back from him all morning, watching where he rode, never drifting too far in his direction so it would look as if she was willing to chat. Now she didn't need to make an effort. Jack looked back at her through the impersonal eyes of a stranger.

Something inside her bled. She tried to reach him anyway.

"Are you crazy? Do you know what we've got heading toward us here?"

"A class-A prairie-type storm."

"No, Jack, no. Look how hard it's coming at us."

Jack did. Already the thunderheads seemed close enough to touch. Where once they had been on the horizon, now they were boiling up, black and violent, nearly peaking over their heads. At any moment now, the thunder would start and the rain would drum down.

At any moment now, everything would start happening.

"I can see that," he said tightly, checking on Scorpion again.

"You can *see*, but you don't *understand*. Don't you remember what I told you that day at the chutes? A storm's one thing, but when one comes in fast like this, then the cold air collides with the hot air and we've got major problems!"

His eyes came back to her, narrowing. "Spit it out, cowgirl. Are we flying to Kansas?"

She couldn't believe this. What was the matter with him? Suddenly fury burned hotly through her.

"Maybe *you* are," she snapped. "*I'm* going to save my daughter and my herd and my guests."

She sawed on her reins, turning her mare around. Before Jack could answer she was galloping away from him.

Scorpion was still sitting close to the wagon. When Carly peeled off, his eyes sharpened on her, like a hawk spying a rabbit in midleap. Jack took off after her and caught up with her just as the assassin began gathering up his reins. To follow her?

She was shouting at the cowboys, trying to get everybody to head for the chasm. Jack reached over and grabbed her reins out of her hands.

She struck him away, enraged.

"Not the cattle, cowgirl, and not the wagon," he said again. "They stay up here. If you're serious, if you think a tornado's coming, then take the people to safety. But you're going to have to leave the rest of this caravan behind."

She fought him, grappling for her reins, her mare skittering beneath her in panic. "No! Not more than three hundred head, Jack! *No!*" Oh, God, she couldn't let that happen!

"They're *cows*, goddamn it!" And he was trying to save her *life!*

"They're steers! Most of them are steers!"

"I don't care if they're leprechauns, they've got to stay up here!"

"I want my herd!" she screamed. "I'm not going to lose 355 animals just because you're some kind of heartless, predatory fool!"

She was beyond all reason. Jack knew that if she lived through this, she would look back and admit that she had been out of control. But now she was wild, crazy. He got the reins away from her again and he jerked her mare around hard. It reared up as thunder boomed out overhead, but she stayed on. The thunder was a single loud reverberation and the confused cattle began lowing.

The cowboys had started moving them at Carly's command, but now they stopped them again, watching her uncertainly. Faced with their argument, Scorpion had paused, too. He was still far enough away that Jack gauged there was no way he could hear them.

"Listen to me," he hissed. "Scorpion has been waiting for this storm so he can get the wagon away. He's going to take the whole wagon, Carly!" *And he's going to try to kill me so he can take you.*

Something in his tone finally reached her. Carly stopped fighting him but she was still breathing hard.

"Fine," she said finally. "He can have my wagon. I just want my herd."

"You can't have your herd, Carly," Jack said more softly. "You can't save them."

"But—"

"Take the people," Jack said. "Take them to low ground. It's going to happen now, cowgirl. Come on, I need you on this one. I need you to do what I tell you and before you know it, this'll all be over." The man wouldn't be able to grab her if Carly was in the chasm and they were on high ground, he reasoned. Then he would literally have to kill Jack first to get to her.

Being needed steadied her a little. But the Draw needed her, too. She shook her head frantically.

"I want my cattle. I *need* them. I have to go to Dodge."

"We'll take care of that later."

There wasn't going to be a later. She finally understood that. There had never really been much of a possibility that they would make it all the way into Dodge. He'd known it, too. It was just something else he hadn't bothered to tell her. In that moment, she purely hated him.

She felt her whole life, her world, slipping through her fingers like sand, and it left her oddly numb. The rain started, a few huge drops at first, then the clouds opened up. The sky rumbled again and water began sheeting down.

"You want me to go in there *alone?*" she asked shakily. "You've been standing guard over me like a pit bull for days." It had something to do with that picture, she realized, and then she finally understood, whether she wanted to think about it yet or not. Her heart stalled.

She was right in the middle of this somehow. Had both Scorpion and Jack come to Oklahoma precisely because of *her?*

Why? Dear God, *why?*

She would have screamed at him for answers, right then and there, no matter how much of her heart it cost her. But Jack was already urging her mare toward the chasm. She twisted around to shoot him one last, wild look.

"Tell Sure-Shot Rawley to keep his gun loaded and ready. If he sees Brad before I get back, tell him to shoot to kill."

Cold washed through her. Then her spine hardened.

Jack watched her shoulders square. *Way to go, cowgirl.* He wondered if he had ever appreciated anyone more, and if he had ever been more terrified of losing them.

"Go on," he went on hoarsely. "I'll cover you until you're down, then Rawley can take over. And for God's sake, don't let your ego get in the way here. If it comes to it, let *him* shoot. I don't care if it chokes you that he's better than you are. I want you to stay alive." Jack didn't add that the only way it would come to that was if he died first. He saw her understanding on her face. She paled and her eyes went a little wild again.

"Go on," he said again. *"Go!"*

She jerked as though he had struck her, but she went.

Scorpion didn't move to go after her this time. The assassin sat in the rain, watching, waiting. He knew how this was going to have to play out, too, Jack thought, and it was long past the time for false identities and disguises.

Carly shouted at the guests to ride down into the chasm. Scorpion still hadn't moved. The wind began screaming. Lightning arced across the sky and this time the thunder was a roll, traveling through the clouds.

Jack dragged his forearm across his eyes to clear the rain from them, then he rode toward the chasm as well. When everyone was down, he went over the lip. Even above the storm, he could hear Carly's voice, strident with nerves as she called out instructions to the others.

Hang on, cowgirl.

Jack dismounted, gauged where the cattle was and climbed back up the chasm on that side to come up behind them. He moved from one cow to the next steer, trying to find the wagon, keeping low behind each animal.

He found the wagon.

He saw Scorpion's horse, and his heart stopped beating for a breath-robbing second. It was already riderless. He didn't see Scorpion.

"Looking for me?"

The voice came from behind him, slow, even, eerily toneless. The skin at Jack's nape crawled. He forced himself to turn around calmly and smile.

"Yeah. And I always find you, don't I?"

"Only when I let you." Scorpion held his gun hand out, his finger through the trigger, dangling the weapon. "Okay, let's do it, comrade. What do you say? One on one. May the best man win, and, of course, take the lady." His face twisted. "You're going to have to die for that, you know. Did you think I was just going to let you get away with touching her like that?"

"She doesn't want you," Jack growled.

"She doesn't have to."

"What are you going to do? Hold her for the rest of her life against her will?"

"She'll come around eventually. And if she doesn't, I'll kill her."

Jack's blood froze. "You're going to have to kill me first."

Scorpion chuckled. "That's what I've been counting on."

The assassin dropped his gun suddenly and charged at him. Jack went for his own weapon, got his fingers around it as they struggled and pulled it free. Then Scorpion struck a chopping blow to his arm, making him lose it again.

The man had another weapon on him. Jack was sure of it. There had been a certain cunning in the assassin's eyes before he'd let go of his own gun, the knowledge that he wouldn't be defenseless without it. Jack figured that his last edge was to attack hard and fast before Scorpion could get to the knife or whatever it was that he was hiding. He brought his right fist upward into the man's belly. Jack was enraged enough, wild enough, that he managed to drop him with that single blow.

He followed that shot with one to the man's jaw. Scorpion rolled, staggered to his feet again, then he came back at him. He crouched down and shot up this time, driving into Jack head-first, his crown ramming squarely into his gut.

It drove the air out of him. Jack managed to wrap his arms around the assassin and drag him down again, wrestling with him, rolling on top of him, even as he gasped for his own breath. He straddled him and smashed his fist into his jaw, once, twice, again. Exhilaration suddenly made him feel unconquerable. Blood flew. He was going to get him. He was finally going to get this bastard and he knew somehow that once he did, he would be free. The consuming chase would be over and he would have nothing left to hide behind, but that was good, cleansing, even exhilarating. He might even be able to plant a few trees.

Scorpion managed to get his hands on Jack's throat. Jack knew a brief moment of triumph. The assassin would try to squeeze and that would be that. It would be fine, because one more punch, maybe two, and Scorpion's strength would be gone, fractured by pain. Jack felt bone crunch and grind beneath his next blow, then he knew that he had underestimated the man.

Scorpion didn't squeeze. The assassin knew better. His fingers probed almost delicately, looking for that single place on Jack's neck that would stop the flow of blood and the oxygen to his brain. When he passed out, Scorpion would use his knife, the knife Jack wouldn't let him get to.

Jack twisted his neck, trying to ease the pressure. Finally he was forced to roll away. He came to his feet again fast, braced for Scorpion again, then he saw the funnel cloud growing behind the man.

He stared at it dumbly for a split second. In his rage, in his driven fury, he had forgotten about the storm.

Like a snake slithering down from the boiling blackness of the clouds, it winded and writhed, trying to reach the earth. The rain had stopped, and it lent an eerie, dreamlike quality to the atmosphere. Then the wind came suddenly, pitching Jack down, barreling into him with impossible force.

Jack felt the ground begin to tremble. Not from the twister, not yet, he thought. It hadn't touched down yet. It was the herd stampeding. The roar of the air became stitched with their bleats and bawling.

The force of the tornado's birth began sucking the air from Jack's lungs. He dragged for more and there was none. If he didn't breathe, didn't find a way to move, the cowgirl was going to die. One of them—either he or Scorpion—was going to seek shelter in that chasm first. He couldn't keep Scorpion up here if he couldn't even stand upright to fight him. He had to be the one to find her.

The earth began trembling more violently beneath him. It shook as though with a horror all its own. The air bellowed. The tornado had touched down somewhere, and he couldn't get up to look. He began crawling toward the chasm.

There was a muted, clanking sound and the wagon team crashed past him. The conveyance rocked wildly over the hard ground as the horses fled in terror.

Scorpion screamed in protest as his money went bouncing away. Jack smiled and felt the immense wind flatten the grin against his face like a grotesque caricature.

He managed to get to his feet. He staggered a few steps and went down again. He got back up to his knees and crawled. He rolled over the rim just at the point where the force of the wind was enough to sweep him away.

Scorpion had been behind him, not even close to the lip, but that wasn't good enough. It brought no satisfaction, no sense of victory.

The bastard was up there somewhere, still alive, and Jack had to find Carly.

Chapter 19

It was so close.

Carly had lived in Oklahoma all her life. Once she had seen a twister pick up a hog shed but leave an elm standing right beside it. She knew they were live, capricious things with unique wills of their own. She had learned to fear them less than she respected them. And she knew, given the millions of prairie acres that they had to choose from, the odds of one coming down on the exact place she stood were on her side.

In all her life, it had never come close to happening. But this twister seemed to be almost directly over her head.

She knew she and the others were relatively safe. The chasm was deep enough to keep them pretty far below ground level—that was why she had chosen it. But when she looked up at the sky, she could see the debris the tornado had claimed spinning by, and fear and awe trembled inside her.

Fear and awe and horror. *What was happening up there?*

They had to be dead, both of them.

Carly knew it with her head even as her heart rebelled. An ugly, clawing pain filled her chest. She'd barely had time to touch him, had scarcely explored him. There was so much about him she had yet to learn, and she wanted to, oh, yes, she wanted to. She wanted to get past the secrets, the lies, because there was a really good man inside.

She realized in that moment that he had *never* lied to her. He had evaded her questions. He had given her half-truths. But he had never blatantly told her anything that was untrue. Though God knew others had hurt him, he would never willingly hurt anybody else. He wouldn't betray anyone.

Not at all like her father and ex-husband, she realized much too late.

A thin, almost mewling sound escaped her throat. She held Holly tightly, but then she motioned at her that they should crawl down the chasm wall. The others were huddled closer to the northern rim.

Myra was dwarfed in Rawley's big arms. Only her dark, disbelieving eyes peered out from the man's embrace. Leigh was lying down, protected by Gofer's long, skinny body. Reggie was stricken and mute, and she thought Winston might actually cry.

"You're all right," she managed. "You'll all be fine."

Rawley nodded and spoke, and Carly realized that she could hear him now.

"It's passing."

She looked up dumbly at the sky again. There was no more debris overhead. The earth still rumbled, but the rain had come back. The tornado sounded more like a freight train than the earth trembling on the brink of explosion.

Rawley was right. The twister had torn past them.

Carly got to her feet, staggering a little when her legs wouldn't quite hold her. "I've got to find him."

She'd thought she'd accepted that he was dead, but now she knew she hadn't. She couldn't give up without looking. She wouldn't accept it until she saw for herself, until she went up there and there was no sign of him.

"Not yet," Rawley shouted at her over the weather. "Don't go up there yet. We don't know where Brad is."

But she scarcely heard him. The twister hadn't come down right there, her thoughts raced on. Almost—yes, it had been *almost* right on top of them, but it hadn't touched down right there. And if Jack was still up on high ground, then he might just be hurt. He might need her.

"Go get him, Mom," Holly urged, not knowing the true danger involved, but Carly didn't hear her daughter, either.

She hauled herself back up the slope. She reached the top and struggled to her feet, looking around. The wind was still strong enough to buffet her, to snatch her voice as she shouted Jack's name. There was no answer.

Carly choked on a harsh, indrawn breath. Everything was gone—the cattle, the wagon, everything, and she could see the tornado's path. It had cut a distinct swath of destruction across the land and her eyes followed its trail. She saw the twister easing up from the earth again, maybe ten miles away now.

Where it had passed there were no rocks, no grass, just churned, scoured mud. And it had passed no more than two hundred yards away.

Two hundred yards. And she had last seen Jack come up out of the chasm right about here. Unless he had ridden in that direction, right at the twister, he could very well be okay. And his horse was down in the chasm. She knew he hadn't *ridden* anywhere.

She shouted for him again. The storm howled and the rain came down harder. Then she felt something sharp prick into the small of her back.

Her heart seemed to stop. Rawley had warned her, but she had forgotten to watch out for Brad, for Scorpion.

"Come on, now, babe, you didn't think I was going to leave without you, did you?" His voice was soft, eerily pleasant. "Your old man's money never came with the condition that I *stayed* away. So now let's find out who's gonna be taking you home from this party."

The rain started again as Jack got to his feet and began maneuvering the rest of the way to the bottom of the chasm.

He heard a horse whinny from somewhere distant, from the other end, around the bend. He started that way, finally dropping to his knees to crab his way around a curve where swells of earth came together in another huge knot. He kept a wary eye open for Scorpion as he picked his way along. He didn't see him, but when he reached the other side of the tangled bend, he found the others.

His eyes flew over all of them. *She was gone.*

For a moment, he was only stunned. Then he was furious. Then he was scared. He would have roared her name but he found he had no voice. The terror that hit him was so deep, so all-encompassing, it stole his strength.

Scorpion wasn't in this chasm. He had never been in here. Suddenly, Jack was sure that the man had found another ditch to shelter in. By now he was back on high ground.

And so was Carly.

The others turned to look at him when he reached them. Most of their faces were still slack with amazement over the tornado. They had no idea yet that they had far worse things to worry about.

"She went up that way," Rawley called out, pointing. "Looking for you."

A fist hammered Jack's gut. She would have done that. Of course she would have. She might be angry with him, she might be hurt, but her heart was far more true than any of her resentments.

"I need a gun," he said hoarsely, and *that* started snapping the others out of their shock.

"A *gun?*" Leigh bleated into the sudden quiet.

"What for?" gasped Myra.

"You're going to shoot something? What in the world are you going to shoot?" Winston cried.

Of them all, only the cowboys and Rawley seemed unsurprised by his request, Jack thought. And Reggie. Quiet, watchful Reggie.

"It's Brad, isn't it?" that man asked shortly. "Something's off about that guy. I've been thinking that for days."

"You're going to shoot *Brad?*" Leigh wailed. "Who *are* you?"

She looked like she was about to faint, Jack thought, but there was no time to explain.

Plank was closest to him. He held out his weapon without question, and Jack grabbed it. Gofer and Josh tried to push theirs on him as well. He took Gofer's for a backup.

"You and Josh need to stay armed," he told Rawley. "The same thing still goes. If you see Brad before you get clear of here, shoot him."

Leigh started sobbing. Rawley's eyes sharpened.

"So where exactly are we going?"

"Ride to the nearest town."

"That'd be Buffalo. We passed it a little ways back."

"Good. Go out that way." Jack thrust a thumb over his shoulder. "Through the back of this hole. Not here. And when you get there, call this number." He gave it to them. Rawley repeated it, nodded, and Jack knew he would remember it. "Don't go together," he went on. "Scatter as much as possible. And take all the horses."

They nodded at him like a row of puppets. They started moving about woodenly, bumping into one another at first. Jack left them and started back down the chasm first.

He didn't dare go up right there. He had a strong suspicion that Scorpion had been right at the top, waiting for Carly. If Jack followed her path, he would stumble squarely into them and lose his only element of surprise.

He reached a good spot and started climbing. Terror sang through him like a thrumming wire and he noticed almost dispassionately that he was shaking.

Carly turned around slowly. Brad had a knife. He moved it just enough so that it came to rest at a place above her navel.

No, not Brad, she thought wildly. Brett.

Brett?

But of course it was him. Who else had taken her father's money to leave her? Who else had ever called her "babe"? She thought wildly that he didn't look anything like what she remembered. Now it was even more difficult to tell, because his face was bloodied and bruised.

How long had she known and hidden from it, she wondered helplessly, because it was just too much, because it was the one truth she found intolerable? *Her child's father.* No wonder Jack had tried to shield her, even at the cost of her hating him for it.

Brett must have kept that picture of her, though she couldn't imagine how Jack might have ended up with it: *All those sly smiles.* No wonder he had passed through Oklahoma on his way to retirement. Dallas, she thought giddily. Jack had said that Scorpion's first hit was in Dallas, where Brett had gone to take that "job." More than ten coincidental years ago. She choked on crazed laughter.

Maybe she'd even known, subconsciously, when "Brad" had said he couldn't swim, when he had been so obviously terrified of that river crossing.

"Why?" she croaked, swaying a little under the terrible magnitude of it.

"That depends on what you mean," Brett said equably. "Why did I leave?"

"That blonde . . . I always thought . . ."

"She was convenient. I left her in Amarillo. I left for the money, really. For the opportunity." He paused and laughed derisively. "What your father gave me wasn't enough to make a difference. I was leaving anyway, and then the old man handed me a few thousand to boot. So why wouldn't I take it? But there was no way he was going to let you go, either, not without a fight. So I figured I'd just get myself set and come back for you later." His mad eyes gleamed. "I never gave up on you, babe. I knew you'd still be here, waiting."

Carly shook her head hard and fast. She felt sick. "Why . . ." she began again, then she trailed off. Why had he killed people? But she didn't have to ask that because she already knew the answer. It had just been a way to get rich. He saw nothing wrong with it.

She *was* going to be sick. She clapped a hand over her mouth, swallowing convulsively.

"So here I am," Brett went on. "Back to claim my wife."

"I divorced you."

"Doesn't matter. That's just a technicality. I need you and my kid so I can retire. Let me tell you—*she* was a surprise." His face darkened. "You should have told me, Carly. You should have told me about her. I would have come back to collect you sooner."

Holly. Oh, sweet God, he knew Holly was his daughter!

Before she could react, he went on. "It was just a matter of getting together enough cash first," he explained. He laughed, shaking his head. "Man, as fast as I earned it, I spent it. You've no idea how expensive it is, running around the globe, looking for work. That's why it took me so long to get back here. Sorry."

He was crazy. But even before she'd known who he was, she had known he'd have to be.

"This last score was big enough to keep us comfortably for a good long while." He scowled, looking around briefly. "I think I can find that wagon. As long as it didn't explode, we're okay. I packed the money in good and solid. And even if I can't find it, I'll raise more cash somehow. The important thing is that I've got you now. Where would you like to go? We can't stay here, in this country.''

A scream finally began working its way up her throat. His eyes sharpened on her.

''Don't do anything ridiculous,'' he warned her. ''Don't make me kill you now. I've waited a long time for this. I want to make it work. I'm even willing to forgive you for what you did with *him*. I mean, hell, I was gone a long time. I didn't expect you to be a nun. And you didn't know I was here. But *he's* going to have to die for it.''

Carly nodded helplessly. *Play along with him.* It seemed the only thing she could do. She had to wait for some chance to get away. He had that knife.

''The others!'' she gasped. ''They'll come. They'll come to help me find Jack!''

Brett pressed the knife into her a little harder. ''I told you not to make me hurt you. Forget Jack. He's history, babe.''

Her voice broke off in her throat. Carly felt the blade prick, turn, and she reeled, knowing without looking that he had cut her.

He had cut her. That was when she understood that he might have come back for her, but he would just as easily go on without her if she proved too troublesome.

She stumbled backward, groping at the spot, her head spinning. Not enough blood to kill her, she realized. Not yet. It was barely a graze.

Brett caught her arm. Pain shot through her shoulder as he began dragging her back toward the gorge. ''We'll join the others,'' he decided. ''Holly's there. Besides, that's where he'll look for you, and I have to take care of him before we can go anywhere.''

''Jack's gone. Jack's already dead.''

''No.''

''You can't know that!''

''I know.''

''How?'' she demanded shrilly, stumbling.

''Because he wants me too badly,'' Brett answered. ''It's just like São Paulo. He can't die. He can't die until he stops me. He's too damned self-righteous. I'm the thing that's kept him going all this time.''

Carly nearly fell again. So he had realized that, too. But then, Jack wasn't really all that complicated, she thought, not once you got to know him.

Brett frowned again. "I always thought he'd fall apart without me, but then he started getting soft on you. That's okay. He's going to lose both of us, but I'll put him out of his misery."

Carly dragged frantically against him, trying to hold him back from the chasm where Holly waited. He jerked her arm angrily, impatiently, and she cried out. *Think! Do something! Don't fall apart!* But she couldn't stall enough and before she knew it, they had reached the edge of the chasm. Carly looked down.

Everyone was gone.

Holly was gone. Her knees nearly buckled with relief. Jack had been here already! He had done . . . something.

She screamed suddenly and plunged over the rim. She took Brett by surprise. He was half a step behind her and reacted too late to grab her. *Where was Jack?* She leaped over an uprooted bush tossed into the chasm by the tornado and landed on her bottom, skidding, tumbling, rolling the rest of the way. When she hit the floor, she scrambled to her feet again and began running.

She heard Brett scrambling down behind her. He would gain on her. He was bigger, stronger, faster than she was, and his legs were longer. Hysteria clawed at her.

Then she realized that she no longer heard his footsteps.

She twisted around, looking back, and fell over a boulder. She landed with a cry of pain, the breath jarring out of her, but she saw Brett go back up the wall again. He was moving *away* from her and she looked after him for a moment, dumbfounded.

Then she got to her feet again and kept running. He would come back. She knew that. But somewhere in here there had to be a place to hide. She scrambled over the rough canyon floor, then she heard the first gunshot.

It came from *inside* the gorge.

Jack was halfway down the slope on the side nearest the bend when he saw her. He hadn't found them on high ground and he had returned to the chasm out of sheer desperation. When he saw them, his heart staggered and air filled his legs. He had to force himself to move again. *She was still alive.*

But what the hell was Brett doing?

Carly reached him, but when she would have gone into his arms he pushed her behind him. She fell just as another gunshot sounded out from overhead.

Carly screamed and cringed behind Jack, but it was a wild shot, pinging off a nearby rock. When she looked up again she saw that Brett had returned to the top of the chasm. Both he and Jack held guns, they had each missed a shot, and for a long time they only watched each other.

Jack spoke first. "That's my gun, buddy," he called out. How had the man ever found it? Clearly, it was what he had gone back for, but Jack couldn't believe that the twister hadn't taken it, as it had obviously taken Brett's own. He wondered if the assassin had some fallen angels watching over him.

It didn't matter, he thought, not as long as he had Plank's and Gofer's both.

"Let Carly go," he called up to him. "Let her leave."

Brett laughed. "She's the prize. That's rich, isn't it? That we end up finishing this over a woman? But then, you've wanted her since you took my picture, haven't you, *Gemini?*"

Carly felt her mouth go dry at that. Her heart started moving too fast. How long had Jack had that thing, anyway?

She looked up at him. He was grinning like a hungry cat who had just found the key to a canary cage. If what Brett had just said was true, if he had that kind of soft spot, then it didn't show now. Jack's expression chilled her to her soul . . . and it bolstered her, warmed her, made her feel safer, because she could only thank God that she wasn't the one on the receiving end of that glare. The man who was was in deep trouble.

"That's right," Jack said. "So let her leave. One of us is going to walk out of here alive, buddy, and he can go get her easily enough. If she stays in here, she could get hurt."

The assassin was quiet for a long time. "Okay," he said finally. "Okay, she can go. I'll hold my fire. You sent the horses away, so I guess she can't get far."

Jack felt breath escape him. He hadn't been aware of holding it. It rushed out of him, leaving him hollow and weak. "Go on," he said quietly, and his voice was strangely thick.

"I don't want to," Carly said from behind him.

Jack's eyes widened. He spoke grimly, without taking his eyes off Brett. "Don't start, cowgirl. Not now. Go. *Get*."

"No. I'm safer down here. If I go up there and you stay down here, he could grab me before you could even think of getting out of here and back to the top." And that, she realized now, was what he had been protecting her against all along. *That* was why he hadn't let her out of his sight. Something inside her melted.

He had just been trying to spare her. He'd been trying to keep Brett away from her.

"I don't want you to climb up right here," Jack explained slowly, holding on to his temper. "Walk back around the bend and do it there. Stay behind me."

"No."

"Damn it, Carly—"

"I'm not going anywhere if you're not with me."

"I'm not going to let him grab you!"

"You might be good, Jack, but I guess you'd have to walk on water to stop him if I leave here. That's assuming that you even *want* to shoot him, and I'm still not sure you do."

He went very still. "I want to. Oh, cowgirl, I want to very much. And as soon as you're clear, I'm going to start firing."

She snorted. "You missed the first time."

"I wasn't *aiming* at him the first time! I was just letting him know that I was in here."

"I don't want to go, Jack. I want to stay with you."

"I'll be *with* you. He'll be dead before you take two steps and I'll follow you."

"How can you shoot him? He hasn't done anything yet. He's just standing up there talking to you. Are you just going to start blasting away at him in cold blood? That's not like you, Jack." She realized in that moment that she knew him pretty well after all. "You need him to *do* something first."

Jack's voice got very quiet. "Do you still have a soft spot for him, cowgirl?"

Carly recoiled, then her eyes flared. "No. Is that why you didn't tell me who he was, because you thought I would *help* him?" She started to come to her feet, enraged.

"Stay *down*. No. I didn't tell you because there was no reason to do that to you."

She knew that. She believed him. Her fury ebbed again almost as suddenly as it had lit through her.

"And," Jack went on, "I don't particularly want to make you watch me shoot him now. This could get ugly, Carly."

"Is she going?" Brett called out impatiently, interrupting them.

"She's going," Jack answered.

"No," Carly yelled at the same time.

"Damn it, cowgirl, if you don't start moving *now*, I'm going to choke you myself!"

"No, you won't. You'd have to take your eyes off him to do it."

Okay, Jack thought, holding on to his temper. He'd just change direction. He couldn't stand here arguing with her.

"You're done, buddy," he called up to Brett. "You're *done*. You can't disappear this time. Even if you killed both of us, you're still trapped. It's a long walk out of here, and you're not going to make it. Before you could manage a mile, a chopper'll come and find you. I gave the others the agency emergency number. Uncle Sam will look for you from up there in the sky, buddy, and he'll find you, too, in all this emptiness. You blew it this time. They know where you are and you can't hide from them and you can't get away."

"What are you doing?" Carly whispered.

"If you won't go up, then I need him to come down. I'm going to try to finish this without guns."

"*Why?*" That sounded even more dangerous. She didn't want Brett to get close to them.

"Because somebody else could get shot if bullets start flying," he snapped. "Namely you, and you won't get the hell out of here."

"What are you talking about?" Brett yelled at them. "What are you planning?"

"Hear the choppers, buddy?" Jack taunted. "Listen. They're coming."

Brett made a sound of derision, but after a moment his gaze flicked up to the sky warily.

"Come on down here," Jack said. "We'll finish this one on one, the way you first said."

The assassin had decided there were no choppers. "No, thanks. I have an advantage up here. Correct me if I'm wrong, but it's a lot easier to aim downward than upward. Isn't that one of the things they teach you guys?''

Jack shrugged. "Maybe so, but *I've* got the lady. I'd think you'd worry about me getting her away before you could shoot me down."

"Don't worry about it," Brett said pleasantly. "I'll manage."

Now, Jack thought. Brett wouldn't expect him to shoot since Carly hadn't left the canyon. Carly didn't expect him to shoot at all. Jack finally admitted that a week ago he might not have been able to do it, not unless it was life or death. Oh, yes, Scorpion had been his security blanket.

And he didn't need him anymore.

He roared a sound of rage and brought his gun up. Brett pulled his own trigger half a breath sooner.

Jack took the bullet near his first scar, and it made his own shot go wide. He felt it as he had the last time, pain exploding, then receding. Cold, then fire, then cold again. It threw him back, sprawling him in the dirt, but this time, painfully, he was able to push himself upright again.

Carly screamed, then she helped him to sit. She was saying something to him. He heard her as though from very far away. But Brett's voice seemed clear, thunderous, growing even louder as the assassin came down the slope toward them.

"Drop your gun, Jack," he said gently. "You can't shoot it. You know you can't shoot me. I've been your 'buddy' for too long now. Drop your gun and hand Carly over. You're at a disadvantage now, my friend. Don't make anyone get hurt. Anyone but you, that is. Come on, be a hero."

Jack dragged his arm up again. At least, he thought he did. But it felt as though there were no bone in there, no muscle inside any longer.

"That's always been your problem, Gemini," Brett went on conversationally. "It's the single thing you really do wrong. You don't shoot fast enough. You always have to think about it first. You're too soft."

He *had* to shoot now, Jack thought. It was all that mattered. If he died later, so be it, but he had to get this one precious shot off. He had to kill him.

His gun was too heavy. Jack couldn't find the trigger. It took all his strength to remain sitting up, even though Carly braced him. She was shaking, and each of her tremors seemed to rock through him as well, bringing excruciating pain.

Jack moved his neck, but he couldn't quite see her clearly anymore. His vision pulsed oddly, graying and fuzzing over with each beat of his heart.

Plant the tree, he thought. *Even if you die, tell her. Tell her you love her. She needs to know that. You both need for her to know.*

But in the end it was still easier for him to find the trigger. He finally shot and a stunned look of disbelief crossed Brett's face as the assassin staggered backward.

"You *did* it!" Carly cried.

Jack shot again, and one more time for good measure. Then he sank slowly back into the dirt, his strength and his adrenaline gone.

Of course he had done it. The assassin had overlooked one very important, very driving factor.

There was no way in hell he was going to let him take the cowgirl.

Chapter 20

Carly watched the minute hand on the desk clock in her office. When it finally slid down to the six, she reached for the telephone again, feeling fragile.

She'd been calling every half hour. She intended to keep calling until they told her what she needed to know.

The line picked up. "Doctor's Hospital."

"I'm inquiring about a patient's condition," she said in a rush. "Jack Fain, and no, I'm not family." She'd said the same thing four times already and knew the routine. But this time she got a different answer. "Mr. Fain has been released."

"Pardon me?"

"Have a good evening."

"No! Wait!" She sat straighter in the desk chair. "Fain," she repeated. "F-A-I-N."

"Yes, ma'am. He's been released."

"*No*. You've got the wrong patient." She dragged in air, steadying herself. "He was still in surgery thirty minutes ago."

There was a short silence, broken only by the click of computer keys in the background. "He was in *recovery* thirty minutes ago," the woman said finally.

"But you told me—never mind." Surgery, recovery, what difference did that make? "People don't walk out of a hospital the same day they're operated on!"

This time the operator's pause was longer. "No, one wouldn't think so."

"So will you please check again? I just need to know how he's doing."

"Hold on." Hollow silence filled the line. Carly eased back in her chair again, trying to relax.

But she couldn't. She had a very bad feeling about this. Had he died after all, in surgery? Everything in her chest clenched.

She should have gone to the hospital with him. She had intended to, but when the helicopters had finally arrived, they had been full of men in suits who'd monopolized her attention. They'd loaded Jack into one chopper and Brett into another, and they'd begun grilling her six ways to Sunday about what she had witnessed. By the time she'd grown angry and exasperated with them, one of the choppers lifted off again, taking Jack away.

They'd brought her back to the Draw in one of the others. Now she sat in a silence that had an eerie feeling to it. It was pure and too perfect, except for the monotonous ticking of the clock.

Carly waited for the operator to come back on the line. *Come on, lady, come on.* But the line remained empty and her mind wandered again.

Holly and all the others were still in Buffalo. Theresa had taken the truck to pick up those who wanted to come back to the ranch. Michael would make travel arrangements for those who simply wanted to go home.

Life would go on, Carly supposed.

In the next moment she knew that hers was going to go on without Jack Fain. The operator came back on the line, and her words sent a jolt through her, the kind that hit her right in the throat then reverberated downward until there was nothing left inside her, no air, just a shimmering, hollow sense of loss.

"My records are correct, ma'am. Mr. Fain is gone from this hospital. He was transferred twenty minutes ago."

"Transferred," she whispered.

"Yes, ma'am."

"Where?"

"I don't have that information."

Carly hung up very slowly, without pressing her. She knew she wouldn't get any more answers. She doubted very seriously if the woman even knew anything more herself. Apparently, Jack's "agency" took care of its own.

There are organizations that only the President knows of.

He'd been transferred.

He was gone, without a trace.

The ache was worse than she had thought it would be. The emptiness was deeper than she had thought it could go. She'd told herself she could handle this, but she hadn't been prepared for this terrible sense of loss.

Michael made a surprise trip to the ranch on the following Saturday to help pick up the pieces of his ill-fated tourist idea. Carly sat in the kitchen, watching him scribble on a notepad. He was fair-haired like their mother, handsome and tight-mouthed, clearly hating the necessity of being back in that house. Carly made a snap decision not to tell him what Rawley had told her about his scholarship. It would only add to his bitterness. And for what? Gabriel was gone.

But there were other things, she thought, that really needed to be resolved and put to rest.

Holly came to her room that night after Michael left. On her way down the hall to her own room, she paused in Carly's doorway. She dragged her bare toe along the carpet and finally crossed her arms over her chest in a belligerent gesture that Carly knew all too well.

Carly groaned inwardly, but Holly's voice was soft, without any of the accusation that usually went with the arm-crossing.

"Do you think Mr. Fain will come back?"

Carly flinched. "I don't know."

"He might come back."

"Probably not, though." Maybe he would find himself another Scorpion to chase. But she knew better than to allow herself to hope he would come back to the panhandle. She knew better than to yearn, to hope, to ache for a man to love her.

"But he liked you," Holly pointed out helpfully.

Not enough. Carly decided to take the bull by the horns. "I think you and I are going to be alone together for a long, long time, honey," she said carefully. "And maybe it's best if we both just...well, you know, look at the bright side of it."

Holly's forehead creased. "That's what he said. He said to make the best of things."

Carly's heart thumped. "He did?" Apparently the two of them had had some cozy chats that she didn't know about.

"Yeah," Holly answered. "So what's the bright side?"

Carly thought fast. "Well, there won't be any whiskers in the bathroom sink after some guy shaves."

Holly surprised her by laughing. "Only a slob would do that."

"There are no tears," she went on. *No laughter.* "No arguments." *So you can never win one.* She blew out her breath and shook her head. "Never mind." Then she thought of something else that really needed to be said.

"You know, I've been thinking a lot lately about your...your father, and, well...I think he really did love me." In his own sick, twisted fashion, she thought. "Holly, I didn't drive him away. I want you to know that. He just...he didn't want to live here in the middle of nowhere, I guess. He had bigger...dreams."

Holly blinked in surprise. "He did? Like what?"

"I'm not sure, but he wanted me to go to Dallas with him."

"So how come you didn't go?" Holly got that accusatory look on her face again.

"Because your grandfather needed me here." And that, too, was true, as far as it went. No matter what else Gabriel Castagne had been, he had loved his ranch, had been fiercely possessive of his family, and Carly knew that he had loved her mother. So she would remember that, and work at putting the rest of it behind her.

"That's *it?* That's all it was?" Holly asked incredulously.

"Yeah."

"So how come you didn't tell me before? How come you just said he left us?"

"I thought you were too young to understand."

Her face turned mutinous.

"And it hurt me to think about it, to talk about it," Carly went on.

Holly's glare flickered, then settled into a more mild scowl.

"And...I had to figure it out for myself."

"I don't get it."

Carly smiled softly. "You don't have to."

Holly finally shrugged. "Well, I'm going to bed."

And that, Carly thought, was that. Oh, to be as resilient as a kid!

Holly turned away from the door, then she paused again. "Mom, I really think Mr. Fain is going to come back. He doesn't like to wear a suit."

Carly sighed. She didn't even want to know where *that* had come from. And she'd scrubbed her heart clean enough for one night. She wasn't going to try to explain to Holly all the many reasons why Jack probably would not return.

"We'll see," she said emptily.

To her surprise, Holly laughed again. "See, I *told* you you always say that. Yeah, I think I'll just wait and see."

Carly was standing on top of a hundred bales of hay on the back of a flatbed truck when Holly proved to be right. She looked up and saw a car pull into the barnyard, and it wasn't a rental one this time, unless the Oklahoma companies were suddenly renting white Lexuses with Virginia tags.

It was the heat, she told herself. That was why she felt faint. It was all this exertion in the dry, thin air. That was why she suddenly found it hard to breathe. She had absolutely no explanation for the tears that tried to sting her eyes.

Jack got out of the car and shut the door lazily. He crossed his arms over his chest and moved toward her slowly. He had shaved, and he wasn't wearing a suit.

It was her first bizarre impression. She had gotten so used to looking at his gradually growing beard all those days on the trail that somewhere along the line she had forgotten what had first appealed to her about him. Now she saw again the jaded character etched into little lines around his eyes, that I've-seen-it-all-and-I-prefer-to-think-it's-funny set to his mouth.

Carly moved carefully to the edge of the hay to look down at him. "Lost?" she asked when she could manage her voice.

One corner of his mouth kicked, then it moved into a full-blown smile. "Not now."

Carly's heart slammed. *Don't read anything into it, don't you dare.* She'd had her fill of seeing what she wanted to see, of hearing what she wanted to hear, and hiding from the rest. She wouldn't play that game anymore.

So what was he doing here?

She tugged her leather gloves up carefully and bent to get a good grip on the wire holding one of the bales together. She had to do something. She couldn't look at him anymore. She couldn't bear it.

"Are you all healed?" she demanded.

He'd almost forgotten the mental dexterity it required to keep up with her. Jack finally grinned. "More or less. It's been four weeks."

"Thirty-two days, but who's counting? Catch."

She swung the bale up and outward. It sailed through the air toward him and caught him squarely in the chest. It barreled him over, landing on his legs, flattening him on the hard, dusty ground.

Jack sat up, spitting hay dust, gaping at her. "What was that for?"

"There's work to be done and no one to do it. So are you just going to stand there—" *looking like heaven* "—or are you going to pitch in this time and do something to help?"

Suddenly he understood. "I'm sorry."

"You ought to be."

He got up, then he ducked as another bale came sailing toward him. She was really throwing them now. He dodged out of the way of the next one and the next. Well, he thought, she had every right to be angry, but not at him.

"I couldn't sway them," he called up to her. "I did try."

"Yeah?" she challenged him. She stopped in midmotion and put her hands on her hips. "Did you point out that the twister—the 'act of God'—couldn't have scattered my herd if I had taken them down into that chasm?" Her temper was building. Oh, God, it felt good. For thirty-two days there had been nothing inside her.

But who was counting?

"You're the only one who can tell them that, Jack," she went on. "And you've been God knows where. They couldn't find you to verify it. That's what they told me. They think I'm trying to cheat them or something, and they won't pay me for anything they don't consider their fault. I've never cheated anyone in my *life!* They said their assassin didn't scatter my herd, that the tornado did it. So that's that. That herd was one of the last hopes I had.'' She had finally been forced to file for bankruptcy, a reorganization plan. Michael was working frantically to use the stay of execution to save them . . . somehow.

Jack understood then that the IRS hadn't been the only wolf at her door. Losing those steers had blown her whole house down.

And she had let him do it. She'd let him keep them on high ground, even knowing it would break her.

"Why?" he asked hoarsely.

She didn't pretend to misunderstand him, but she wouldn't meet his eyes. "Well, I sure didn't do it for your *employer*."

Yeah, Jack thought, he definitely loved her.

"We'll get it back," he managed.

"What?"

"The money for the herd."

"It's too late now."

"No." It was never too late, and you were never too old. If nothing else, he had learned that. "We'll just threaten to sue and raise a general clamor. They need an excuse before they admit culpability. That's the way it works."

We? No, she definitely wouldn't read anything into that. Carly felt her eyes begin to burn again. She shook her head and snatched her gloves off to rub them.

"Forget it. You can't beat Uncle Sam."

"Uncle Sam is just like everyone else. He won't give an inch until he has to."

"Whatever."

Jack cautiously closed the distance between himself and the truck again. "Are you okay?" She looked different, he thought. Thinner than usual. And there were dark smudges under her eyes.

Carly shrugged. She wanted to touch him. She balled her hands into fists and hugged herself, sticking them under her arms so she wouldn't leave the flatbed and give in to the urge.

"Is it money?" he asked. "Is that what's wrong?"

She hesitated, shook her head. "Not entirely."

"What then?"

Why were they talking about this? she wondered wildly. She didn't want to talk about her father. She wanted to know why he was here. But she heard herself say, "Maybe I've just been wondering if all this is worth the fuss." She waved a hand.

All this? The ranch? "You never struck me as a quitter," he said cautiously.

"You don't know me."

"Sure I do."

"No. You were the one who said you couldn't get to know somebody—" *love somebody* "—within a few days."

She didn't love him.

She didn't need him.

She started to cry.

At first Jack was just appalled. Then he was stunned. She had cried before. But not like this. Never like this, in great chugging breaths, fighting it, dragging her arm across her eyes. He climbed up to her, but she scrambled away. He finally caught up with her near the cab, pinned her down on the hay and leaned over her to look down into her green eyes.

"Where is everybody?" He struggled to hold her.

"Who?" she snapped.

"Holly, Theresa, the cowboys. Everybody."

"Here and there."

"On the ranch?"

"No. Laid off, in town, all over. Why? Get off me."

Good enough, Jack thought. He closed his mouth over hers.

Carly fought him harder. "Are you *crazy?*" she demanded, tearing her mouth away.

"Nope. I might have been, but then I found you."

"Leave me alone!" She wouldn't listen to this. She didn't dare.

"Is that what you want?"

No, no, no! She set her jaw stubbornly, refusing to answer.

"I didn't think so," he murmured.

He found her mouth again, and this time she didn't twist away. There was so much he needed to say, so much he had to tell her. But he'd always been rotten at putting his heart into words, and he didn't want to change. He just wanted someone who understood him in spite of it. Someone who knew him better than he knew himself. And now, he thought, he had found her.

She began moving underneath him. It wasn't in protest. He took that for the response *she* wasn't willing to speak aloud, and he couldn't blame her. He knew that she needed more than sex. But sex had always been a pretty good place to start before.

He pushed his hands beneath her hips, pulling her against him, and felt everything inside him strain to get still closer to her, to get inside her, where everything was warm and safe and good. She finally started kissing him back, hot and fast. Her mouth skimmed over his face before latching on to his lips again. He heard a groan catch deep in her throat.

It still wasn't completely assent, but neither was it denial. He took her mouth again and again, desperate, feeling raw and needy and wild. He shoved up her T-shirt and her bra and gathered her breasts in his hands. She shuddered once, hard, and groaned again.

"Not here," she managed. And if he stopped touching her long enough for them to move somewhere else, she thought, then maybe she would get sane again.

"Now."

"The others—"

"If they come home, they'll just blush and look the other way."

Holly would probably cheer, Carly thought. She gave up. No one was expected home for a while anyway.

She wrapped her arms around his neck and gloried in the feel of him pressed against her again. She groped for his belt, but she couldn't manage to do anything with it because her hands were trembling too badly. She finally settled for wrenching his shirt free from his jeans.

She slid her hands beneath it, over the hard muscles of his back, so clenched now, so tense with restraint. For whatever reason, Holly had been right. He had come back to her. It was enough. For now, it was enough.

She twisted beneath him, splaying her legs so she could wrap them around him. His mouth dived to take in her nipple. His hands were alive, touching, coaxing, urging her on, and she didn't need any more urging. She never had where he was concerned.

He slid his hands down over her tummy to cup her through her jeans, rubbing, the weight of his body deepening his touch until she cried out. "Now!"

He wouldn't argue with her. Not this time.

His hand moved, sliding her zipper down. She grappled with his belt again and this time she won her battle with it. She managed to tug his jeans down at the same time his fingers—his wonderful fingers—slid beneath the cotton of her panties.

Jack shuddered. She was wet, hot . . . his, still his. It was all the proof he needed.

She got his shirt off. Her mouth skimmed feverishly across his chest. Her fingers found his new scar and she explored it, remembering, then she passed it by because the memories of that day struck cold into her heart. There was no room for cold now. Her hand searched for his hardness, and when she found him, Jack made a strangled sound and fought not to explode at her touch.

He had missed her so much.

He felt her hand tremble on him, stroking, taking away the last of his control. The hay scratched her back, her bottom, and Carly felt nothing but the warmth of him against her palm.

Jack eased his mouth away from hers and clenched his jaw. He worked her with his fingers but it wasn't enough, her hand was too much, and he finally pushed it away so that he could sink into her. She stiffened and quivered and he held her hips, just savoring the feel of her before he moved inside her.

She gave a breath that was half sigh, half gasp, and wrapped her legs tighter around him. She wouldn't let him go this time. She wouldn't let him slip away.

He found the band at the end of her braid and tugged it free. Her hair spilled into his hand. He tangled his fingers in it and felt a wave of tenderness, so new, so terrifying that he finally lost control.

He pumped inside her, harder and harder. He wanted more. More of her, more of them, more of this sheer sweetness of mating, matching, joining together. He had never wanted it so badly in his life. He kissed her swollen mouth and drank his name from her lips. Then her breath started coming in short, little pants that drove him the last of the way over the edge.

Carly climaxed hard and fast and completely, crashing over that edge with him.

Finally, she lay still and caught her breath. For a while they watched the wind puff a single white cloud across a clear blue sky. Jack wanted to savor this new peace, and he knew that, as always, she wouldn't let him. There were still those words left to be dealt with.

She sat up and started grabbing her clothing. Her motions were fast and jerky. Never a dull moment, he thought, grinning.

"What's the matter now?"

"I don't know what your story is, cowboy, but you didn't have to come—what?—two thousand miles? You didn't have to come all this way to tell me how to get money out of your powerful men." She was perilously close to crying again. "I'm sick of chasing carrots, Jack. I'm *sick* of having all of you hold them out to me like some kind of ... of promise, but no matter how I try, I can't run fast enough, I can't collect the prize, because none of you ever intended to give it to me in the first place!"

She was dressed, scrambling down off the hay again. Jack stared after her. Where had *that* come from?

"Hey! Wait a minute!"

She spun back to look at him. "I want the *truth*, Jack! Not excuses, not lies, *just the truth*. What are you doing here and why?"

He scrambled for a response, but she didn't wait for an answer. By the time he got his jeans back on, she was halfway across the yard. She veered for the closest barn. Jack went after her. His gut was sinking fast.

Something had happened while he was gone. Something that had smudged the shadows beneath her eyes. Something that had hurt her badly, and it didn't have anything to do with him. Maybe something had even happened before he'd left. He'd been so preoccupied with Scorpion those last couple of days, he couldn't say for sure.

He ran into the barn, then stopped, out of breath, trying to let his eyes adjust to the darkness inside. He heard her before he saw her. Soft sniffs were coming from the back of the barn. He ran a hand along the wood, guiding himself toward the sounds. He found her sitting in a stall, her legs drawn up, her head down on her knees.

"What is it?" he asked. "What happened?"

She dragged a hand over her cheek and shrugged. "I've been five kinds of a fool," she muttered.

"You?" He moved carefully to sit beside her.

"Yeah, me. You can't get to know somebody inside a few days. You were right about that."

He took a deep breath. "No. I was wrong."

Carly snorted, but her heart chugged.

"I know you well enough to know that you're no fool." She was dogged and feisty, he thought, but she wasn't stupid.

He watched her tilt her head back to look up at the rafters. Her tears had been short-lived, as usual. Now there was a grim set to her jaw.

"My father was a lot like you," she said finally. Her voice was just bitter enough to scare him. "You're both so damned good at moving people around like chess pieces, putting them where you want them, telling them only what you think they need to know. And like a pathetic puppy, I guess I just panted and wagged my tail and gave the best of myself to both of you."

"Yeah, but it's a hell of a tail."

She didn't even smile. His throat closed. Had protecting her hurt her so much? It seemed safer to ask about her father.

"Who'd your father move around? How?"

"Me."

She told him everything Rawley had told her. She'd tried to come to terms with it, but she hadn't been able to. She didn't give herself any benefit of doubt in the telling, but he knew she never would.

It took Jack a long time to find words. "So what?" he asked finally.

She turned wide, green eyes on him. "So *what?* I've been *killing* myself for this ranch, for him!"

"Not for him. Not anymore. You've been killing yourself for you. And for Holly. Maybe Theresa."

"What do you mean?" she asked stiffly.

"Your father's dead, sweetheart. This ranch is yours. If it sinks, you're the one who loses. If it floats, it's you who triumphs."

She closed her eyes weakly. "I hate you," she breathed.

The response took his breath away a lot faster than he liked. "Why?"

"Because I needed you to say that thirty-two days ago."

He shifted his weight, suddenly uncomfortable. "I was in the hospital thirty-two days ago."

"Hmm. Nice tan you've got there. Let's try seven days ago."

He had been in Florida, searching, not finding, but then, he'd known he wouldn't. He had only done it as a symbolic gesture of putting things behind him. If his father had stayed in the state, he was gone now. Jack could have looked elsewhere, and he had realized that he really didn't need to bother. The man had left him. Now he could let him go as well.

As for his mother, she was no longer in the system. She wasn't receiving any government aid. Jack found he wanted even less to look through other channels for her.

He'd been born in Florida and abandoned there, but now it was just another place with palm trees. Happiness and hope, home, hearth and family were here in the Dust Bowl.

"I had some traveling to do," he said finally. "I had to wrap some things up for myself. What do you want from me?"

Carly took a deep breath. "The truth," she said again. No matter what it was, she knew she needed to hear it. "I thought you were different. That maybe you didn't actually *betray* me, that I was just being paranoid and blaming you for what everyone else did. But then you just . . . vanished. And if what we had was something . . . anything . . . you wouldn't have just gone away, Jack. Tell me," she said again. No more delusions, she thought. No more chasing after carrots. "I want to know why you came back here. It wasn't because of Uncle Sam, and it wasn't for a roll in the hay. So to speak."

He wanted to smile, but he saw that she had braced herself for a blow. That made it easier to say what he needed to say. He enjoyed jolting her for a change.

"I came to ask you to marry me."

He got more or less the reaction he'd anticipated. Carly came to her feet in one lunging motion and stared down at him.

"What?"

He stood as well and watched her. "Marry me." It was so easy to use words after all.

"Why?"

"I love you. You love me. Makes sense, doesn't it?"

Her heart was slamming. Her breath was gone. She shook her head frantically. "I never said I loved you."

"You said you needed me."

I did. I do. Always. "I did not."

"Yes, you did. You said you needed me thirty-two days ago."

"I had a moment of weakness thirty-two days ago."

"That's garbage," he said mildly. He leaned a shoulder against the stall door, watching her. He enjoyed her panic and loved the flare of longing in her eyes.

Such expressive eyes. Her whole heart showed there if you looked at them just right. They were really much better in reality than in the picture.

"So what do you say?" he prompted her.

"No." It was a gasp. Carly felt herself starting to shake.

"Why not?"

"Because . . . well, we're not good at it. Neither one of us. There was Zoe, and Brett—" She broke off to shake her head hard. "No, Jack, no."

"I don't like blondes, I have all the money I need, and I've always had a hard time pulling the trigger. Brett was right about that. So I'm not like him, and trust me when I tell you that you're not anything like Zoe."

She stared at him. "You're crazy."

"No," he said quietly. "I'm just finally willing to settle down. But it has to be with you, cowgirl. No one else."

That shook her like nothing had yet. And she needed, wanted, to believe it so desperately that it was a physical ache. So she tried one last time to remember all the reasons it might be wrong.

"We've only known each other . . . days. Really, it was just a week."

"Those were some action-packed days, cowgirl. We lived *lives* in the space of those hours." He moved closer to her. "Think about it, Carly. I saw you under the best of circumstances and the worst. I know what you're like when you're under pressure and I know what you're like when you're in pain. I know how you react to pleasure. I know what you *are*, and you're everything good. I never thought your kind of simple, basic goodness was out there." Hearth and home, he thought. "I just never looked in the Dust Bowl. I was sort of preoccupied with Florida."

Florida, she thought. Palm trees. Her heart spasmed.

She let herself touch him, laying her palms flush against his chest. His heart was beating hard.

Words could be lies, she thought again. But he'd never really told her lies. And his heartbeat . . . his pounding heart had to be the truth.

He *wanted* her to say yes, she realized. He wanted it badly. Her head swam and she felt a strange, tingling sensation run over her skin.

"Jack," she said softly, "just exactly how long *did* you have that picture of me?"

He hesitated only a moment. "Six years. And Brett was right when he said I wanted you before I even saw you in the flesh. Your heart showed right there in your eyes. For six years, I hated that a woman like that, like you, could love *him,* while I was falling in love with you."

Her head spun. "Then why didn't you come looking for me right away?"

He thought about not telling her that he—that the agency— had kept tabs on her, because he wasn't sure how she would take it. But she was right—he had never deliberately told her anything that wasn't true, and there was no reason to evade her questions any longer.

"I did."

She blinked. "You did?"

"We knew who you were and where you were, and that you were Scorpion's woman." She winced at that. "We just kept an eye on you, in case he came back here."

"Don't ask me yet, Jack," she burst out finally.

"What?" She'd done it again, he thought. She'd veered, jumped subjects, and he rushed to catch up with her.

"To marry you."

"When then?"

"I don't know. Later. Just . . . later. I need to think about it. I need to...be sure." Oh, God, the *fear,* she thought. The fear was so great.

Did she dare take a chance again? Could she give another man all her heart?

"Can I hang around in the meantime?" he asked, half-smiling.

Yes, please yes. "Try to leave before we've finished this and I'll break your legs."

He gave a bark of laughter. She moved out of the stall, braiding her hair back up as she went. She got as far as the re-paired back porch before she stopped and looked at him eye to eye. He had stopped on the step below her.

"So did you retire?" she said suddenly.

Jack scowled. "Technically, I haven't decided yet. I've taken a leave of absence. What are you getting at, cowgirl?"

"I don't want to go to Virginia," she said bluntly. She looked around at the ramshackle fences and outbuildings of Seventy Four Draw. He was right. Her father was dead. This was *hers*.

"Virginia, huh?" He grinned slowly. "Now where could you have gotten the idea that I'd want to settle there?"

She almost flushed, then she pointed to his license tags with a triumphant expression. Jack laughed aloud.

"And here I thought it might have something to do with you snooping through my wallet when I left it in the sofa. Here I thought you might have had occasion to see my driver's license."

Her eyes widened deliberately. "Snooping? *Me?*" She sniffed righteously. "Uncle Sam lives in Washington, right? And I was merely thinking that he might get a little testy if your wife sues them for the lost revenue of three hundred and fifty-five cattle. You might get fired."

Jack's heart chugged. Slammed. He forgot about the wallet. He had no secrets from her anymore anyway.

"Is this later?" he asked cautiously.

Carly barely hesitated. She nodded.

"Is this yes?"

She nodded again.

His knees felt weak. "I'll retire."

Carly breathed again. "You will? Really?" She was amazed. The government had something he needed. She'd finally figured it out while he had been gone. He hadn't been avoiding commitment with his work, not exactly. He'd been replacing something. He'd been replacing family, home, love...with Scorpion, with his powerful men and his agency.

And a man like that valued family, love and honesty too much to give in to betrayal.

Jack nodded. "I'm entitled. I've put in my time. And I wasn't really sure I felt like starting all over again on another project anyway. I was on Scorpion for so long, it feels like he *was* my job."

Eleven years, she thought. "So what will you do?"

"Need any help around here, cowgirl? I work cheap."

She wrapped her arms around his neck. "Yes. Oh, yes." Then they both looked up sharply when a truck came into the barnyard.

It was Holly and Theresa, back from the market in the city. Holly got out, stopped dead in her tracks when she saw Jack. She grinned slowly.

"I knew it! I *knew* it! You're back! Are you staying?"

Carly glanced at Jack. She answered for him, grinning. "We'll see. That's sort of up to him."

"Yeah," Jack said without hesitation. "And now your mother has to go take a shower and get cleaned up." He gave her a little push up the steps. "Come on. There's one more thing we have to take care of here."

"What?" Carly asked, startled.

"I believe I owe Rawley Cummings a very fine bottle of bourbon." At her surprise, he grinned. "Hey, I'm a man of my word."

* * * * *

Watch for THE MARRYING KIND,
Beverly Bird's next intriguing novel,
coming in August 1996
from Silhouette Intimate Moments.

* * * * *

In July, get to know the Fortune family....

Next month, don't miss the start of Fortune's Children, a fabulous new twelve-book series from Silhouette Books.

Meet the Fortunes—a family whose legacy is greater than riches. Because where there's a will...there's a wedding!

When Kate Fortune's plane crashes in the jungle, her family believes that she's dead. And when her will is read, they discover that Kate's plans for their lives are more interesting than they'd ever suspected.

Look for the first book, *Hired Husband,* by *New York Times* bestselling author **Rebecca Brandewyne.** PLUS, a stunning, perforated bookmark is affixed to *Hired Husband* (and selected other titles in the series), providing a convenient checklist for all twelve titles!

FREE
Keepsake
Bookmark

Launching in July wherever books are sold.

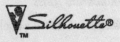

This July, watch for the delivery of...

An exciting new miniseries that appears in a different Silhouette series each month. It's about love, marriage—and Daddy's unexpected need for a baby carriage!

Daddy Knows Last unites five of your favorite authors as they weave five connected stories about baby fever in New Hope, Texas.

- **THE BABY NOTION** by Dixie Browning
  (SD#1011, 7/96)

- **BABY IN A BASKET** by Helen R. Myers
  (SR#1169, 8/96)

- **MARRIED...WITH TWINS!**
  by Jennifer Mikels
  (SSE#1054, 9/96)

- **HOW TO HOOK A HUSBAND (AND A BABY)**
  by Carolyn Zane
  (YT#29, 10/96)

- **DISCOVERED: DADDY** by Marilyn Pappano
  (IM#746, 11/96)

Daddy Knows Last arrives in July...only from

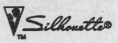

DKLT

by
Cathryn Clare

The Cotter brothers—two private detectives and an
FBI agent—go wherever danger leads them...except
in matters of the heart!

But now they've just gotten the toughest assignments of
their lives....

Wiley Cotter has...
THE WEDDING ASSIGNMENT: March 1996
Intimate Moments #702

Sam Cotter takes on...
THE HONEYMOON ASSIGNMENT: May 1996
Intimate Moments #714

Jack Cotter is surprised by...
THE BABY ASSIGNMENT: July 1996
Intimate Moments #726

From Cathryn Clare—and only where
Silhouette Books are sold!

CCAR1

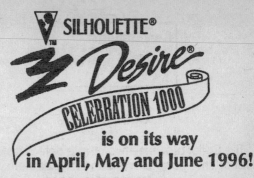

SILHOUETTE® Desire® CELEBRATION 1000

is on its way
in April, May and June 1996!

Join us for the celebration of Desire's 1000th book! We'll have

- Book #1000, *Man of Ice* by Diana Palmer!
- Best-loved miniseries such as **Hawk's Way** by Joan Johnston, and **Daughters of Texas** by Annette Broadrick
- Fabulous new writers in our Debut author program

Plus you can enter our exciting Sweepstakes for a chance to win a beautiful piece of original Silhouette Desire cover art or one of many autographed Silhouette Desire books!

SILHOUETTE DESIRE CELEBRATION 1000
...because the best is yet to come!

DES1000TD